DALE MATHENY

A Door Opens

# Contents

# Prologue

*Pan-STARRS telescope, University of Hawaii, Haleakala, Hawaii, October 2017*

Dr. Damon Garcia pushed his glasses up onto the bridge of his nose. "I'll be," was all he could say while staring at the new contact he just found with the Pan-STARRS telescope. A few minutes passed as he typed on the observatories' control console in the small office below the one-point-eight-meter primary lens. Research papers and thick books of astronomical observations lay scattered around the office.

"Wow, it can't be." Damon brought up the previous night's observational data for the area of the sky he was studying. "You missed it!" he spoke to no one, but referring to the Pan-STARRS computer program that was supposed to find moving objects in the observatories' data.

Damon measured the object moving at a tremendous angle above the ecliptic, the common plane that planets travel in the solar system. The program's purpose was to sift through gigabytes of data and find near-earth objects. It had missed the object Damon was tracking.

Damon always wore a sports jacket and white shirt, making him feel comfortable, even while sitting for hours doing

1

his research. His peers knew him as a quiet man who had infinite patience and a researcher's talent for attention to detail and observation. To Damon, data told a story; it was like breadcrumbs leading to great discoveries of the natural world. He was good at knowing how to spot and patiently follow the crumbs.

As he was leaving for the night, Damon sat and wrote in his notebook, "I've got an amazing find! My data says the object is only four-hundred meters wide but moves at twenty-five kilometers per second, coming at a severe angle to the ecliptic, higher than I've ever seen. It can't be an asteroid or a comet, as far as I can tell. It's got to be coming from outside the solar system."

*Three days later*

"We have designated the object A/2017 U1. Dr. Garcia has given it the name Oumuamua, which means what, Damon?" The director of the Minor Planet Center in Cambridge, Massachusetts, was hosting a call with a hundred scientists and reporters. The center in Cambridge recorded all official observations of near-earth objects in our solar system.

"It means *scout* in Hawaiian. Given it's the first object coming from outside our solar system, it seemed appropriate." The science reporters ate it up. Not less than one-hundred observatories around the world were tracking Damon's sighting.

"Dr. Garcia, you said it wasn't an asteroid or comet, what is it, an alien spaceship?" the reporter from Scientific American asked.

Damon didn't laugh, "We know that it is narrow, long, and

doesn't have a cometary tail. The object has moved rapidly and sling-shot around the sun, passing relatively near Earth on its way out of the solar system. It's heading to the constellation Pegasus. Oumuamua is the first interstellar object we've identified moving through the solar system."

Another reporter commented, "Holy mackerel, it could be a spaceship."

\* \* \*

Damon stretched and cracked his neck to the side. He had worked late for the last few weeks, tracking Oumuamua and coordinating with his peers at other observatories worldwide. He got up and walked around his telescope's office, exercising a bit. His console beeped loudly, and Damon rushed back.

"What's this?" Damon typed into his keyboard to zoom in on the objects being tracked coming out from Oumuamua. "Whoa…" he breathed as he saw two objects shoot out and take up different courses than Oumuamua. The probes, what else could they be, he thought, accelerated. Damon set up his software to track each and waited to see where they were headed. They were going five times faster than Oumuamua itself.

After three hours, he had tracked the first probe toward an asteroid in near-Earth orbit. "Anteros, why Anteros?" he asked no one. He couldn't find any indication it crashed, leading him to believe that it landed. The second probe took up orbit close to the sun.

Damon sat back and took off his glasses. He had been reluctant to be baited to call Oumuamua an alien spacecraft. But damn! he thought. It really is. He stored his recordings carefully and left for the night, deep in thought.

The next day Damon talked with NASA executives and other researchers to coordinate how to verify and possibly release his findings. The meeting was scheduled for tomorrow, and Damon was back at work in his office, preparing.

His phoned beeped and he answered it.

"Are you Dr. Damon Garcia?"

"Yes," Damon replied hesitantly.

"Your recent discovery about Oumuamua is dangerous. They won't allow your findings to go public. "

"Who is this?"

There was a pause, then the man continued, "We can help. I am now encrypting this call, Dr. Garcia. We are a group that works on behalf of people in developing countries. We are called Fuerte. We are not like those who are pursuing you. They only care about protecting their vast assets and want what you have learned for their financial interests. Consequently, they don't want the public to know about it. We are going to give you the address of a safe house; if you can make it there, we can protect you."

Damon hastily scribbled down the information the man from Fuerte gave him. The man ended the call saying, "Please, be careful." Damon sat back and stared at his pad of paper.

There was too much to do to prepare for his briefing tomorrow to deal with this. But he had to do something.

Damon looked up the number of an old college buddy, who worked at the FBI. They talked for a few minutes, then Damon called home. "Hi, Matti! It's Dad." Damon smiled. His daughter was the best twelve-year-old in the world. He adored her. Damon talked with Matti for a few minutes, happy to take his thoughts away from his work's stress and the phone call from Fuerte.

Matti asked, "Are you coming home for dinner? We're having mac-n-cheese, our favorite!"

Damon sighed, "I'm sorry, honey. I won't be home, but it sounds delicious. I've got to go, love you and see you in the morning."

"Ok, love you, dad. I hope you get to come for dinner soon."

Damon ended the call, feeling more guilty than ever. He tapped his wife's cell entry on his phone. "Hi, Honey. I have to work late again. Sorry. My day was disturbing. I got a phone call from a group named Fuerte warning me that my research is being watched and that a hostile group didn't want it getting out. I called Justin, my college buddy, at the FBI. He had heard of Fuerte, the group that called me. He said it was a secret organization in the developing world. They are benevolent, but he didn't like how secretive they were and promised he would look into it."

Damon listened to his wife for a minute, then continued, "No, I don't think I need to call the police. I'm not sure what they could do since no one has threatened me. The call just made me super-paranoid. I can talk to NASA security tomorrow." Damon talked a bit more and then finished the call, feeling better.

As he worked, his mind ruminated on the odd call. *Your discovery of Oumuamua is dangerous. We are Fuerte.* By the time he finished creating his presentation, he felt confident about what he would share. The more he reviewed his videos, the more he thought he was sitting on proof of an alien spaceship.

\* \* \*

Matti woke with a start and squinted at her clock. It was three am. Why was she up? Something had startled her awake. Was daddy home yet? She pulled the curtains back from her bedroom window and peeked outside. She didn't see his car like she usually did. She walked down the hall to her mommy's bedroom.

"Where's daddy, mommy?"

Carol woke and yawned. She reached over and patted the empty bed beside her and sat up, wide awake. "I don't know, honey. He should be home, even with working late. I'll call his office."

Carol called Damon's office and just got his answering message. She hung up and looked worried.

Matti got worried too. "Is daddy ok?"

Flashing lights appeared outside on the street and got brighter as a car pulled into their driveway. Carol jumped out of bed and grabbed her robe. "Come on, honey, someone's at the door." Carol was afraid now and quickly ran down the stairs. She reached the door just as the doorbell rang. Unlatching and opening the door, she was startled by a policewoman standing just outside. The woman looked down at her clipboard.

"Morning, mam. Are you Mrs. Carol Garcia?"

Carol nodded her head and put her arm around Matti, who held tightly onto her mother's robe. The red lights of the police car in the driveway flashed harshly on the doorway.

"Is Damon ok? Why are you here?"

"May I come in?"

Carol opened the door wider, and the officer stepped inside.

"Mam, your husband was found by security twenty minutes ago. His head was bleeding from a bullet wound, and they took him directly to Riverview General. If you'd like to follow me, I can escort you there." Carol and Matti quickly got in their car and drove to the hospital. Three hours later, Damon died with Carol and Matti at his side.

By morning all data from Damon's research was missing from LX1 and NASA servers. But not before Fuerte was able to make a copy of the videos Damon took of Oumuamua.

* * *

*Thirteen years later, Lajitas, Texas*

Playing golf at Black Jack's Crossing in Lajitas, Texas, was Texas Senator Richard Barrister's favorite way to conduct business. He loved the expansive views of the mountains. The food at the lodge was a great draw, also.

His West Texas ranch was nearby. He could drive for hours and never leave his two-hundred-thousand acres. But for a business meeting, he preferred golf at Black Jack's instead of his ranch. The ranch was his sanctuary. He went to the ranch when he needed time out of the limelight. He tried to keep it exclusively for him and his family and not use it for business.

Paul Manning, the CEO of Space Industries, flew in from Houston that morning to meet with Barrister. They were on the green at the first hole. Paul took in the view. "I'm glad we met here; the view is unparalleled." Black Jack's was at the southwest edge of Big Bend National Park, and the twenty-mile views of massive pines, limestone cliffs, and mountains rising in the background were spectacular.

The love of wide-open expanses was one thing that both men had in common. It gave them a sense of freedom and progress they couldn't get sitting in an office. The senator craved the openness of West Texas. Paul worked to open access to the asteroids' infinite mineral resources, just waiting to be tapped. Wide-open spaces symbolized bountiful resources and endless opportunity, growth, and prosperity. Activists and scientists in the climate change debate argued for constraint and limitation. The senator and Paul couldn't accept that. Both would rather die than give up the notion that America couldn't expand itself into a higher state of prosperity through old-fashion American ingenuity, grit, and above all, technological growth.

"I do love this view," the senator remarked. "I'd love to come here every day to revel in this view of America, wide, open, and free."

Richard looked every bit the powerful US Senator that he was. He was elected at the age of twenty-seven and served fourteen years in Congress, twelve as a senator. He was short at five-foot-seven, bald, and always wore a cowboy hat and boots. He compensated for his lack of height with a strong, commanding voice. He bragged, to anyone who would listen, that he never lost at anything, ever.

Paul was taller at six-foot-two. He had a full head of wavy brown hair and an actor's bearing, handsome, and confident. His parents had encouraged Paul to pursue acting, but he was driven to entrepreneurship and space exploration.

At twenty, he started a business in his college city of Boston, Massachusetts, to provide more affordable student housing. He made his first million building and renting cheap apartments that students loved.

He loved to talk about his 10x mindset, which he defined as always trying to improve whatever he tackled by ten times. He would say, "No one wants slight improvements, but they think you're God if you can deliver something ten times better." He had always delivered a ten times improvement in his business ventures and was rewarded financially for his abilities.

It wasn't until Senator Barrister teed off at the fourth hole, and after a perfect shot down the fairway, that he turned to look at Paul to give him the good news.

"Our board met yesterday and approved full funding of Space Industries' expansion. We agreed to your proposal for one-hundred billion dollars in exchange for twenty-five percent ownership and a seat for two of our members on your board."

Paul looked over at the senator and reached his hand out to shake on it. "It's great to be partners, sir. The space station is going to provide many opportunities for excellent financial returns."

The senator responded, "That proposal you sent us is the answer to many of our problems. Your technology will save the world from this so-called global warming! We'll just keep expanding past the open plains, past those mountains, and right out into the vastness of space. There'll be no limits to growth on my watch! Climate change will not mean business stagnation for us."

"Amen to that!" He was proud that he secured tens of billions of dollars for his company in federal tax waivers and grants from the senator's committee and the consortium of companies to which the senator was tied.

Paul had worked on bringing his space expansion vision to fruition his whole adult life. He spent years buying additive manufacturing and smaller rocket companies. Space Industries recruited the best engineering talent they could find from space programs and aerospace startups. He was relentless in securing patents to protect his new technologies. This new infusion of capital would supercharge his dream of building a space economy.

They played through the next hole, then the senator stopped and looked earnestly at Paul, "One more important point. We want you to pull in the Anteros asteroid and explore it."

"Explore it?" Paul was confused, "Why, Anteros?"

"We want you to mine it to build the space station, but you must *explore* it first. We have solid research that tells us it is an object of extreme interest for many reasons. I think we'll all be surprised at what we find there," the senator added mysteriously.

Paul looked thoughtful, "I'll run it by my folks. If it checks out, we'll certainly prioritize it."

The senator's smile vanished. He looked straight at Paul with a practiced, stern look.

"Paul. This isn't a *wish*; it is a stipulation of the agreement. You will bring Anteros to lunar orbit and explore it, or the deal is off. It must be the first asteroid you bring in."

The senator didn't trust well. He loathed putting risks with substantial consequences into other's usually incapable hands. He also thought about the effort his group had spent finding out that Anteros was where Oumuamua had sent a probe a dozen years ago.

"So, are we in agreement?"

Paul thought about the herculean changes to Space In- dustries' priorities to mine Anteros first. The funding was everything. He consented, "Yes, we are. We have to build the Lunar processing station first, which will take five years, but Anteros will be the first asteroid we bring in."

"Perfect," the senator smiled. He held out his hand, and Paul grasped it and shook.

# Space Pioneers

Year:2030
Earth Population: 8,279,899,930
Population off-earth in Solar System: 35
Temperature increase due to global warming: +2°F
Yearly population decrease due to global warming: 90,000

The sun was bright in the blue Texas sky as Logan Conover drove his convertible up to the NASA training center. He parked in the lot and walked up to the center reveling in the beautiful day. One-hundred and fifty new astronaut trainees reported to the Johnson Space Center in Houston for their first day of training.

Until 2029, NASA and the Russian Yuri Gagarin Cosmonaut Training Center were the only organizations in the world that trained astronauts. All US astronauts were connected to the NASA astronaut corps, even if they flew spacecraft owned by private companies. But now, the astronaut corps was making a giant leap forward in size and scope to support the hundreds of new astronauts being recruited for the commercial space economy. Jobs in asteroid mining, space station, space elevator construction, pilots, and even food-service workers needed extensive training to survive in space.

To support the influx, NASA, Space Industries, and Roscosmos, the Russian space agency, and the Chinese National Space Administration teamed up to create the International Space Academy. The Academy was a six-month program based in Houston and the Yuri Gagarin Cosmonaut Training Center in Moscow. It was a subset of NASA's and Russia's previous legendary astronaut training programs.

Space Industries was poised to send one-hundred recruits through the new Academy program. Logan Conover was one of the recruits. He spent the day checking in and taking a tour, then entered the dining hall the night before training was to start. All the recruits were having a welcome dinner. Looking around the lobby, he saw Mike Fitzgerald, a buddy from flight training in the military.

"Mike, good to see you!" Logan reached out to shake his hand.

"Logan! You made it. I saw you on the list of trainees. A long way from our days at Lockheed flight training, huh?"

"Glad you made it, too. Now I know how I can get through training!"

Mike was a giant of a man with Norse and Irish heritage and the red hair to prove it. Unlike Mike, Logan was of average build, five-foot-ten, one-hundred-eighty pounds, a full head of dark brown hair, and bright blue eyes. His eyes were his most distinctive feature. Logan was a retired Air Force pilot completing twelve missions during the six-year China Sea war.

They found a table as the dinner began and were joined by two other trainees. "Hi, I'm Matti Garcia. Did you two know each other before coming here?" Matti said, looking at Logan and Mike. She couldn't help but think the two were too friendly for having just met.

Mike smiled, "Yes! I knew this crazy guy back in military flight school. Hi, I'm Mike, and this is Logan."

The other recruit that had joined the table reached out her hand and introduced herself as well, "I'm Emily Watson. I'm local here in Houston and will be working in space construction."

Matti spoke up, "Glad to meet you, Mike, Logan, and Emily. I'm here as a strategic analyst. I worked a while at McKinsey and just passed the bar."

Logan raised his eyebrows. McKinsey was the world's most reputable management consulting firm. "Wow, nice. Welcome aboard to you both, even if you're not pilots!"

Matti smirked, "Ha! In case you hadn't heard, it's not all about going fast and high anymore; we have to build things and make a profit now."

"She put you in your place, buddy!" Mike shot back at Logan. They all laughed.

As the dinner went on, Logan was intrigued by Matti. She was funny, witty, smart, and beautiful. It was an intoxicating combination. He enjoyed listening as she enthusiastically related a story and wondered if he was falling for her. What a crazy idea, he thought. They had just met.

The four spent the rest of the evening at the same dinner table together. When the evening wound down, they all agreed they should form a team and meet up for dinners.

The next day, the first session of training started with a keynote talk from Paul Manning, Space Industries' president. Logan met with Paul when he came aboard Space Industries and liked his enthusiasm and vision. Mike, Logan, Emily, and Matti met for breakfast and then sat together for the opening talk.

Paul walked into the session to a standing ovation. "Welcome! Thank you! It's great to be here with you all on this first day of training! I see you are ready to start on our tremendous adventure!"

Paul changed the projection screen to a picture of Earth from space with a prototype LoadStar asteroid mining ship hanging in the foreground. "I love this picture of our LoadStar spacecraft. Just floating up there. Welcome to your new home!" The audience loved it and started cheering.

"I'm so glad you're here. You've joined the most important race in humanity's history. The race to create a space economy that will generate new business opportunities and pave a pathway for humanity to expand beyond our limited resources on Earth. Will humanity bury itself in social, political, environmental, and population crises that threaten to overwhelm the world every day? Will the acceleration of these problems surpass our ability to address them? Will the rampant effects of global warming and resource degradation overwhelm us? Serious issues."

Manning paused, just the right amount for theatrical effect. He gazed at the audience. All hundred new trainees were riveted to their seats. "Or," he advanced to a cool graphic of a space station with a space elevator extending up from the earth, "will we be able to use amazing technology to climb out of the crib?" Manning loved using the metaphor of humanity growing up, "Will we get the opportunity to launch ourselves into a boundless future based on unlimited resources out in space?"

Logan sat in the audience, whispering to Matti. "Heady stuff, huh?"

Matti slapped his arm and whispered back, "Haven't you seen the news? There's a major disaster every day. He's not kidding!"

Mike leaned over, "What do you suppose he's leading up to?" he asked.

Paul continued, "We, here, are the only ones at the gateway to the solar system, the only ones that will birth generations of explorers and pioneers." Another pause. "So."

"Here it comes," Logan whispered to Mike, Matti, and Emily.

"Space Industries has just received an additional one-hundred billion dollars from our investment group." Whistles from the audience. "We are triggering our long-awaited expansion plans to build our own resource processing facilities in orbit around the moon and then a true, permanent space station in Earth orbit. Over a million people will live and work at the station!" More hoots from the audience.

"All of you are a major part of it. You have all been hired into three new corporate divisions, which you will join after finishing your NASA training. The three divisions are space mining, construction, and future logistics."

"Future Logistics?" Mike, Logan, and Matti mouthed to each other, raising their eyebrows.

"So, buckle up, we're on an amazing journey. I will see you all individually over the next six months of training, and I look forward to being at your graduation in November!"

The remarks ended with enthusiastic applause, and everyone got up, excited to start the program.

Matti, Logan, Emily, and Mike made their way to the new main Academy building. It was six stories high and covered five acres. It contained classrooms and a dorm complex around the central courtyard where all the trainees could go between classes. Having just emerged into the courtyard, Mike and Logan stared in awe, a big grin on each of their faces.

"So, we're like the first Star Wars cadets or something, right?" Mike joked.

"We're the first space miners," Logan quipped. "Not as glamorous, but still pretty cool! Hey, check this out!" Logan jogged over to a sizable glassed-in area that held spaceship simulators and looked like a kid in a candy shop.

Meanwhile, other Space Industries recruits were finding their way to the courtyard. Most were Logan's age, with some fresh out of college and a few older men and women in their mid-forties. Major Tibbets, the lead instructor, entered with Captain Sandy Pulaski.

"Ready for a new batch of recruits?" Sandy asked Tibbets.

Tibbets smiled back, "Absolutely, I've been looking forward to getting real classes going for awhile. We've been preparing long enough."

Sandy shouted across the courtyard, "New trainees, front and center! Bring it in folks, no time for sightseeing."

All of the students hustled over to where the Major and Captain were standing.

"I am Captain Pulaski, your new instructor. This is Major Tibbets, the Lead Instructor for your program. We graduated from the old two-year astronaut training program, but we will be training you in six months because we've learned so much at the International Space Station. So, get ready for six months of hard work that will keep you all alive when you get to space."

Major Tibbets stepped forward.

"I look forward to working with all of you. I know you

will come out of this program ready to take on the dangerous tasks related to asteroid mining."

Mike leaned over to Logan and Matti, "Why is he so nice compared to the Captain?"

At that point, the major gave Mike a hard stare that could freeze boiling water. Mike shut up; lesson learned.

The Major paused and looked over the group of recruits. "So, let's be clear. Not all of you will make it through training. Some of you will wash out. But if each of you commits to forming an effective team around our common mission and purpose, you have an excellent chance of making it through the program. You will need to focus, listen to the captain and me, and you will accomplish something no one has ever done before, start the new space economy and help Earth move into a new era."

Logan, Mike, and Matti glanced at each other with mixed emotions. Pride and excitement were first and foremost and a growing realization of what they had signed up for. Others in the group raised their hands.

"I'm sure you have lots of questions which we will answer tomorrow at our first training class. You will wake at 5:30 each morning, have physical training, *PT,* and breakfast. Classes start at seven and last until four when you have two hours of simulation training or pool time before dinner. And, FYI, pool time doesn't mean swimming. It means you'll be suited up in our six-point-two-million-gallon neutral buoyancy tank to simulate weightless conditions in space.

We will be repeating this schedule in six-day weeks with Sundays *all yours*. Your apartment assignments were emailed to you with your acceptance packets, so you're welcome to settle in, and we'll get started first thing after lunch."

Logan and the group said good-bye to Matti and Emily. Matti started leaving and called back to Mike and Logan, "Meet you for dinner tonight at six-thirty?"

Mike smiled. "Sounds great, Matti. Come on, Logan." He looked over at Logan and motioned with his eyes to the hallway that led to their dorm block.

The next week was a blur. It turned out that Sundays were busier than other days as they were the only time everyone could catch up from the grueling schedule during the week.

A week later, Matti remarked to Mike, Emily, and Logan at dinner, "I really wish we had one day just to appreciate the craziness of where we are. Why can't we slow down and smile and just go to a movie or something?"

Mike was more philosophical about the academy training schedule. "That's the thing about great moments; they don't look like it when you're in the middle of it all. I mean, here we are training for the first massive push into space. One hundred of us will be the first large-scale industrial and space construction effort. Way bigger in terms of expected results than Apollo or the International Space Station, and you'd think from our classes we were all going to go working on an oil rig. Classes on mineral deposits and ore samples, chemistry." Mike looked over at Logan, "Why are you so happy? Aren't you worn out or stressed about this crazy schedule?"

Logan finished a big bite of cheesy mashed potatoes and smiled. "No way, man, this is my thing. In the Air Force, we loved being in the zone, you know, flights, prep, fixing stuff, just doing our jobs, and no time to think about the ramifications of anything. Just give me a plane or a spaceship, and I'll be happy for the rest of my life. The key is not to think about it too much."

Matti wasn't buying it. "The rest of your life, you're going to be a happy-go-lucky fly-boy?"

Mike was laughing now too. "Wow, you two are hilarious."

"Hey, everyone quiet down, look at the newscast!" shouted Huang Chou, a programmer from Shanghai.

With images of flames in the background, the BNN news reporter was saying, "This firenado is unprecedented. A mile-wide wall of destruction has engulfed the mid-size California city of Brentwood, population fifty-one thousand. This city has thirteen thousand homes, and almost every single one has been destroyed in just the last two days. While rescue efforts continue, scientists clearly point to the Global Burn and say this is only the beginning of new levels of destruction we can expect." It seemed to Logan that there was a more intense 'new normal' every year due to the global burn effects.

Will Bonalado shouted from a few tables away, "Oh, man! I live only ten miles from there. I gotta call my family!" then ran out of the room. Logan had met Will last week, a brilliant guy. He graduated with his Ph.D. in physics from Caltech when he was twenty-one. Logan made a mental note to invite Will to join their group.

Matti turned back to the dinner table, a new look of determination on her face. "I guess my problems are small problems. I can't wait to start planning how to take people off this planet and make ourselves a second home. This one is crumbling beneath our feet."

Logan was still looking at the images on the screen. "Agreed. That looks like something out of Dante's Inferno. Those space stations we're supposed to build might actually be life rafts."

* * *

Logan started Astrophysics and Navigation the next day. Will Bonalado was in the class, so he made a point to sit with him. When the teacher assigned their first project, Logan leaned over to Will, "Hey, want to team up?"

Will nodded, "Sure, I'll handle the physics, and you can do the navigation. It sounds like a great partnership! I assume since you were a pilot, navigation should be easy for you."

Logan looked through the assignment, "Well, I've been finding navigation in space is a lot more complicated, but, yeah, I can handle it."

The project called for each team of two to design a flight plan between three celestial objects, including an asteroid. The trick was a severe fuel loss due to an emergency, and they were to find a solution using what was available on the spaceship and asteroid. They were to travel from a low-earth orbit to the asteroid Adorea and return to moon orbit, a typical route once Space Industries started production flights.

Logan and Will met in the courtyard later that day to discuss the project over a soda. "So, it says here in the instructions that we will have a complete loss of fuel, that has to be wrong. How can we get back without any fuel at all?"

Will thought about it. "We will have to build a machine that extracts water from the asteroid. Our engines are water-propelled." Will furiously typed on his keyboard. "Here's an article from MiningUniverse.com on how to extract water from asteroids. It says it is possible to use lasers to vaporize the rock. This lets the water-gas out, which can then be collected."

Logan laughed. "So, all we need to do is fashion a powerful laser from what we have on the spaceship and somehow collect the water vapor."

Will typed furiously again. "Here is a list of all the materials available on our spacecraft. Give me an hour, then meet me in the lab."

Logan replied, "OK, I'll go get the weight and engine specs and work on the navigational issues."

When Logan arrived in the lab, Will was climbing on the mock Loadstar spacecraft. "Pass me an 8mm socket wrench, will you?" Will waved toward the tool cabinet that held all of the tools typically available on a Loadstar for repairs.

Logan passed him the wrench. Will detached a communication device from the outside of the Loadstar. "This, my friend," Will waved the device in the air, "can be converted from a simple communications laser to a high-powered spalling laser that will get us our water."

"No way!" Logan couldn't believe it.

"Way!" Will shouted as he was climbing down. He spent the next hour trying out different communications laser modifications, then shouted, "Presto!"

"You did it? It works?" Logan asked.

"Yes, please go to the geology lab. Ask the teaching assistant for a pound of simulated asteroid rock that has ice content, will you?"

"Sure, be right back." Logan jogged down to the geology lab and returned in a few minutes with the rock. He deposited it in a storage bin Will had retrieved from the Loadstar.

"Step back," Will said, then pointed and turned his laser on the rock for a full minute. At first, nothing happened. After a few more seconds, the stone started off-gassing. "Quick, get that bag, and cover the rock." Logan grabbed a plastic waste bag and held it for another minute over the hissing rocks. He was amazed when he started seeing droplets of water forming on the inside of the bag.

They ran the process for fifteen minutes and were able to generate a cup of water. Logan did a rapid calculation. "We need twenty gallons of water, so it should take us a day to generate that much. Do we have the electricity to run the laser that long?"

Will looked up the electrical capacity of the Loadstar, "According to this, we would if we were fully charged, and the assignment said nothing about the emergency destroying the batteries."

"So, we did it!" Logan shouted, "you did it! It's brilliant!" Logan was impressed by Will's ingenuity. They spent the next four hours documenting their device, writing up the navigation solution, and then turning the whole project into the professor a day early.

The next evening, Will was eating with Logan, Matti, Emily, and Mike at dinner. Will and Logan's phone beeped simultaneously. They glanced at their phones and smiled.

"100 on our project!" Logan said to the group, "all because Will is a genius. Our teacher wrote 'Innovative solution.'"

Mike turned to Will. "Welcome to the team Will! Now we have an ace pilot, a magnificent engineer (me), a construction specialist, a crack lawyer, and a brilliant scientist. There is no task we can't accomplish."

\* \* \*

It was quiet as Logan walked down the hall of their facility. He had just left a study session for his asteroid chemistry class. All of the courses were making him antsy. He loved the freedom of being in the air—the speed. Logan's eyes lit up with an idea.

Logan ran down the hall, "Hey Uli?" he queried as he reached the simulator room. Uli Gurgen ran the simulators. "Any simulators free? I have a few maneuvers I want to practice." Logan loved spending free time in the simulators, and he had an idea he wanted to try out.

"Sure, come back in five minutes, and I can get you in for a half-hour."

Logan came back in thirty minutes and strapped himself into simulator four. "Launching now," he informed the computerized controller. The simulator launched him out of a space station orbiting Earth, and Logan looked around. He couldn't wait to really get to space, but the simulation was convincing. It would have to do for now.

The view of the stars was inspiring. Logan oriented his craft toward the Earth and entered the atmosphere, approaching the Himalayan mountains.

When he got to the Alps, he punched the afterburner. The simulated Loadstar pushed him back in his seat as it accelerated with a punch. Two-gravities. *More acceleration!* Logan thought.

He stopped increasing the acceleration at three-gravities. The mountain tops flew by. He dipped between them and had to swerve to avoid the peaks. *Lower, faster.* Logan imagined his hair whipping back in the wind. *More speed.* All of his classes, all the stress just flew by and was left behind. *No future, no past, just now*, he thought.

A warning signal went off, and a computerized voice came on, "Craft has exceeded maximum safe velocity for this altitude." Logan pushed it harder. More speed. A siren went off. The ground flew by at three-thousand miles per hour. More speed. He leveled off across a glacier and was flying so low the snow blasted upward from the ground.

Then Logan pulled forcefully back on the stick to climb rapidly. The Loadstar rocketed upward in the sky, gaining orbit in a matter of a few minutes. *Wow, these babies can haul.* He just let the Earth glide by, the imagery surprisingly detailed. He could pick out storm lightning over Italy as he passed one-hundred-twenty miles overhead.

After five minutes of gazing, he stopped the simulation and jumped out of the simulator, grinning at Uli, who smiled back, "You always fly like that, Logan?"

"All the time. It's my thing, man!"

\* \* \*

Logan, Mike, and Matti had agreed to be a team in the official simulated LoadStar flying competition at the Academy, which was the program's highlight. The competition was intense because the winning team would get a weekend in Austin and a decent cash bonus. They were deep into the final simulation in the contest.

"Mike, I'm getting a faulty engine indicator on number seven," Logan shouted as he rolled and spun away from the asteroid, careening toward them at three-hundred-fifty kilometers-per-hour.

"Ignore it!" Mike was tired of all the faulty indicators and had more significant repair work to deal with. "Your right stabilizer should be working now."

Mike, Matti, and Logan were in third place after seven simulations over the last week. Their current mission was for the championship. Their task was to attach to and propel a small asteroid to lunar orbit. Several tedious hours had ended when a surprise asteroid field hit them from behind as it moved through their path.

Matti was on communications, talking with their contractor. "Boeing Space control, we require assistance. Can we get detailed scan navigation data for our location?"

"Ah, that's a negative, Loadstar twenty-three," the controller immediately responded.

Matti looked shocked, then angry, and slapped the communication toggle off. "We're on our own guys, sorry."

Logan focused on navigating through the asteroid field, in some cases missing asteroids by mere feet. He navigated them around the last killer asteroid, and they all started to relax.

The simulated space station came into view. "Whew. OK, now we just have to get over to the dock on time, " Matti summarized and requested clearance from the station. She finished and then spoke to her team, "The assigned dock is around the other side of the space station, dock L52."

Logan applied additional thrust. They reached their assigned dock almost on time. "Dang, two minutes late!" He powered down the craft.

The controller came on the line, "Loadstar 23, you're two minutes late, you're not getting paid for this one."

Matti was livid, "What?" she screamed and typed furiously on her terminal, "this isn't right; I know what our contract says."

Logan looked over at Mike with a hopeful expression, "If anyone can navigate *this* problem, it's our lawyer."

"Got it!" Matti shouted and toggled her comm line on. "Boeing Control, please refer to section one-ninety-five of the shipping contract, line five. Our shipment was freight-on-board *shipping point,* so you guys have owned this shipment since our departure. You're paying *us* to deliver. According to the manifest line two, a shipper working for you has a tolerance of five minutes on delivery. Please deposit our funds for our *successful* delivery, plus bonus, into our accounts."

The lights came back on.

"Simulation complete," came the computerized voice.

Logan looked over at Matti. "Oh well, it was worth a shot."

"Thanks," Matti smiled up at Logan.

They stowed their helmets then left the simulator. All the teams were standing around big screens at the front of the simulator room.

"Here come the results," Mike called over his shoulder and ran closer to the big terminal, which started scrolling up final contest standings beginning from the twentieth place. Matti was anxious with anticipation; she knew she called it right, but would that be reflected in the standings? Would the instructors agree?

"Ok, we're not in the bottom ten," Mike commented. Over the next two minutes, the results scrolled by. Most of the other teams turned away from the standings, dejected. Occasionally, a shout would fill the hall from a team that placed better than expected.

Fourth-place came up, and they still hadn't seen their team name. They started getting hopeful; they were in the top three! The last three teams all huddled around the monitor, taking furtive glances at each other. Third place went to Loadstar 5, captained by Michelle Thomas, the best American pilot Logan knew in the group. The Loadstar 5 team chanted "Whooooyah!" three times when they placed third. They had been fifth until this last run.

Second-place scrolled into view. The room started chanting for either Loadstar 23 or 2, depending on who they thought deserved top honors. Loadstar 2 was commanded by Boris Yavonavich, the leading Russian pilot in the world. When second place was displayed, they saw Loadstar 2 had placed second. Loadstar 23 was first!

"Woohoo, we did it!" Logan high-fived Mike and Matti. "What a team! Matti, they were trying to trick us. You nailed it."

Matti was grinning from ear-to-ear. "No one out-contracts Matti Garcia!"

Logan, Matti, and Mike turned to face the room where all the teams were chanting, "23! 23!" Boris held up his hand for quiet. He came over to Logan and shook his hand, "It was close, but you earned it. We saw the replay before the results. That was great flying and teamwork. Congratulations." Boris then turned to the whole group, "First drink is on us at Murphy's!"

The rest of the academy training flew by. They fine-tuned critical space skills such as low-gravity survival, spatial navigation, and communications, all skills they would need soon.

One evening, Logan walked into the dinner group, "OK, I am officially water-logged. I've been in the Johnson Space Center pool for the last forty-eight hours repairing attitude jets. I can't wait to deploy for space in one month, no more water."

"Wait, space in a month?" Matti exclaimed.

Matti wasn't going with the first deployment since she was in the strategic planning group and staying in Houston and joining Space Industries' executive team.

The others looked at each other. Logan asked Matti, "Would you like to take a walk?"

Logan and Matti had grown close. Logan could see Matti was sad at their group's inevitable break-up as they were assigned to different company operational divisions.

"Listen, Matti…" Logan began.

Matti turned to Logan, "It's just so fast; we were all just getting to be a close team."

Logan continued, "I know it's only been a few months, but I was hoping…" Matti gave Logan a closer look. He was getting at something else. Matti thought she knew what it was. "I was hoping we had something worth continuing, even when we go to our new postings. Maybe we could…"

At that point, Matti put her hands on Logan's chest and kissed him long and hard.

"I never planned on giving you up. In a few months, I'm sure you'll be back from the first mission. We'll have time together then."

"You're the best," Logan beamed. He slipped his arm around Matti, then leaned over and kissed Matti. That told Matti all she needed to know.

# Deep Remote

Year: 2037

*Earth Population: 9,554,132,018*
*Population off-earth in Solar System: 54*
*Global warming temperature increase: +3°F*
*Yearly population decrease due to Global Warming: 285,000*

Loadstar 1729 majestically and silently flew fifty-million miles from Earth with its two-astronaut crew tucked into its command module. Faint sunlight glinted off of its shiny new titanium-alloy hull. Loadstar spacecraft were the workhorses of Space Industries Mining Company. At eighty-five feet in length, the Loadstar Harvester was a long cylinder equipped with a grappling hook at the front. A solar array ran down its entire length. At the rear, an engine fanned out. Its purpose was to seek out and push high-value asteroids into lunar orbit.

Logan Conover and Mike Fitzgerald sat in the command module, the lights glowing from the various instruments showing that systems were operating optimally. Spending months in the most remote locations from Earth, pushing multi-billion-dollar asteroids from space to the Moon was their new job. They had trained in space for the better part of a year and were finally on their first real mission, to acquire the asteroid Anteros and bring it to lunar orbit for Space Industries to mine it. Materials gleaned from mining Anteros would allow Space Industries to start building the first permanent commercially operated space station in earth orbit, Earth Space Station One, or ESS One. Anteros was overflowing with precious metals, which would generate revenue for Space Industries and provide critical resources for buyers on Earth.

Logan was commander; Mike was the engineer. Logan liked being in the command chair. He had the best seat on the whole ship. To his left was a small window where he could see the stars. Logan finished his daily report, typing in the password that would beam it fifty million miles back to the company processing station that orbited the moon. He picked up his half-eaten burrito and bit off a huge bite, a few chunks of processed cheese floating off to the top of the cabin. His thoughts turned to his wife and daughter.

*I wonder what they're having for dinner. Whatever it is, I'm sure it's better than this.*

Mike interrupted his thoughts, calling from the kitchen that was next to the command module, "You dog, you took the last chicken! The only burritos left are those flat cheesy things."

Mike and Logan were best friends since they met at the Academy. Mike filled his seat. He reached the outside limit of height for a pilot at six feet and five inches. Logan felt at ease with Mike, especially appreciating his sense of humor, a critical ingredient on long flights millions of miles from Earth. They were a great team.

"Early bird and all that," Logan said between bites. "How's that firmware package upgrade coming along?"

Being the first asteroid mining ship built and launched by

Space Industries, LoadStar was unique. It could capture near-Earth asteroids, those found less than 1.3AU or one-hundred-twenty million miles from Earth. The ship was all engine. Its thrust powerful enough to push asteroids across space into new orbits that would bring them back to the moon for mining and processing.

"Loaded and spun up." Mike checked the software upgrade instructions, "You'll be pleased to know we now have a fix that allows us to fly straight."

"What's the fun in that?" Logan joked with Mike.

They operated in deep remote, as the pilots liked to say. Traveling up to one-hundred-and-fifty million miles away from Earth, they flew farther than any human being had ever ventured. Their ship, Loadstar 1729, was one of three Loadstars that comprised the first fleet. Logan and Mike had taken two test flights out to asteroids, but this was their first capture mission, and the stakes were high. The squadron was flying three months to Anteros with only a five-day window to break the asteroid out of its orbit and nudge it into a lunar orbit where the moon's gravity would capture it.

The mission was historic and watched by many on Earth. If they were successful, space mining would enter a new phase of profitability and progress. If they weren't, Space Industries wouldn't be profitable for another year and their schedule set back significantly.

"I am locking in our course adjustment now," Logan confirmed. It was a considerable effort to push an asteroid back to Lunar orbit, but once there, another team in Space Industries would break the asteroid down into water and metals.

The only sad part about his job, thought Logan, was he would be away from his wife, Matti, and daughter, Kira, for six months, an eternity for a six-year-old.

Logan checked his instruments methodically and communicated with the other two Loadstars that made up the Anteros mission, synchronizing their courses. Afterward, he set the craft back to automated mode and settled in, casting his thoughts to his time with Kira and Matti just before he left on the mission three weeks ago.

* * *

Sweat dripped from Logan's forehead, stinging his eyes as the wrench slipped from his grip, ramming the hand holding the pole in place. Even though it was six o'clock in the evening, it was still 102 degrees Fahrenheit in Portsmouth, New Hampshire. Portsmouth was the new Atlanta now that the *Global Burn* was in full swing. People stopped calling it global warming decades ago. Warming was benign compared to the throes of environmental violence and extremes the planet was currently experiencing. Logan had just a few more bolts to tighten on the swing set. His goal was to complete it in the next hour so Kira could come outside and play. The forecast said it should drop down to 85 degrees by seven o'clock that evening.

Matti and Kira were looking forward to the evening when they could go outside and enjoy their new backyard after weeks of hard work moving in. "Daddy is almost done with your swing set," Matti encouraged patience in Kira as she pressed her nose against the hot glass, watching her dad build her swing set. Kira had long, curly, dark hair, which her mom was braiding to keep it cooler and off her neck so she wouldn't get heat rash.

Logan wiped the sweat from his forehead and waved to his wife and daughter. "Kira, look at this!"

"I think it's cool enough outside now. Let's pop out and see how Daddy is doing."

"Is it finished yet, Daddy?"

"No pressure, Dad," Matti smiled at Logan gently. This time Logan held on to the socket wrench, and the last pole stabilized as he turned it.

"Ta-da! May I present your new swing set."

"Yippee! Yippee! Thank you, Daddy!" Kira shouted as she jumped on the swing and pumped her legs, reaching for the stars which were just beginning to appear in the dusky evening.

2037 had not started well. Matti and Logan had hoped moving to Portsmouth would be better than Houston, which had chronic severe water shortages and horrid heatwaves. It was too much.

They decided to move north to mitigate the heat, droughts, and hurricanes and to be closer to Matti's sister, Rosalyn, especially since Logan spent so much of his time away in space. Matti wanted her sister's companionship since she would be raising Kira alone so much of the time. They knew they were lucky to move as most people couldn't. Matti worked remotely from home as a strategic planner for Space Industries. Logan spent most of his time in space, so it didn't matter where they lived.

"This is great, Daddy!" Kira exclaimed as she pumped her legs up and down on the swing to gain more height and with it a cooling breeze, "The bestest!"

Matti smiled at Logan; they hadn't been so happy in years. Going out of the Houston heat, and having everyone home as a family for a few weeks was incredible.

Kira spent an hour on the swing while Matti and Logan watched her play. "Rosalyn told us the school she teaches in is the best in New Hampshire," Logan offered. Rosalyn was a third-grade teacher at the same school Kira was going to attend. He was happy to be out of Houston. "We're on a new track," Logan added, lifting his cold soda. He took a long, well-deserved drink. "Things are going to be great."

\* \* \*

From inside the Loadstar, feeling all alone in space, Logan sighed. Six months away from his family. Such was the life of a space explorer. It was like being on deployment for the military. How many soldiers were away from their families for six months or more at a time? Every one of them. He looked out the thick glass window, which was the size of a dinner plate. The view was amazing. With so many stars, space was hardly dark. He loved space and being a pilot, but it was hard missing his family so much.

To distract himself, he ran a full diagnostic of the command systems. There was a lot of spare time on the trip to Anteros that was filled with idle work. Mike was doing the same in the engineering area for the engines and electrical systems. Logan's thoughts drifted again. He reflected on a memory of his father, back when he was a boy.

\* \* \*

It was 2015 when he first gave serious thought about where the world was going.

Logan was ten. He was standing by his dad looking at the sunset over the Appalachian Mountains, over a set of rolling hills near Big Meadows campground. They were on a road trip to New York City from their home in Roanoke, Virginia, to attend an appliance convention. Roanoke was nestled at the foothills of the Blue Ridge Mountains. Stopping at Shenandoah National Park with its scenic Skyline Drive was the highlight of the trip so far. They walked part-way down the Appalachian Trail, which ran along the ridge of the mountains. That hike with his dad was magical.

Logan sighed, remembering how his dad promised they would hike the entire Appalachian Trail when Logan was older. It never happened. His father, already in late middle age, owned an appliance shop. He was too busy to take extended vacations. Life took over.

Walking along, his Dad said, 'Look at those hills, Logan. Boundless. You can do anything with your life.' He was so full of hope.

Business executives of the early 2000s thought the world was wide open—that economic growth would last forever. Logan's dad lived in a time when businesses tapped into the planet's resources and didn't factor in that they could be depleted. Economists held onto this view until climate change became undeniable. Now, continuous economic growth theory was recognized as a myth in a world of severely limited resources.

In 2037, the population was nine and a half billion, four times when his dad was a kid in the 1960s. Natural resources were no longer abundant. Oil was running out. Other critical resources were also running out. For the past eighty years or so, people on Earth used resources two to three times faster than the planet could sustain. Many environmental organizations built awareness by forecasting an annual Earth Overshoot Day, which in 2037 would be June 25. Overshoot Day was when humanity used up all the resources that the Earth naturally produced in that year.

Scientists estimated critical resources would be gone by 2100 or earlier. This would precipitate an economic, biological, and sociological world crash. Humanity might not survive to see 2100.

The signs of the crash were already present. The only salvation was if the planet could be replenished using resources from asteroids. This is what motivated Logan and Mike, the knowledge that they could make the difference; they could contribute to the solution.

Logan missed his dad. He passed away in 2026 while Logan was fighting in the China Sea. He received the news one evening after a mission and could not get back to Roanoke for the funeral. The war was too intense at the time for personal leave to be granted. He grieved alone.

After having another bite of the burrito, Logan forced himself away from going down that rabbit hole of sadness.

# Anteros

Logan commed the three Loadstars in the squadron, "We are two minutes from Anteros intercept. Fire thrusters on my mark."

They had endured the tediousness of the past ninety-two days of flight to the Anteros asteroid. The two other Loadstars, 1322 and 958, that joined them on their journey arrived within minutes of each other. It required three Loadstars to push the asteroid into lunar orbit, and all three had made it without a mishap.

Anteros was spherical, two kilometers in diameter, and rotated once every three hours, a slow spin. Approaching the asteroid, Logan mapped the surface carefully, matching the asteroid to prior maps from an exploratory robotic mission that had initially mapped the asteroid two years ago.

Logan commed the other Loadstar captains, and they synchronized their systems to pre-assigned landing sites to gear up for the 'big push,' when all three spacecraft would fire at full thrust for a week, changing the asteroid's orbit. Once the asteroid came close to the earth's moon, the moon's gravity would help capture and slow it down into a lunar orbit.

Mike spent the day going through engine check-lists.

"Hard to believe that rock is worth over four-hundred

billion dollars," Logan commented on the radio while talking with the other Loadstar captains, Zia Hu and Michelle Thomas.

Zia responded, "Too bad we just get paychecks. Maybe we could divert it somewhere else and start our own company."

Michelle chimed in, "Yeah, like I want to mine rocks. I don't mind delivering the rock; just don't make me mine it. I'll take piloting any day." Michele's cousin, Shaun, was on the mining crew back at the moon. She was glad he liked what he did, but she couldn't find joy in breaking up big rocks into small rocks.

Five hours later, Matis, the engineer for Loadstar 958, was out on an extravehicular activity (EVA) to fix a directional thruster damaged on the trip. It was a standard repair job. As commander, Michelle was monitoring the EVA when a jolt shook the Loadstar. She saw a bright flash from where Matis was working.

"Matis, your vitals just spiked on my monitor, report!"

Matis didn't respond. Michelle switched her monitor to an outside view. She saw Matis floating away from the Loadstar. "958 declaring an emergency. Matis is untethered and moving away from 958, unable to contact him. Possible explosion."

Logan was asleep in his cabin when the loud squawking of the emergency signal went off. He jumped up, lurching out of his cabin. Grabbing the handrails to pull himself the short distance to the command module, Logan propelled himself feet-first into his chair, then scanned the monitors and found they were close enough to 958 to help. "1729 responding," Logan commed while giving his thrusters a slight jolt to maneuver closer to 958. He saw Matis. "Mike, are you at the airlock? You're going to need to go out and grab Matis.

He's spinning away from 958."

"On it." Mike commed. Logan could hear heavy breathing from Mike as he struggled into his jetpack suit. The jetpack would allow him to go beyond tether range and maneuver.

"In range in 3, 2, 1, launch," Logan broadcast.

"Launching." Mike pushed himself out of the airlock toward Matis and fired a burst of propellent to give him extra momentum. He came up rapidly to him. It didn't look good; Matis's faceplate was cracked. He was ready with a patch and took a few seconds to apply it to the face mask. He then latched a belt onto Matis and jetted back to 1729 with Matis in tow. It took twenty-five agonizing seconds to get into the airlock and pull Matis behind him. Another five seconds to cycle the airlock.

Mike unfastened Matis' helmet. He checked Matis's vital signs. "Matis isn't breathing," he shouted as he applied CPR. Matis didn't respond. Logan pulled himself into the airlock and grabbed the defibrillator off of the wall as Mike struggled to get Matis suit off enough to put the electrodes on his chest.

"Clear!" Logan shouted as he applied the pads to Matis' chest. Nothing happened. He tried two more times and then stopped, breathing hard. He informed the others, "He didn't make it. His face mask was cracked, and he was exposed too long."

In 958, Michelle screamed in frustration. She hit the wall of her command module. "No! Damn!" She spent the last ninety-two days with Matis, and he was the best mission specialist she ever had. She couldn't believe he was gone. It just wasn't possible.

"I'm sorry, Michelle, we'll do the honors here on 958 if you wish."

It took a few more seconds for Michelle to respond. "Yes. And thanks 1729, I know you did your best," was all Michele could manage.

Lisa Mulvany, the mission specialist on Loadstar 1322, transferred over to Loadstar 958 to allow Michele to go over to 1729 to attend the ceremony.

Mike and Logan welcomed Michelle. She was clearly shaken by Matis's sudden death. Logan took her hands, "I'm so sorry, Michelle. I know you and Matis had become good friends. He was a good man."

"Thank you, Logan. It's such a shock."

Logan and Mike had cleared their lab and kitchen areas, which were next to each other. Matis was on a table with a flag draped over his entire body. Logan tapped a button on a display, starting a recording so that Matis' family would have a copy of the service. The service was also being broadcast to the other two Loadstars so all of the five remaining mission crew could participate.

Logan spoke briefly, honoring Matis, then read a few passages from the Bible as Matis was a Christian. Michelle spoke of Matis's bravery and friendship. Logan then ended the service by playing a recording of taps. As the last notes from the bugle ended, they all stood straight and saluted Matis.

Mike stored Matis' body safely for the return home so he could be transferred back to his family on Earth when they got back.

They all shared a solemn meal together, and then Michelle headed back to her Loadstar. They had ten hours before the burn to reposition Anteros.

Logan laid on his bunk in his small room off of the command module, unable to sleep. He lay staring at Matti and

Kira's picture that was on the low ceiling over his bed. Was it worth it? His head told him yes, but the emotional impact of losing Matis was hard to deal with.

Logan recalled meeting Matis' wife, Rebecca, and his two daughters who were around Kira's age. He met them at the pre-launch party for this mission just three months ago. It was scary how fast the repair had ended in disaster. Logan reflected back on the several friends and peers he knew that had been killed. It never got easier.

Hours later, Logan woke up. He felt much better physically. Emotionally, losing Matis still felt horrible. Logan said a short prayer then stood up straight and took a deep breath.

After a breakfast of powdered eggs, the five astronauts aboard the three Loadstars went to work ten million miles away from Earth. They had a two-kilometer wide asteroid to move. It took them two hours to maneuver into the precise positions needed to synchronize their rocket burns to push Anteros. At three symmetrically and strategically spaced points on Anteros, they had buried each of their LoadStar's large grappling arms deep into the surface of Anteros, ready to push the asteroid out of its orbit.

Logan was monitoring the systems. The navigation and firing of the engines were all automated. Suddenly, five seconds before they were set to ignite the rockets, Zia, commander of Loadstar 1322, spoke urgently, "I'm getting a fault light on my navigation panel. Resetting now, hold countdown."

Logan acknowledged, "Holding site A countdown," and Michele responded, "Holding site C countdown."

The reset was disconcerting. There was a window of four hours to fire the rockets and start moving Anteros. Outside of that, they would miss their mission parameters and would have to declare the mission a failure. But they had practiced a false start many times in Houston before the mission and were prepared.

"Cause?" Logan asked.

Zia commed, "Checking. There is a discrepancy between my navigation coordinates and both of your computers. I don't understand. We synced our nav systems two hours ago. I'm running a recalibration routine now to resync our systems." Any deviation between the three systems could unevenly fire the rockets and throw off the direction they pushed Anteros.

Five long minutes passed, then Zia announced, "Confirming reset. Navigation in sync. Restarting countdown."

"Confirm countdown restart," Logan and Michele verified.

This time there were no malfunctions. The rockets fired without incident. It was a beautiful sight, three large rockets all firing at full thrust. The asteroid started, ever so slowly, to move to a path that would intersect Lunar orbit.

Logan took off his headset and looked over at Mike, "That is a beautiful burn. We just captured our asteroid and are taking it home. Wow!"

"It is amazing," Mike smiled but then felt sad, "it's just bittersweet what with Matis and all."

Logan nodded. Success wasn't as sweet as he hoped; it carried a high price.

# The Object

March fifteenth, the ides of March, started like other days in space, with the humming of the systems aboard Loadstar 1729. Logan yawned as he went through his morning system checks. They were only a few hours from the Moon now after a three-month journey back. The time shepherding Anteros on its way to its new lunar orbit hadn't been eventful, which was good, but it gave them way too much time to think about Matis and how he had died.

Logan checked in with the lunar command center, orbiting above the moon, "Lunar Command, this is Loadstar 1729 requesting final approach coordinates."

The command center was twice the old International Space Station size and orbited above the moon between nineteen-hundred and forty-three thousand miles. Space Industries had purchased NASA's old Artemis program's Lunar Gateway station, used in the late 2020s for a moon landing, and enhanced it. It was now named Titan2. It took the first five years of Space Industries' operations to ferry components from earth to build its fleet of six LoadStars. The station consisted of five modules, all powered by a vast solar array. The modules were crew quarters, that currently housed eighteen astronaut workers, a large dock for the six

LoadStars, a life-support and computer systems module, a small manufacturing module, and a command module. All of Space Industries' current operations centered around the station.

"Loadstar, 1729, Titan2. Sending your approach data now. How's it going, Logan?"

"Hey Tim, just us space cowboys and girls, herding our big rock back to the corral."

Tim laughed, "Ok, good to hear. It will be great to have you all back and the corral filled with our big rock. Just a minute, I need to answer an internal flash message."

Tim pressed the flash message light on his console. "Controller, this is Systems. We're experiencing an estimated two-hour downtime on server one and two. Please be advised as this may impact flight operations."

Systems was the module containing all of their communications, power, and computing systems. Tim Haynes ran flight operations and coordinated all of Space Industries LoadStar flights.

"Systems, say again? We have two redundant mission servers. Are we completely down on both?"

"Affirmative. We just had simultaneous failures on all systems and need to do a full reset."

Tim sent a quick message back, "OK, terrible timing, you realize we're coordinating the arrival of our first asteroid, right?"

"Affirmative. We're doing our best, Tim. Standby."

"Please send ten-minute updates. We have inbound in three hours. I am declaring this as an emergency. Get whatever help you need and get it fixed now."

"Affirmative Tim, we're waking up backup personnel now."

The two navigation computers didn't impact the station's communications but eliminated the sophisticated navigation control the station provided to the incoming Anteros mission.

Tim sent another message to the three inbound flight captains pushing Anteros toward the moon, advising them of the potential disruption.

Logan acknowledged the message. He couldn't believe the timing. They spent three months babysitting Anteros back to the moon, and the station picked now to have a system failure.

"Loadstar 1729 to Titan2, what is our alternate plan if they can't get systems rebooted?"

Tim addressed all three LoadStars on the Anteros mission, "Captains, I am having LoadStar 1524 launch. They will act as a backup command center until we are back online."

"Affirmative, we will synchronize with 1524 as alternate once they are in position," Logan confirmed. The other two Loadstar captains acknowledged as well. Logan spent a minute keying the backup connection to 1524 into the Loadstar navigation computer.

Plan B's seemed to be the norm lately. Luckily, he hadn't needed a Plan C yet. Plan C's usually involved rescue vehicles.

Tim noticed a slight deviation from Loadstar 1729's planned trajectory and spoke to Logan, "1729, please note your nav variance and correct."

Logan re-checked his plot.

"Titan2, we're showing we are on the correct course. I'll re-check against 1524's data." Logan flipped his nav signal to the readout from LoadStar 1524, and the plot shifted five degrees.

Mike noticed the change and looked up from his work on the other side of the command module, "I'll run a diagnostic on our equipment. Give me twenty seconds."

Logan checked the mission profile, "We've got two minutes before the critical detach maneuver."

Mike shifted to the central computer console and ran several maintenance programs to check their navigation systems hardware.

"Hardware systems check out ok, it's in the software. Readings don't match. It's the last upgrade. It subtly changed our reference point coordinates." Mike compared several other readings to Titan2's signal. "This isn't random, Logan. Either this bug was lucky, or someone intended this discrepancy."

"Titan2, this is 1729. We're detecting an issue with our nav upgrade and switching to your signal."

Titan2 responded, "Negative, we are still in maintenance on our server. You'll need to go switch to 1524's and we'll guide you through it. All LoadStar's stand by in thirty seconds for your main detach from Antaros."

Logan was sweating. He wasn't sure their detach would be clean with the navigation issues. He switched their navigation reference to the signal from LoadStar 1524.

"Detach in five, four, three, two, one…detach." All Load-Star's released the connections to Anteros and started floating away from the Asteroid. The Asteroid would now enter its correct orbit around the moon.

As they and Anteros drew apart, Logan watched his plot and noticed the deviation again, and tried to manually correct their position.

Just then, Titan2's and 1524's signal cut out.

A sharp jolt slammed Logan against his harness. The craft was thrown into an intense spin toward Anteros. They were three-thousand meters away and closing fast.

A severe shake and a horrible screeching noise started. Logan announced, "Titan2, 1729 declaring an emergency, we're diving into Anteros."

Logan then punched the repeat button on his comm panel to automatically repeat the emergency call while he manually wrestled 1729 so they wouldn't crash into the asteroid. His control stick was shaking wildly. Logan was focused on his radar and using what thrust he had left to slow their descent to a survivable one-point-five meter per second velocity from their original speed of twenty-meters per second. Mike read out altitude, "200 meters …120 …80 …60 …30 …10."

There was a loud crunch when they hit. Then the landing gear buckled. A more deafening bang occurred when the main body of the LoadStar hit the ground, then all was still except the sirens blaring. Logan smacked them off.

Logan turned and looked at Mike. He had hit his head and was bleeding, "Mike!" he shouted. Mike was strapped in his seat but appeared unconscious. "Mike!" Logan shouted again while unbuckling himself. "Mike!"

"Dang," was all Mike could manage as he regained consciousness. He shook his head and looked around. The acrid scent of hot metal and burnt electrical connections hung in the air.

Logan looked over at Mike. "You ok? Do you know what the heck caused that explosion? Can you check the nav log for what happened?"

Mike was slowly regaining his senses. He started scrolling through the log for the time of the explosion, checking performance readings.

"Aft tank shows a strong electrical spike at t-minus-two seconds, right after the maneuver. That led to a sudden increase in pressure and a valve blowing out. I'm checking what would cause that spike now." After a few moments, Mike looked up at Logan. "The upgrade, the damn upgrade. The log shows a new updated electrical routine sent the spike."

The radio rebooted, and Titan2 space station came on, "...9, come in, this is Titan2. 1729, come..."

Logan spoke up, "Titan2, 1729, we had an explosion."

"Thank God you're ok, Logan," was all Tim could manage. "1524 is coming over to rescue you. Are you injured?"

"Mike is bleeding, but he says it isn't serious, and we're still in shock, but we can function."

"What happened? One moment you were correcting your course, and the next, you had spun toward Anteros."

"We have an initial log scan. The last software upgrade sent a severe electrical spike on our aft tank two seconds before the explosion."

"OK, got it. I have a call from security coming in now. I'll let them know what you've found. And Logan," he paused, "just glad you two are alive."

"Amen to that."

Logan signed off and took a deep breath.

Loadstar 1524 touched down two hours later, two-hundred meters from 1729. Fletcher, the commander of 1524, was on the line in seconds.

"Guys, need a lift?" Logan heard chuckling in the background.

Fletcher and his engineer, Juan, could joke through anything.

"Really glad to see you," Logan commed.

"Least we could do, 1729. It's going to be a tight fit over here. No gravity on this rock, so you're going to need to use grappling hooks for safety on your trip over. Take your time,

Logan. I'm sure you're both pretty shaken up."

"Yeah, understatement of the year. We're exiting once we hand crank the airlock, emergency power only over here."

"Do you need assistance? Juan could come over."

"Negative, but Juan, stand by in case we need you."

Juan chimed in, "You got it, Logan. We'll deploy a tether out toward you for thirty feet. I'm suited up near the airlock if you need me."

"Thanks." Logan started shutting down the systems and pulled the computer core to take with him. Mike and Logan suited up. Logan strapped the computer core into a backpack. They went to the airlock, and each packed ten grappling hooks, a hammer, and several bottles of water into their packs."

They entered the airlock, which was just large enough for the two of them. Logan secured the door to the main cabin.

"You ready?" Logan asked Mike who did a last check on his helmet and gloves, then responded, "All secure." Logan clipped a tether onto each suit then checked that they were secured to the craft. He then flipped open the safety lock and cranked the red emergency handle to open the outside door. "Door unsealing in three, two, one."

A hissing sound came as the outer door opened, and their air was vented. They climbed out and did a quick exterior inspection of the LoadStar. The craft loomed above them, and they could see one of the rear engines had exploded.

"Wow," Mike exclaimed in awe. "Glad we survived that. Let me get a picture." Mike walked down the hull and snapped a few shots from a camera that was in his suit.

Logan turned from the damage and looked out over the dimly lit asteroid, "I've never been in such an ancient feeling place. So still." The dust on the ground kicked up when they moved, then ever so slowly settled back. The gravity was so light.

Logan secured a grappling hook into the surface of the asteroid and saw the dust was thick and pristine. It felt weird that they were marring its surface. Logan was startled by this feeling. It brought him back to his childhood in Virginia after a snowstorm. He and his brother would want to go build snow forts, and his sister would beg them not to mess up the new snow. He chuckled to himself. Now he knew how she felt. Good to get on the same page with his sister. Too bad it took him thirty-five years to understand her feelings about the perfectness of the snow. Next time he talked to her, he'd have to tell her about being here. I wonder if she will remember that slice of their childhood?

They secured a new power piton every thirty feet that, when pressed, drove a pin into the rock and kicked up a puff of dust. The pitons buried two inches into the surface and had a short cable to attach the tethers. Logan went ahead of Mike, and they were tied together with another cable. When Logan reached the end of the tether, he would drive a new piton into the rock, then Mike could unhook his tether from the last piton and move forward. In this way, they were able to work their way across to Loadstar 1524. Two hundred yards was a lot when they had to move so carefully. Both men fell silent as they made their way, ensuring each line was secure before moving on.

Clunk. They were half of the way to 1524 when Logan felt his latest piton hit something unyielding. "Mike, I'm hitting something really hard here. The piton won't penetrate."

"Here, let me clear it," Mike offered as he worked his way beside Logan. He took a trowel out of his backpack and leaned down to where Logan's hook was. He cleared a few spades full of dirt.

"Holy crap!" Mike jumped back.

"What?" Logan leaned in to look. "What the heck?" He was looking at a small section of smooth metal buried in the asteroid's surface.

"Probably one of our probes from the initial survey," he stated as he recovered.

They radioed 1524 to report their find and spent a few minutes clearing the area.

"This doesn't look like a probe," Mike concluded as he brushed dirt from the object. After a minute, three square feet was exposed. The metal was as smooth as the original section they had seen. It looked like a box, all of it the same shiny silver color.

"Is that a handle?" Logan bent down to look at the surface closer. "Looks like marks and a divot a few inches long in the metal."

Mike was sending a live video to Titan2 via the LoadStar 1524's communication link.

"Guys, please don't try and open that," Tim ordered from control, where several engineers and administrators were monitoring the discovery. The engineers were talking excitedly in the background.

Tim went on, "There is no record of any craft landing or losing any debris at that location of Anteros. Can you uncover the whole object?"

Logan and Mike checked their oxygen tank levels.

"Fletcher, we have another two hours of oxygen. We can work here for thirty minutes, but then we must get to 1524."

Fletcher commed, "Ok, we're standing by," and then added,

"But if little green men start firing ray-guns, we're outta here."

Tim responded, "Can it, Fletcher. Logan, that's affirmative, work on the object for thirty, then get out of there."

Logan left Mike to uncover the object to explore something twenty feet away that glittered in the side of his vision. When he got to the spot, he reached down and used his shovel. He hit something else and pried another, smaller object out of the surface. It was made of solid glass, a tube four inches long with a marble secured to the top.

"Hey, look at this," Logan called out and lifted the tube so Mike could see.

Mike was focused on uncovering the bottom of the first object and didn't look up. "Logan," Mike called, "can you give me a hand lifting this? I've got enough exposure to get a hold on it."

Logan shoved the small object he had found in his pant leg pocket, zipped it in, then shuffled over to Mike to help him.

When they dug the box out, Mike noticed marks on the box, "There are weird marks etched into the metal. Nothing I've ever seen before. It might be writing, not sure."

Logan leaned in and blinked twice. The marks were slowly scrolling in a pattern, stopping every few seconds, then repeating.

"I must be seeing things. It reminds me of an ancient script, but my eyes must be having a problem. I could swear it's moving." A cold shiver went down his spine.

"Titan2, you seeing this?" Mike shifted the small camera so they could see the marks.

"Affirmative Mike. Paul Manning is on a delayed signal from earth but just told us to have you leave the box and come back. We'll have another Loadstar land and secure the box."

Logan looked over at Mike, who shrugged, "Let's get back. We've done what we can here. This box isn't going anywhere." They resumed their careful walk over to Loadstar 1524.

When they were thirty feet from 1524, Mike commed, "Fletcher, we're almost to your tether."

Juan was waving through the airlock window, "I have a visual on you. I'm ready to open up and get you guys aboard."

"We gotcha covered, you alien artifact finders, you," Fletcher added. Logan chuckled, rolled his eyes, and secured the next grappling hook on the surface of the asteroid. In another thirty minutes, they made it to 1524's airlock. Juan opened it. There was a hiss of escaping air. Mike climbed in first. Logan handed him the backpacks and climbed in. Sitting in the airlock as it cycled was a huge relief. Going through the emergency was stressful, but then finding possibly alien artifacts was intensely exciting and draining at the same time.

When Mike and Logan were both aboard, Juan commed, "Ok, Fletch, you can lift-off. We're all aboard, safe and sound."

# Shock

*Three weeks later, Houston, Texas*

The lights were blindingly bright at the press conference in The NASA briefing room in Houston. Logan squinted from his chair, the lights right in his eyes, making him feel more dazed than he already was. Surreal was the word that came to mind when he thought about the last three weeks. This was the first time they were officially announcing the discovery on Anteros to the world. Logan and Mike stepped to the podium with Paul Manning, the head of Space Industries, Jessica Watkins, the current NASA director, and Michael Zatz, a Colonel in the United Nations Space Force.

To say the room was crowded was an understatement. Logan looked out over all of the lights and cameras. He could easily imagine over two-hundred reporters and VIPs were present. He recognized Senator Richard Barrister in the front row, who was a big supporter of Space Industries.

The room was a typical NASA briefing room, with bland tile floors and bright white LED panels. No windows. After being transferred back down to NASA headquarters on Earth, they were subjected to constant 'debriefings' which Mike correctly called interrogations. Now the thought of the press conference going out to billions of people worldwide made Logan feel humble and quiet. This was a big deal.

Jessica Watkins read a prepared statement.

"Ladies and Gentleman, the UN, NASA, and Space Industries have a joint announcement."

Logan was suddenly nervous. This was about to become the event of the century, and he hadn't come to grips with that.

Paul continued, "On March fifteenth, one of Space Industries' Loadstar crews," Paul nodded to Logan and Mike, "the crew before you, after an emergency landing on the Anteros asteroid discovered an object we have now determined is not of human origin."

Paul pulled back a curtain. There, within an atmospherically controlled clear Perspex box, was the object that Logan and Mike found on Anteros. Power was applied. A purple glow appeared around the object. This evoked an immediate collective gasp from the audience.

Reporters started shouting questions. Jessica moved over for Paul to read the next part of the announcement. He stepped to the podium and dramatically raised his hand for them to wait.

"Our scientists and those from NASA and the UN's National Science Council examined the box once it was brought securely to Houston. We have made this determination: the material used to construct the box is unknown and not manufactured anywhere on earth. The power generation of the box before you is radically different and in advance of any currently known power source or generating method. These facts and the extreme location of the box on Anteros supports the radical conclusion we have put forward."

Paul paused for effect. "Further, upon opening the box, all of the contents are of unknown or *alien* technology and construction." The presentation slides changed to show black tubes that were emitting a powerful orange glow from the ends.

The word alien did it. Reporters were furiously trying to ask questions.

Paul continued, "We'll entertain questions in a minute. The high power glow you see was achieved when we applied a 240-volt power source to the ridges on the far end of the box. We measured power output from the box at one megawatt, a substantial amount of generated energy from such a compact device. There does not appear to be any harmful radiation or other outputs detected, as was our initial concern. Given such a significant find, our intention is to study and possibly reverse-engineer these devices as soon as possible. We will now answer your questions."

Paul pointed to the well-known reporter, Katherine Winters, from the New York Times.

"Who owns the technology and, if it is Space Industries, do you intend on sharing the technology?" she asked.

Michael from the UN stepped forward and cleared his throat.

"Ownership has not been determined, but both the United Nations, NASA, and Space Industries have put forward legal briefs claiming ownership. This will be resolved soon for obvious reasons. Right now, all three groups are sharing scientific research on the object and what it contained."

Katherine followed up, "Shouldn't the technology belong to all of mankind, given the nature of the find?"

Paul responded, "We'll have to let the courts figure that out."

Paul pointed to the Boston Globe's reporter.

"Logan, what went through your mind when you first saw the object?"

Logan came forward. "I thought at first it must have been debris from a probe, but after we determined that wasn't possible, I began to think it must be alien. There really are no other options given that we found it on an asteroid millions of miles from Earth. I'm still coming to grips with that conclusion."

"As we all are," Paul added with nods from most in the audience.

Mac Easter, the International News Network's science editor, was next.

"You mentioned it registered a one-megawatt output. Have you tried increasing the input power to the object?"

Paul looked nervously over at Michael, who took the question, "We have not finished our complete analysis of the object, which is complex, as you might imagine. So, we aren't prepared to release detailed technical findings yet. We will release the findings when our science team is finished, and they are substantiated by multiple scientific sources."

Logan thought Michael had been a lawyer before going into the military. He and Mike happened to be present when the scientists applied a 480-volt charge to the box. The meters on the output blew up. They practically brought the lab down on top of everyone. Logan noticed the readout top out at twenty megawatts before it blew, so he knew they were sitting on top of a significant find that could change the course of the world's energy industry if they could replicate the technology.

Caroline Maddox from Scientific American asked, "You mentioned you're trying to reverse engineer what you have found. Have you been able to understand any of the conceptual workings of the box and how it generates power, or what source that power comes from?"

Paul stepped forward.

"Not yet, but we are relocating the box after this press conference to a lab in Nevada to continue research."

This caused a whole new round of shouting reporters, given that any lab in Nevada was automatically linked to Area 51 and aliens. Paul raised his hands and smiled, anticipating the question. "No, it is not going to Area 51, in case you were wondering."

The press conference lasted another ten minutes. Technicians started loading 'The Object' into a lead-lined safe that was then loaded onto a helicopter for the trip to Nevada. Logan had never seen so much security. Afterward, he went straight to his home in Portsmouth, New Hampshire. After six months in space and three weeks being questioned about the artifact, Logan was on a one-week vacation. He wanted to spend every minute with his family before having to report back to Space Industries' headquarters.

# And Awe

*Year: 2038*
  *Earth Population: 9,902,224,665*
  *Population off-earth in Solar System: 235*
  *Temperature increase: +3.2°F Yearly population decrease due to Global Burn: 350,000*

"We find this discovery so enthralling. But whoa! Scary. Were you scared all alone on that dark asteroid, once you figured out the artifact must be alien?" Rory Pintar asked Logan, his live internet audience fascinated with the discussion.

"So, we're up there, we were shaken up from the accident, Mike was still bleeding, and we started uncovering this silver box. When you're in survival mode, the last thing you expect to find is an alien artifact, right?" His audience laughed. "So we were not scared at the time. Once we got back to earth and had time to reflect, it was hard. I mean, we were prepared to deal with accidents but world-changing discoveries? Not so much."

Rory turned to his audience, "There you have it, folks. Logan Conover, astronaut and the first human to discover an alien artifact. Thanks for coming on, Logan. We appreciate your calm approach to life in the face of terrifying events."

The show ended, and the production crew starting packing up.

Rory turned back to Logan, "Thanks for coming in. They loved you. Your boss, Paul Manning, was a guest a week ago. He's all official, just couldn't loosen up, so we appreciate you just being human and telling us a good story."

Logan had heard similar comments on other shows. He wished Paul could relax. Logan enjoyed the spotlight and spent the three months after the artifact announcement traveling from one news or talk show to another. His enthusiasm was contagious. Audiences loved his retelling of the discovery.

News shows asked Paul to appear for two weeks after the incident, but Logan became the star and was still popular. Logan sensed Paul resented his success, but he didn't know how to change that. Space Industries was the ultimate benefactor, so he imagined Paul was basking in the company's success even if he didn't personally get recognized.

*Three months later, Secret NASA Base, Nevada*

Paul Manning swiftly created a special research team to study The Object for commercial benefit. The team was led by Will Bonalado, Logan's friend from the Academy.

Will and his team worked in a secluded area in Nevada's desert. Their lab was in an old research hanger purchased by NASA from the military. Logan walked into the hanger and looked around. Many researchers were working on various aspects of the project. The main focus was in the middle of the hanger, where The Object was surrounded by a ring of cameras, recording every experiment done from ten different angles.

After his talk show appearances, Logan switched from being a pilot on the asteroid team to a logistics resupply pilot. He loved blasting off in big rockets from Kennedy space station in Florida to the moon station. In between shuttle flights, Logan was able to spend more time at home with his family. Logan had a few days between trips and decided to pilot a resupply ship to Will's research site to visit his friend and check out what was going on with the artifact.

Logan found Will, "Hey, good to see you, buddy!"

Will was surprised, "Great to see you too. Hey, check this out. This current experiment, which just started, measures a new metal alloy we fabricated to see if it will conduct quantum electricity. We determined that the box operates on quantum principles, so we need to replicate the material exactly."

"Do you know how it works?" Logan asked.

"We are starting to! The Object is a quantum conductor that is entangled with a quantum energy transmitter somewhere else. Amazingly, all this device has to do is conduct electricity that is generated at the other end. The trick is to entangle our receiver with the transmitter. It's like we have to tune the conductor to listen on just the right radio station over a practically infinite number of frequencies. But since we have a working conductor, we can use it to tune other conductors to the same frequency. If we can replicate the entanglement, we should be able to pull power out of our material and make any number of new generators, all pulling power from the same quantum source."

Will pushed the start button on his computer, and an intricate program started adjusting the electrical current of the conductive metal. Hydrogen gas was used to tune or change the metal's frequency in tiny increments, testing each time for results. Hundreds of tests were run per minute. Suddenly the output meter jumped to ten-thousand volts for a microsecond and then back to zero.

"Repeat that exact frequency," Will instructed his technicians.

"Where does the power come from?" Logan asked.

"Ah, the question of the millennium. From another similarly tuned quantum source. Probably in our solar system, although we don't really know. Our best guess is that whoever put these samples on Anteros put a quantum power source in our sun. It's really the only place to get practically unlimited power like this device seems to transfer."

"So, forget solar panels and conversion, just go to the source. Instantly transfer it to the place of need. Sweet."

"Yeah, it's elegant and not complex, at least on the user end. We just have to get the quantum material tuned correctly. It's beyond sensitive. We'll get there soon. Having a working example means it's possible. Imagine if Thomas Edison was given a working light bulb to invent with. It takes the fun out of it."

"Amazing, what is the upper limit? Could we have ten-thousand of these around the world?"

"We just don't know, and I'm not sure we will know. My guess is we'll make thousands, then someday we'll find out the hard way what the upper limit is. Then we'll have to limit the usage. As simple as they are, Paul wants to meter every single watt of output and charge like an electric company. It will take a while to manufacture the quantum material, though. That part isn't easy."

Logan told Will, "I'm taking a large load up on the next

flight. With the start of the space station project, I'll be making a couple of regular runs a week. Let me know if I can do anything for you, ok?"

With all of the public support to develop space due to the alien artifact, Space Industries secured a contract to start their ultimate goal, a vast space station. A station that would hold up to a million residents would be the anchor for a new space elevator. He was thrilled to be a part of it.

Will responded by singing a few bars of Rocketman from Elton John, teasing his friend. Will knew about every 1970s and 1980s rock-n-roll song there was.

Logan chimed right in and finished with Will. He knew the lyrics by heart too.

"How's Kira doing?"

"She doesn't like mom and dad being gone so much. We're thinking of taking her up with us when the station gets more complete. Probably in about ten months. Hopefully, she can last that long with her Aunt. She stays with her a lot and loves her, but it's not the same, you know? I'll say hi for you." Logan squeezed Will's arm affectionately, "Take care, buddy."

Will smiled, grasped Logan's arm, and then walked back to where his technicians were discussing the latest test.

*Ten months later, ESS One, Earth Orbit*

Logan, Matti, and Kira were carrying lots of bags to the rocket. The ESS station's outer ring was finished, and they were moving up to the station. Logan was recently promoted to the commander of all construction support craft in space, so they would all live in space. He supervised twenty other pilots.

"Wow, dad, that is a big rocket. I had no idea you flew these things. I mean, I knew you did, but wow, it's huge." Kira stopped to look up at the rocket. She was moving away from her friends to space. It was a lot for a nine-year-old to take in.

"It's ok, honey, hundreds of people now go to space every month. This rocket holds twenty-five people, and your dad flies every week. So, sit back and enjoy. We'll be at our new home in no time at all. You have a whole week off before attending school."

"Ok, I'll try. I commed Sam today. He's going up too, did you know?"

"I heard he'll be there in a few weeks, right?"

Logan chimed in, "Mike is so happy he and Marisa are coming up. We'll all get together. It'll be like old times." Marisa attended the Academy class after Mike, Logan, Will, and Matti. Mike and she dated and married up in space. The first orbital romance.

"Here we are. You two strap in. I'm up front, co-pilot for this flight."

"Ah, dad, you aren't staying with us?"

"Sorry, Kira, but I'll be thirty feet away if you need me. I'll check in on the radio with you."

"Ok, cool." Kira still wished her dad could stay with her, but she understood he was needed to fly the rocket.

The rocket blasted off with its usual intense g-force. Nothing like the old Apollo missions since new technology allowed a less severe launch, but you still knew you were launching into space. Matti had gone up several times, not as much as Logan, of course, but she knew what to expect. On lift-off, Kira's eyes grew huge, but not from fear. She was thrilled! Matti smiled, grateful Kira was taking it so well.

\* \* \*

The growth of Space Industries was exponential. They purchased Lockheed Martin and then purchased Boeing Space Corporation, making Space Industries the first trillion-dollar space company. Airbus changed its name to SpaceBus and then jumped into the space race as well.

Paul Manning followed the wave of successes and was now the head of the enormous Space Industries conglomerate. He was in charge of four-hundred-and-fifty engineers and pilots on the newly constructed Earth Space Station One, or ESS One, a joint Space Industries, Spacebus, and Chinese effort.

At the heart of ESS One was a much larger version of The Object, which was now named Quantum-Power Generators or QPGs for short. Twenty QPGs were on the station, providing power to all aspects, including the construction bots that 3D printed new sections of the station every day. The end goal was a station that could hold one million people, an enormous challenge. Twenty more ESS stations were planned, with every major country on earth planning to expand into Earth orbit. ESS One, though, was unique and was the only station jointly owned by the US, China, Japan, India, Russia, and the European Union.

The successful cooperation between global rivals surprised everyone. It was made possible because the six countries' space agencies were used to cooperating when they worked together on ISS, the International Space Station, in the early 2000s. But now, it seemed everyone was jockeying to build political power by committing to build out a space station of their own. A new territorial contest was beginning.

Logan, Matti, and Kira had been on ESS One for ten months

now. Now ten years old, Kira was one of the initial children to attend the first permanent school in space, the ESS One Jimmy Carter Academy. The family's apartment was on the outer ring. They could see Earth every rotation, and it was amazing, better than any photo. Seeing Earth in all of its blue and white glory always inspired them during their hectic workdays.

Having settled in, their routine was now set. Matti dropped Kira off at the school on the outer ring, not too far from their apartment. She then took a lift inward to the inner ring, the work ring. Matti was running a briefing for new employees, one of her duties as a senior future logistics analyst. Once all the new recruits were settled, she started.

"Good morning, my name is Matti Conover. I'm going to give you an all-morning briefing on the mission and status of ESS One. It should give you a clear goal of why we're all here, which you can use as context when you start your training over the next few days in your specialty areas."

She went around the room, and the recruits introduced themselves. Many were construction workers, but a few were assigned to future logistics, and she encouraged them to see her 'for the inside scoop' after the meeting. Matti started the main briefing with an overview of the mission and then started reviewing the current status with a 3D projection of the construction schedule.

"As you can see, we are on track for completion of ESS One by December 2044, four years from now. When complete, the bigger picture is that the ESS One effort will have perfected a workable design for massive space stations, hold one-million people each, and complete infrastructure to build more stations. Specifically, we are building two large sites in orbit around the moon, a materials processing station and a 3D-printer manufacturing site that can create anything, including 3D-printing robots that manufacture the space station girders and coverings.

"These sites will support the build-out of our nineteen new ESS stations that will be starting, two at a time, early next year with a finish date of 2065, twenty years from now. This is an aggressive schedule, but one we can meet with the infrastructure build-out we've done and what we've learned from ESS One."

At this point, she paused, and Mary Ellison, a new robotic specialist asked, "It will take almost ten years to build ESS One, how can we possibly build nineteen in just over twice the time?"

Matti smiled and responded, "Exponential learning curves. With our new power sources, space-based infrastructure investments, and especially our robotics and 3D printing advances, we have enabled a radical decrease in construction times. But the biggest reason is that we don't have to bring anything up from Earth except people. This reduces costs and time astronomically."

"Amazing," she replied, clearly excited about the possibilities awaiting her in the robotics area.

Yollin Vischaky, a construction specialist, spoke up, "But we still need lots more people, and when we finish, how can we even bring twenty million people up to space in twenty years? I think it would take twenty years to come up as we did on rockets given the launch facilities we have."

Matti smiled again; she was always impressed with the intelligence of the newcomers.

"Yollin has asked a most perceptive question. The answer is

the Space Elevator. Few realize how important the Elevator is to our plans and how fast we intend to build it. Within two years, the elevator, mankind's largest and greatest engineering feat, even compared to all these stations, should be complete."

As Matti continued to explain all of the projects, Colonel Logan Conover was in a critical meeting of his own in the pilot's ready room. "Gentleman and ladies, the space elevator is our most critical project. It will enable us to bring personnel and equipment up to the station economically and send critical resources down to the Earth. It will be anchored by this station. As you know, we are in a geostationary orbit above Singapore. Who can tell me why they need pilots to help with the space elevator?"

Jack Kimble, a hot-shot pilot Logan knew since his days of ferrying near-earth asteroids with the Loadstars, offered, "Because we need to catch all the construction geeks who fall off of it into space?"

Everyone snickered. There had been more than one rescue mission performed over the last two years during the construction of ESS One when the workers floated off into space, usually because they hadn't been adequately tethered. There had also been ten deaths due to accidents and impacts from space debris.

"No. Anyone else?"

"We need to fly the cable down to earth?"

"Close, we get to gently move a five-hundred-meter graphite-rich asteroid directly over ESS One that will be used by huge 3-D printers to produce a forty-thousand-mile graphene cable that will be dropped down to earth and be secured to the ocean floor."

This got the other pilot's attention. "So, boss, you want us to position a five-hundred-meter asteroid this far," Yang Li held two fingers up close together, "from the Earth, without, of course, hitting the planet and killing everyone."

"Precisely, think of the asteroid as an enormous satellite we need to put into orbit. We have the next two months to get it done." Logan declared.

Yang nodded thoughtfully and looked like he was happy to have the challenge. They all started putting their heads together, devising safety procedures and strategies to do the task. Never been done before was the new normal.

# The Wrath of Ida

*Year: 2042 +3.3°F*
  *Earth Population: 9,962,999,625*
  *Population off-earth in Solar System: 9045*
  *Yearly population decrease due to Global Burn: 850,000*

Ida was a monster storm that no one was ready for. Ranked a category seven hurricane with sustained winds of two-hundred-thirty miles-per-hour, it was essentially a five-hundred-mile-wide F4 tornado.

The United States was evacuating half of the East Coast with little hope of moving the fifty-four million inhabitants in its path far enough inland to prevent catastrophic death tolls. The storm surge was forecast to be a staggering fifty-two feet, enough to roll over and wipe out every structure in its path for miles inland, at least the buildings that the winds didn't blow away first.

Mag Soren was the head of the Washington DC FEMA operations center. She was currently shouting into two phones at once.

"Sir, I don't care if you can't cope with five million new residents," she shouted at the governor of West Virginia, Bud McCaulic. "In case you hadn't noticed, Virginia is going to

71

be your new beachfront in 72 hours. You're getting everyone, whether you like it or not. So you need to mobilize not just your national guard but your entire population!"

Mag was damned if this storm was going to wipe out Washington D.C., but there was little she could do. A category seven hurricane just wasn't something anyone thought possible.

"Yes, you heard me, all of DC is to be evacuated. Every office building, the White House, Capitol, everything, in 48 hours." She was able to communicate better with Richard Stevens, the new Joint Chief of Staff of the US military. The military was made for this sort of thing and already mobilized D.C. using twelve thousand buses and trucks. It wouldn't nearly be enough to get every person and critical document out.

When the hurricane hit, the inhabitants of ESS One looked down on Earth from space, knowing that devastation was taking place on the East Coast of America. A feeling of change and a new mission settled on those working at the space station, a seriousness of purpose in contributing to helping save mankind from increased devastation due to the *Global Burn*. Could more people be saved by going to space?

After the hurricane, the U.S. Congress, Supreme Court, and the White House were temporarily relocated to Philadelphia. The Congress was first established in Philadelphia and resided there until 1800 when it moved to Washington, D.C., so that felt appropriate to everyone. The Capital in D.C. was covered in thirty feet of water. The mall in D.C. looked like the bottom of the ocean with mud as deep as eight feet. The White House was buried in the muck.

When the death toll reached ten-thousand people, everyone knew fixing the Global Burn was taking on new urgency. The symbolism of a destroyed Washington galvanized congressmen and leaders in the U.S. like never before. The world was grateful they started taking action. Some leaders turned to the possibility of escaping to space.

ESS One was the center of the movement to get to space, and a conference call with ESS One had been set up to explore the possibility of expanding its goals.

"We have always known that the effects of global warming were coming. That is why we have so much urgency to build the space economy, and in establishing this station," Paul Manning was saying to the group of corporation chairmen and government officials on the strategic conference call. "We are breaking records for the pace and safety of the construction. Billions of dollars are being well spent. But we are still pioneers. In twenty years, we will, ambitiously, have twenty ESS stations finished and be able to host a productive population of twenty million, which is a great goal, one we should be proud of."

At this point, the president of the Save the Earth Foundation, Sir Reginald Temple, shook his head then made his appeal to the group.

"Recent events, as all politicians and those with the public ear can attest, have forced upon us a new urgency for solutions to humanity's problems. While I realize Paul's group is breaking records and achieving miracles with the progress in space, we are at nothing less than a crossroads for humanity's survival. Miracles are going to have to be the new normal. This is no longer a theory or some future graph showing the dire effects of the *Global Burn*. People are dying by the tens of thousands.

"While the original ESS mission was economical and scientific, we must take advantage of the wonderful breakthroughs

73

Paul Manning and his crew are making to expand the mission to a global effort. We need a life preserver. A migration into space, not a science outpost, or an escape resort for the rich! If we do not act, well, chaos will mark the beginning of the hell we receive from a revolting population, one that no longer can survive in our world. Gentleman and ladies, we are one generation away from global destruction. So we need to be thinking bigger."

Matti marveled at the bold words. She was also excited by them. Several years ago, the speaker would not even have voiced such viewpoints, but current events were forcing industrialists and investors into action to help humanity. A twenty-percent drop in the stock market also put added pressure on many. No one could argue with the devastation of the images seen. After Ida and the loss of ten-thousand people, tens of millions of people joined Save the Earth Foundation. They were demanding action.

Paul spoke up, "Space may become a lifesaver for humanity, eventually, but we are already breaking construction records to get to twenty million in space. We can accommodate millions, but it will be one-hundred years, another order of magnitude of development, before humanity will be able to expand its billions into space. And," he added with a warning tone, "if you push us any harder, it may all fail."

"That is not the answer we are looking for," Temple stated, "you're the innovation folks, innovate! Millions of lives depend on it. And think beyond just NASA and Space Industries. We need many more people doing what you're doing. I'd request that your future logistics team pull all necessary resources together to envision a radical increase. In *twenty* years, not a hundred, we need one billion people brought to space."

Most of Space Industries personnel looked around with an incredulous expression. One billion?! Their expressions said it all: impossible! But Sir Reginald went on.

"We are literally on fire, and may God help us all when all the people start running for the exits. It will not be pretty."

The chairman of the committee closed the session, scheduling the next meeting for later that week.

Paul closed his eyes to try and calm himself before his next meeting. The ESS project was hugely successful and, yet, he never thought success would be so complicated.

He called over to Matti, "You better ramp up your team. I think that request Sir Reginald made will get approved by the President given the current political environment to find a solution."

Matti observed, "Why does it take a catastrophe for people to wake up? They knew back in 2020 this was going to happen by 2050."

"Human nature, Matti. We just are linear thinkers, and short-sighted at that. If something doesn't keep us from getting to work tomorrow or paying our mortgage payment, we just don't care."

# This Changes Everything

It was quiet down in the ESS pilot's briefing room. Logan was finishing his flight report in his office, which was right off of the briefing area. A private office was a perk of being the squadron commander. He typed for a few minutes; the lights dim as he liked them. The light felt more like what he was used to in his cockpit.

Logan's office was a mess, the accumulation of two years of working non-stop without enough time to organize himself properly. Matti joked his office was really a shed, and it looked like one too. Logan sent his report and leaned back in his chair, taking a minute to calm his thoughts from the day.

Bing! Another message. Logan glanced over it. A request from a reporter from BNN to talk about his alien artifact discovery. Those didn't come in too much anymore. Paul liked him to grant the interviews as it gave Space Industries more publicity. Like it needed more. Logan reread the request. The reporter wanted to do a step-by-step walk-through of his discovery and wanted Logan to wear the suit he had worn when the discovery took place. Wow. That was new. No one had wanted to go that far before.

Logan got up and dug through his closet. He had never opened the box with his uniform from that day. It was sealed by technicians and sent to him. He found it on his bottom shelf labeled *Cpt. Logan Conover, Anteros Mission, Personal effects.* He broke the seal and shook out the uniform. Memories and emotions of the day came back to him in full force. It had been the most traumatic mission he had ever been on. The fear of the crash landing came back for a moment, and sweat began to form on his forehead. He shook his head to clear it. It was years ago, he reminded himself, and took a deep breath. The tightness in his chest took a moment to loosen. He tried the uniform on and wasn't surprised when he couldn't zip up the front of the suit. It would have to do.

He noticed a bulge in his leg pocket and unzipped it. Reaching down, he pulled out a glass tube. Hmm. Logan held the glass tube up. There was a marble attached to the top. Suddenly, he froze. Could it be? Oh my gosh. He remembered now. He had put this object in his pocket when he was on the surface of Anteros and totally forgot about it. Holy glass tube alien artifacts! He was in so much trouble.

Logan lifted the tube up and detached the marble from its position on top. It looked like it was the tube's size, and he dropped the glass marble through the tube.

Odd. It didn't fall through immediately but took a few seconds to emerge from the bottom. He looked down the tube, and it was empty. He tried dropping it again and counted one-thousand-one, one-thousand two, one-thousand three before the glass ball came out of the end. Then he dropped the marble outside of the tube into his hand and counted one-thousand one. How strange.

This was something he knew Will would want to see and left his office with the tube, tossing the marble up and down with his hand as he walked to Will's lab.

Will Bonalado had finished the fundamental physics research needed on the power generators, turned it over to the manufacturing folks, and now managed ESS One's materials lab. Will received a massive bonus for his work on the generator, but money never meant much to him, so he had returned to what he loved, research and innovation in the quiet of space.

"Hey, Colonel, good to see you!" Will exclaimed when Logan walked in. He hadn't seen his old friend in months. "What can I do for you? Or is this a social call, and you're going to invite me to dinner with you and Matti so we can catch up on old times?"

Logan laughed.

"Wow, I'd love that. How long has it been since any of us has have gotten together? We'll call you and do it," Logan promised, "but..."

"I know you have something for me to do, and no one else can figure it out."

"Exactly," Logan showed will the glass tube, how it was hollow. He positioned the glass marble above it with a lot of fanfare. When Will was ready, he dropped the marble over the open end of the tube. Will cocked his head to the side in a puzzled look when it took a full three seconds for the ball to fall out the other end.

"Hmm. Let me do that."

He took the tube and looked through it, then took a metal rod from a table, and tapped the tube, looked through it again, then dropped the marble himself. It still took three seconds for the ball to come out.

"Holy crap! Where the heck did it go? Logan?"

Logan knew he was asking where the heck did he get this

tube. Having worked together for a long time, they could communicate short-hand speech.

"So, you know when Mike and I found The Object."

Will's eyes bugged out.

"You didn't."

"Well…"

"Ok, let me run some tests. It's fascinating." Will said

Logan replied with a relieved tone, "Thanks, Will."

Two weeks later, Matti and Logan went to the lab after Will casually left a note for them to stop by. Will was engrossed at a long table with all sorts of instruments. The glass tube was suspended in the middle. Will beckoned them over. He turned toward his monitor and motioned with his hand to replay a vid.

"This is exciting stuff. Watch this."

The vid was black for fifteen seconds and then showed a landscape with some sort of shrubbery. Then it was black again.

"And?" Logan queried, but Matti got it.

"Camera on the marble?" Matti knew the short-hand too.

Will smiled, "Weird?"

"Totally," Logan admitted. "Where?"

Will replayed the vid. This time they could make out a red sun on the horizon but dimmer than usual.

"No!"

"Yeah, I think so."

"Weirder and weirder. Is it real?"

"I thought the same thing, so I sent a small puff of air out of the camera, see it?"

They reviewed the video a third time and saw the sand move when the puff occurred. "Wow!" Matti mouthed.

Logan tossed the marble up and down in his hand, "Can you replicate any of this, maybe bigger?"

"I'm going to try."

"Bring Carol over Friday at seven, OK? We can talk over dinner." Will nodded and went back to his work.

Logan and Matti left the lab, looking over at each other with a *wow, this is really crazy. I wonder where this is going* look.

By Friday's dinner, Will was full of excitement. They knew he had found out more about The Tube. Kira was out with friends trying to create a zoo for the station.

Matti opened the door, and Carol, Will's wife came in. Carol had been Matti's friend from the Academy.

"Matti!" Carol gave Matti a hug then hugged Logan as well. Will came in next and gave Matti a small bottle of their favorite drink, Berry Blast, an energy drink they used to buy by the crate while studying at the academy.

Logan was amazed, "How did you get these up here?"

"Special order," Will winked.

They settled into the tiny but neat living room with Berry Blast in glasses. Will jumped right in. "I was able to determine a bit of how The Tube works!"

Logan smiled, "I knew you could."

"It uses the same source of power as The Object, so it pulls power directly from the sun. At least, that is my best theory so far. Both devices transfer energy using a quantum bridge. I think that whoever left The Object on that asteroid also put a matching probe in our sun, both tuned to the same 'energy frequency.' The Tube, I am guessing, is tuned to a similar Tube on a 'transfer' frequency so that, essentially, there is no distance between the two quantum objects and a transfer can occur. But it's one thing to pass energy over a quantum gate and another to move complex objects."

"Wow," Matti commented, "this is so sci-fi and crazy. Any idea if we could make the quantum transfer than that ball?"

"That is the thing." Will smiled. "The energy needed should increase as a power of three in ratio to the volume. But it's not that easy. There is a ton of circuitry in that tube. It only looks transparent, but it's a whole new level of technology than the power generator. It also relies on another matching quantum device at the target, which we can't get to or determine how big it is or where it is."

That led Logan to the question he had been waiting to ask. "Where is the target quantum location of this small device?"

Will got a massive smile on his face and looked at both Logan and Matti, "Well, another star, another planet, of course."

\* \* \*

Matti sat at her desk, running through the various proposals to meet the new goal of supporting one billion people in space in the timeframe before the earth couldn't sustain them. In other words, before they all died because of the short-sightedness of her parents' generation, she thought glumly. The proposals assumed a limit on the cost of ten percent of GGP, gross global productive capacity.

She tossed the various plans from her team around the digital table, keeping the most promising three in front of her. The projects focused on construction since they figured they would need to build several more space elevators to get everyone up to space. So, the space elevator part of the proposal was pretty firm at two to three trillion dollars.

*Option 1: Artificial Moons*

The artificial moon proposal envisioned twenty spheres that would contain three internal concentric rings. The pro of this design was to maximize living space and population per habitat. These were estimated to be fifty million people per twenty-mile diameter sphere or the size and density of a modern-day New York or Shanghai. One-gee of gravity could be achieved with a slow spin around the core, which wouldn't have any gravity. The center would contain services such as power, water, and transportation facilities. Food would be grown throughout the super cities. The disadvantage of these super cities was also the advantage—super population density. It was cheaper, but everyone would be living in a city denser than any on Earth today. Matti wondered if this solution was as bad as the dislocation and disruption the *Global Burn* itself would impose.

*Option 2: Populate the Moon*

The moon's surface area is not even one percent of the Earth's, but there are no oceans. By virtually covering the entire moon with living facilities, it could hold one billion people. There were lots of pros to this design, Matti thought, including a lot less construction since the fundamental structure was the moon itself instead of a completely artificial structure. Having one-sixth gravity was the downside. People would mostly have to live underground. Matti imagined a whole new generation of eight-foot-tall thin humans and wondered if the social effects would be too radical.

*Option 3: The Ring*

The Ring was a space station one mile in width that wrapped

around the entire earth. It would be so spacious that it could accommodate one billion people in a single continuous structure. It was the best solution for gravity as the ring's slow turning at the same rotational period as the Earth allowed for one-gee gravity and great sight-seeing. It would handle the social elements and living conditions better than any design and was extensible as new one-mile rings could hold additional population. Matti sighed. It was the most expensive design and would take the longest to build—one hundred years for the full ring, although habitable parts could be finished in twenty years.

The Ring was Matti's favorite design, but she wondered if she liked it because it was right out of her favorite science-fiction book, *Ringworld* by Larry Niven.

The one option Matti thought of but hadn't developed was the underground option. Basically, it focused resources on building an earth-based city enclosed and underground that would isolate mankind from their toxic environment. She already heard of many small groups on Earth building large doomsday bunkers, many that could hold hundreds of people. She discounted the idea, though, knowing that Space Industries did not want to hear about a solution involving only ground-based resources. In essence, Space Industries was the *space-based solutions company,* as their advertising always pointed out.

At dinner that night, she talked to Logan about her options. Logan whistled at the magnitude of the Ring concept. After thinking about it, Logan felt taking people to the moon was the most practical and least risky option. Something about having soil under your feet was comforting.

Logan cocked his head and then told Matti, "You know I've been thinking about the numbers, and it isn't adding up. It's not just hard technically to house a billion people in space. I think it's a whole new magnitude of a problem *getting* one billion people to space."

"I get we could never do it with rockets, but we have the space elevators. Just add more elevator cars!" Matti protested.

Logan went over to the screen on their living-room wall and flicked the control that made it a white-board. He then scribbled numbers on the board. "Ok, rockets are out. Even if we built and launched ten-thousand rockets per year, we could only get, say, two hundred people on each for a total of one or two-million per year. No one is going to launch a hundred-thousand rockets. So, rockets are definitely out."

He crossed out his rocket math that was on the whiteboard. "Now, let's assume we get another couple of trillion dollars and can build three more space elevators. With three space elevators, each lifting two-thousand people per day, we get," Logan did the math and gave Matti a look, "only two-million people per year. See, it doesn't add up. Even with twenty space-elevators, there is no way to get a billion people up to space in less than a hundred years. We don't have a hundred years with category 7 or 8 hurricanes sweeping over the planet. For twenty years, it looks like fifty-million people can get to space."

Matti was suddenly depressed, "Then why are we bothering with this design work? It's a long-term solution that will take hundreds of years to make an impact."

Logan answered, "Because no one gets just how many a billion is, and they don't have any better ideas."

Matti finished the thought, "And the politics demands they

have a solution."

Logan then got a far-off look in his eyes that Matti recognized all too well.

"Oh no, that's the mad scientist look. Nothing good comes from that, and usually, it entails draining our bank account."

Logan was excited and barely heard her.

"Matti, what if Will can figure out the tube I found? What if we could build a mile-wide portal on earth, and millions of people could just walk right-through to another world every day? That would solve everything!"

Matti was simultaneously inspired and in shock at the implications.

"No. That will never fly. Do you think I can present the option of no option? Of killing our entire space presence because we're just going to walk to another star? Through unproven magical technology? We don't even know if we could breathe over on that other planet. They would fire me for even suggesting it."

"OK," Logan agreed. "But let's just blue sky the idea, wouldn't it solve the problem in the most elegant fashion? You wouldn't have to be an engineer or a kid of a rich dad—which you *know* is who will get tickets to come up to space, at least for the first twenty million people. All you would need is to gather your family, your suitcase of belongings, and cross right over to a new land, like a pioneer that gets off a ship that lands in a new land and knows he never can go back. We'd have to build a colony, infrastructure, and bring tools but no new mammoth space structures. We know how to build buildings. It would certainly be the least risky! And the math works."

"Oh, boy!" Matti was shaking her head, "I don't like where

this is going."

"But what if?" Logan grabbed on to the idea. "I'm going to call Will. Maybe he can come over. We need to figure out how to present this." And how to figure out how to disclose that I found another device and forgot all about it, Logan thought wryly to himself.

Now Matti was worried. How would the administrators react to that news?

"Are you sure? I think we should get rid of that device before we're all kicked off the station, or worse."

Will came over an hour later. He and Logan talked until one in the morning. Will was excited too. He was already thinking of the lab he needed to really take this research to the level Logan was envisioning. "It's a lot more complicated, but with the right equipment and a few years, we might just be able to replicate the quantum material and process on a larger scale."

Will was the type of person who didn't give up trying to make it happen once he saw something was possible. Seeing a working prototype and building the real deal was just a factor of time and money.

\* \* \*

Logan looked out the window as he and Matti descended to earth from ESS One on a shuttle. An orange glow from the heat shield was visible. Ida did not, amazingly, hit Florida. So, Disneyworld is safe, thought Logan with wry humor.

The coast from North Carolina to Maryland was wiped out for forty miles inland, and Logan could see the massive devastation on the way down. It was like a giant hand came down and wiped the ground with a big swath of mud and downed trees.

Logan shook his head and leaned over to Matti, "As a kid, I flew over Mt. Saint Helens in Washington State in a private plane. The mountain was a volcano, and its top blew off. The land looked like this, just an endless wasteland with thousands of trees blown over and stacked up like they were toothpicks. It was just heartbreaking."

Matti nodded. It was one thing to think about how devastating hurricanes could be or see their devastation on the news, but seeing acres upon acres of land flattened and lifeless was horrific. Especially since she knew that many people hadn't been able to get out before it hit. If this was the new normal, she was terrified for the future.

As they approached the Cape, Matti looked over and smiled at Logan. He knew she was thinking the same thing. Not too long ago, they had taken a flight up to the space station from this same location. They were much more confident now. At the time, the ESS program was just beginning. It was routine to come back to Earth every year or so, and soon the space elevator would make it a regular trip.

Matti was coming for two weeks to work with the UN, NASA, and other international agencies to hash out the best approach to solve the 'one billion challenge' even though they all felt the goal was still out of reach. Since the initial push to design a solution, no country had committed more than a few billion dollars to the project. The trillions of dollars to really get people into space just wasn't happening.

The designers all felt they should re-focus on the first challenging goal, getting twenty million into space. But politics was politics.

Logan was on a public relations tour since he was still well known as the discoverer of the first evidence of alien life in the solar system. He was also there to promote the new power generators the Space Industries joint venture with the UN was introducing based on The Object.

They rode together in the limousine. Matti was going to the airport and Logan to a press event in Orlando.

"I'll see you in a week!" Matti shouted as she hopped out at her terminal at Orlando airport.

"Good luck, sweetheart," Logan shouted after her as she ran to catch her flight.

The driver looked back to Logan.

"On to the Ritz-Carlton, sir?"

"Yes, please."

Logan looked out at the green palm trees on the way, the pleasant day hiding the underlying tragedy that Logan knew was on its way to all of Florida in just a few years. Already house after house had water lapping at their foundations. The for sale signs were everywhere. But who would buy vacation homes and condos now when everyone knew they'd be underwater in five years?

The limo pulled up to the Ritz for the press conference. The place was mobbed with reporters. There were picketers outside with signs proclaiming, 'The end is near' and 'Space Industries is our savior.'

Logan was met by the companies' press secretary, Lana Downtree. Logan knew Lana since they had worked together when the news of The Object first broke.

"I hope your flight was smooth?" she asked, then, without waiting for an answer, told him, "Here are the briefing points. Please look them over. We're having the main event in thirty minutes. Come on in here."

She opened the door to a large conference room already crowded with Space Industries executives, both from the ESS station and landside support centers.

Lana shouted out to the room, "OK, Logan is here, we can get started with our internal meeting before the press conference, and we don't have much time!" Everyone started to turn towards her.

"Welcome, everyone. Thanks for agreeing to attend the press conference before you dive into your planning meetings. As you can see, the heat has risen Earthside, and I mean more than the temperature outside. There is a new level of crazy here on Earth after Ida. People have finally realized the *Global Burn* means a major loss of life, and they are terrified. The good news is Space Industries is the new savior. People are looking to space to save them."

Rich Mayer, the head of planetside logistics for ESS, spoke out, "Don't they realize we've been working all out for years as it is to just get to our twenty-station goal? We're not going to be saving everyone."

"People aren't too rational anymore," Lana responded. "They want a global effort, not just an international group of space agencies. That is what we're going to be hit with in thirty minutes. We need everyone to keep out of politics. Please *do not* talk about the numbers we can help. That commitment is above your or my pay-grade. Rave about all our successes and wow them with our technology, but refer all policy questions to me or Paul, who will start off the press conference with a short statement."

Logan had a bad feeling about this conference and wondered how Matti's meetings must be going if this was the tone here. He hadn't realized, up in space, how intense things were. Would the panic on Earth derail the significant progress that Space Industries was making?

He knew that there was no real way Earth could get to the billion-person goal in less than a hundred years, let alone twenty. He and Matti talked a lot about it. None of the projections could support the increase.

You just couldn't skip technological steps and jump to a mammoth build out from where they were at. It would be like building modern-day New York City just as the first skyscraper was being finished. You just don't know enough and don't have the infrastructure in place. It takes time. The commitment to build twenty stations over twenty years was already a stretch goal.

Everyone was beginning to see Earth had used up its twenty to thirty-year climate warning window. Now it was too little, too late, and people were angry and demanding solutions. It made Logan really worried about his family, even if they were the lucky ones and were already living on ESS One.

\* \* \*

Matti couldn't believe the noise in the room. A UN conference, for the first time in recorded history, had the backing of all countries. She hadn't seen so many scared ambassadors in a long time. Unfortunately, there was more urgency than sanity.

There were representatives from ten space agencies and thirty contractors, adding to the one-hundred ninety-three country representatives in the room. The chairman of the new Joint Earth Space Migration committee was speaking.

"Every representative here is aware of the monumental mission before this committee as well as the extraordinary and unprecedented backing this mission has received. It is with this unity of purpose that extends around the globe that we launch our efforts. We shall not fail the citizens of…"

Matti tuned out the speech. She couldn't wait until the subcommittees took over, and they could make real progress. It was clear that the bureaucracy had taken over. She was sure she wouldn't like the result. Paper was usually the only output of a bureaucracy.

The luncheon of the subcommittee on design oversight was much more enjoyable. Matti sat next to Rans Larsen, the CEO of Bech Corporation, the largest construction company globally, and the prime contractor for the space elevator's Earthside facilities.

When the usual conversation died down, and only a few people were left at the table, Rans leaned over to Matti and said quietly, "Are you aware of the motivations of most of the people at this conference? They don't care if we ever finish The Ring or any of the designs. They just smell a huge project. Huge means lots of waste, lots of ways to pad their profits."

Matti gave him a surprised look.

Rans went on.

"Bech will get its slice, of course, a huge slice, but I wish to gain your trust because I believe hard times are ahead. I think you know this more than others. If you or your famous husband and family ever need a refuge, a favor, please look me up."

With that, he smiled, pressed a card into Matti's hand then left to go drink with several other CEO's he knew well. Matti was taken aback. Did Rans know something she didn't? She was sure he knew more than anyone in this room about where things were headed. It made her start questioning alternative views of the project. Crisis and change meant different things to different people.

It was late afternoon in Orlando. Logan was just getting back to his suite after giving eight interviews to various networks. He pushed eight for his floor and had only traveled to the fourth floor when the elevator stopped. He jabbed the button for his floor, but it wouldn't go further. The screen in the elevator lit up with the number 412, then displayed, 'If you would, Mr. Conover,' and then went blank. Mysterious. It reminded Logan of a spy movie. He went to room 412 and knocked. The knock left the door slightly ajar, so he let himself in.

"Hello, Mr. Conover," a deep voice spoke from the balcony. "Come on in, we've been expecting you."

Logan slowly entered the room and edged over to the balcony. The man was smaller than he imagined from the voice: Five-eight, a movie-star haircut, an excellent suit.

The man extended his hand to Logan, "Good to meet you finally. I'm Ruiz. We have mutual friends, Mr. Conover."

He smiled mischievously. "More importantly, mutual enemies. Enemies that you, perhaps, aren't aware of yet. But you will become aware of them soon when they find out about your new discovery. The one you and Will have been quietly working on in your ESS lab."

Logan stood straighter. He turned to leave, but Ruiz continued in a reassuring voice, "It's OK, Logan, you have nothing to fear from me. I very much want you and Will to succeed. I think you have a significant discovery with your *tube*. If you give me an hour, I think it might enlighten you, might even change your viewpoint."

Logan panicked. How had this man penetrated Space Industries' security? But he was even more intrigued that someone was interested in what he had found or even knew it was of importance.

He walked back, "Go on."

Mr. Ruiz held out his arm, inviting Logan to sit. A woman with silver hair was in the kitchen, preparing light refreshments.

"Please, sit. Would you like a drink?" Ruiz asked.

Logan hesitated. "I have no reason to poison you," Ruiz answered the question in Logan's mind. The woman came in, handed him an iced tea then put hors d'oeuvres on the table.

"Have you ever heard of the Fuerte Group, Mr. Conover?" Logan shook his head no. "Yes, well, it is the wealthiest club of the poorest people in the world, invitation-only, of course. We represent the interests of developing and emerging nations. We represent the forgotten. A few of the most successful people within this group of nations, the ones who have gotten wealthy playing the West's game, and have never forgotten where they came from, have been waiting and watching for a solution. They seek a way for the developing nations' peoples to survive this coming onslaught due to the *Global Burn*. Because, as you know, the West isn't going to help us even though we're taking the brunt of the impact. I am the organization's representative that interacts with the public when necessary. I help Fuerte put pieces of the grand puzzle together. Are you following?"

Logan frowned.

"You're their hatchet man."

"Exactly! In the best possible way, of course. Anyway, your

work is exciting. It opens many *doors*, yes?" Ruiz laughed at his joke. "We could use those doors to help with the current problem the world is having. You may have the solution the Fuerte Group has been waiting for. In fact, I'm sure you do."

At this, Logan snorted. "We've only just begun figuring out what the device is. I'm not sure I can imagine what to use it for."

"No? You haven't imagined what a practically free pathway to another world could do for us? It's utterly revolutionary."

Logan thought back to his vision of thousands of migrants walking from one world to the next. How could they have seen it too? It would make sense for those in developing nations to see the possibilities where the first world would only see risk. Why waste precious resources if their goal was only to bring the wealthiest to safety?

"You do see, don't you?" Ruiz went on. "The West, really the wealthy, have always seen the world through the vision of wealth. Of affluence. It is a narrow view that unfortunately excludes many. When the world wants to go in a different direction, they are driven to fulfill their singular goal, more wealth. Even if it involves destroying the very world giving them wealth, yes? Even now, you and your wife are working for this cause, did you know? The same cause that has created the mess and seeks now to escape."

The man stopped to take a long drink and looked expectantly at Logan to see if he was following.

"Yes, I see you are perhaps sympathetic?" he continued. "That is all I ask for now. It is a different viewpoint, but one you must now confront—an ethical dilemma. You know, as well as I, deep down, the vision of a new world in space is, can be, only for the few. For the few hundreds of thousands at the top, not the bottom billions."

Logan felt amazed that he hadn't articulated this viewpoint himself. It was like a veil was being lifted. His heart went out to the billions who would be left behind. But surely, in time, they would be included in technological progress? He was finding the source of the niggling thoughts and doubts he'd had. It was because a fundamental ethical challenge lay at its core.

"Yes, you do understand, I see." Ruiz pointed out. "Once you see it, you can't go back. Not if you have any kind of conscience, which I know you of all the people at Space Industries has." He took another long drink. "The *elite*, if you will, figured out a long time ago that they must perpetuate a vision that held hope for everyone, even though all the financials, all the effort, indicated that only a few at the top would benefit, would be saved. Most of the rest will drown or starve, I'm afraid. We have the models to support this if you wish to see them. The bottom billions cannot be saved in the short-term, which is all we have. But those in space will have made such glorious technical progress, yes? Your discovery, on the other hand, is beautifully *disruptive* to the whole system. It provides an elegant solution that these elites would never support."

Logan was confused. "Why is that?"

Ruiz frowned. "Because it doesn't generate wealth. It doesn't keep them at the top. It provides a solution to climate change that no wealthy person wants because it comes at no cost, and no-cost means no profit, yes? Why would they want that? A trillion-dollar space station is a marvel, not because it would save millions of people, but because it *costs trillions*. The bigger, the higher the cost, the better!

When it was developed, the internet drove these wealthy absolutely crazy, at least until they could figure out how to profit from it. It proliferated before they could respond. The same will happen now. Disruption is our friend. They won't ever know what happened until it's too late. Until all their customers are saved. It really will drive them crazy," Ruiz reflected, then nodded, looking keenly at Logan, trying to gauge where he was at.

Logan was following until that point.

"How do you mean saved?"

Ruiz smiled his biggest smile.

"Well, we're going to help you implement your vision, Mr. Conover. We're going to march many millions of people off Earth onto another world. We're going to do it under their noses!"

Logan was stunned. It was one thing to dream, but did this group think it was possible to do? And right while Space Industries and others kept building out the technological vision in space? Was there really a better way than expanding out into space?

"A lot to think about." Ruiz put his hand in his pocket and pulled out a thumb drive, "One more thing. Give this to Matti. Her maiden name was Garcia, right?"

Ruiz handed Logan the thumb drive. "It is an odd coincidence, but her father was responsible for all of us being here today. Be sure to tell her we are sharing this with her to prove we were not involved with the 'accident.'"

Logan was taken aback, "Dr. Garcia? He died when Matti was a kid."

"We know. Review the contents of the drive with her. If you like what you have heard today and want to do real good in the world, text this number a message saying you want to use your coupon and buy the goods at a discount. We'll help you get out, set up the necessary labs. You'll feel you went down the rabbit hole, but you'll be making history, not just saving the few rich and watching the waves roll over the rest, yes?"

Logan took the card from Ruiz. He was ushered out of the apartment and back to the elevator by Ruiz's associate. The elevator now went up to his floor. Wow! Logan's head was spinning. He thought about Matti and called her up.

"Hi! Logan, how are you holding up? This place is beyond crazy," Matti told him when they connected.

"Beyond crazy here too. It seems like we're either the new savior or the people in the way."

"I know what you mean. This is beyond beyond, you know? I'm worried, so much change, so much money involved. I'm worried about Kira on many levels."

Logan agreed. He told her he loved her. They talked about small things they needed to get for Kira and their apartment before they returned. Logan felt more grounded after the call. Talking with Matti made him feel like everything would be ok.

The rest of the week was exhausting. Logan hardly thought about Ruiz and what was discussed. He still wasn't sure he wanted to even consider the offer. But no matter how hard he tried to get back to his old life, he knew Ruiz was right. The world was rapidly getting to a point where people would have to start making hard choices and taking stands, not trying to hide in a quiet place. There weren't going to be any more peaceful places to hide.

# New Priorities

*Year: 2046 +3.5°F*
  *Earth Population: 10,386,155,620*
  *Population off-earth in Solar System: 12,044*
  *Population in other Star Systems: 1 Robot*
  *Yearly population decrease due to Global Burn: 950,000*

Logan wasn't used to cloak and dagger, how to keep conversations secure, but Matti was. They arrived back at the shuttle twenty minutes before it was due to depart, just enough time to get prepped and strapped in before it blasted off from the Cape. Matti, having worked in communications, overrode the standard communication protocols and engaged her own secure connection. They were now talking on a secure line with the roar of the shuttle engines in the background. Logan related his conversation with Ruiz. Matti, oddly, wasn't too surprised. She told Logan about her several encounters with corporate executives.

"It's like a big rift is widening right now between space-based and ground-based actors, depending on their interests."

Logan nodded, "We are in the middle of it."

Logan paused. Matti was thoughtful, "I've felt the divide. Does space-based technology, being so exclusive, divide the haves and have-nots? It's an age-old problem."

Logan continued the thought, "but The Tube changes everything."

Matti countered, "Might. There is the dilemma. Part of me wants to keep the status quo, let Kira grow up in peace. Just become one of the 'haves' and shut-out what the world is going through."

They sat silently for a few minutes. Logan suddenly remembered the thumb drive Ruiz gave him for Matti. He pulled it out and handed it to Matti. "Here is the strangest part, Ruiz gave me this for you."

"For me?" Matti was confused.

"He said it was from your father and that your dad was responsible for everything that has happened. Very weird."

Matti's eyes grew big when Logan mentioned her father, "My dad? What the heck?" She loaded the thumb drive into her laptop and selected the first video from a series of videos. The video was dated back to 2017 and displayed the name Dr. Damon Garcia. A few seconds played. Suddenly Matti's eyes went even wider with comprehension, "Oh my gosh, this must be his last work. How did Ruiz get this?"

They reviewed all the videos, the last one showing how Oumuamua sent a probe to Anteros. Logan and Matti were both floored. "Wow, this changes everything," Matti breathed, "My dad must have been murdered because of what he found out about Anteros. My mom told me of the last phone call from him the night he died. She always blamed herself for not convincing him to go to the police."

Logan was also slightly in shock, the truth dawning on him. "Finding the artifacts on Anteros wasn't an accident. They knew all along there was something there." They sat for a couple of minutes, absorbing the bombshell Ruiz gave them. Logan spoke again, breaking the silence. "Life always pulls in strange directions, doesn't it?"

Matti looked seriously over at Logan and knew his mind was made up. He had always gone one hundred and ten percent into what he felt a conviction for. If mankind mined asteroids and created a space-based economy, he was totally and completely on board. Now...she left the thought hanging. Looking out the window at the beautiful and peaceful view of the Earth, Matti didn't feel peaceful at all.

The videos disturbed her greatly. Lots of pieces were coming together from her past. Knowing more about her father's murder circumstances to keep his discovery from being made public made her angry. It also made her afraid.

"I want to find out who killed my dad."

"It must be someone else connected to the space program. Now we know that 'accidentally' finding artifacts on Anteros was no accident. Ruiz was right. Your dad was responsible for everything that has happened. We just have to find out who decided to go after Anteros in the first place, and you'll have your dad's killer."

Matti looked determined and shared what was now evident to her, "We're going to have to leave ESS and go in with Ruiz." Logan nodded.

As the shuttle pulled into the ESS One dock, they couldn't shake the feeling that it would never feel like home again. At ESS One, there was a straightforward goal: building a new space station and growing the space economy. Pursuing research around the second artifact, The Tube, would be more complicated.

Logan and Matti exited into the central corridor after going through the standard decontamination routine of a full-body air, and chemical wash and clothes change. Kira ran into her mom's arms when she saw them, although now, at twelve, she practically knocked Matti over.

"Mom, you won't believe what I did in science lab," she exclaimed. "We were doing low-gravity experiments with animals. I brought Andromeda in. I taught her how to do somersaults in zero-gravity!"

It still amazed Logan they were able to bring their cat, Andromeda, up to the station, but such was modern space living. It took a while to train Andromeda on how to use the zero-gee litter box.

"That's wonderful, honey. She didn't get dizzy?"

"No, she loved it, and she could get the treats that I floated in the air by twisting and pushing off me."

Colonel Tibbets, Logan, and Matti's instructor from the Academy came down the hall. Tibbets was now the ESS One security chief.

"Colonel Conover, welcome back. Paul wants to see you at 1530 in his office, then we have a staff meeting at 1600." Tibbets took Logan to the side. "And Colonel, I came personally to tell you because you should know there is some heavy stuff going down on our base in Singapore."

"OK, thanks, I'll get to the meeting. All else quiet up here?"

"Is it ever? Just be at the meeting."

Logan felt Tibbets was more severe than usual. Something must be up. Given his last week on Earth, he wasn't surprised.

Paul Manning's office had expanded over the years. Logan was let in. Paul rose up from his desk to greet him. The center was an old walnut desk that must have cost a fortune to bring up from Earth. The view was amazing out of his

Plexi windows. Logan could see a broad swath of blue and white as Earth rotated below.

"I heard you represented us well at the press interviews. Thank you. Have a seat." Paul seemed particularly busy and agitated. "Logan, we've done amazing work here, haven't we? Just amazing. The world doesn't know the breakthroughs we've made in construction and robotics. But I don't have to tell you that things are getting dicey on Earth. We have a full staff meeting to address problems at our Earthside bases. Some people think it would be better if we hunkered down there, maybe took the funding from our program to build massive underground bunkers instead, but you and I know that approach is flawed, right?"

Logan totally believed that.

"Absolutely, if there was an end game or a period that they could just wait it out, it might make sense, but I don't think anyone thinks the extreme weather or the *Global Burn* itself has an expiration date. It could be this way forever."

"Exactly, we're on the same page, good to hear. Now there is just one other thing we need to talk about. Colonel Tibbets and his folks said you and Will have been working on a lab experiment in your spare time?"

Logan swallowed hard. He smiled and tried to act like it was nothing. "Just some interesting materials research that Will thinks might help us make stronger spacecraft."

Paul looked Logan in the eye.

"It's more than that if Tibbets is getting intelligence reports from Earth saying groups are talking about it. But look, Logan, I have my hands full. So, do you. How about you and Will put whatever you've found on the back burner? We're developing all sorts of new tech up here that have applications on Earth.

Will is already getting royalties on the power equipment. I can offer a bonus to you and Matti, but can you cease and desist and focus on our important work? I'm counting on you to keep all of our pilots safe, a huge responsibility."

Logan relaxed a little. Paul was assuming he and Will wanted to carve out a future empire in high-tech applications. He looked Paul in the eye and nodded.

"You have my word, sir, we won't start a company to go after wealth. Maybe in ten or fifteen years when all this settles."

Paul relaxed as well.

"Good to hear. OK, let's get into this staff meeting and try to inspire our Earthside suppliers? You can give them the alien artifact save mankind pep talk you always give. I'll threaten them with lawsuits if they break their contracts."

Paul led them both to his adjoining conference room, and they got on the conference call.

Logan wasn't able to come up for air until late that night. He entered their apartment at midnight. Logan took off his uniform and got into bed when Matti woke up and gave him a kiss.

"I got in at ten," she told him. "Kira's fine. Suzie took good care of her."

Suzie was Kira's caretaker and was the daughter of a construction worker. She was fifteen and Kira's hero. She could do no wrong. Suzie was an absolute godsend to Logan and Matti.

Over the next three weeks, Matti was buried in work with the UN design team. Logan spent hours with his pilots in construction tasks, ferrying vast amounts of raw material from the moon asteroid processing orbital to earth's high-orbit positions where two new ESS space stations would be constructed. After they started pre-positioning the raw materials, a swarm of robotic 3D printers arrived and started building station trusses at three hundred feet per hour.

Earth had never untaken such a monumental construction project. It was all happening quietly two-hundred kilometers up in the sky. In a decade, twenty new stations would be visible in the night sky. Millions of people would start coming up with the space elevator. That is, Logan thought if everything stayed together down on their land-based supply stations. Massive amounts of electronics and gear were still more economically built Earthside and sent up the elevator. If these supply chains started failing, there was nothing they could do to keep on schedule.

Logan found time to tell Will privately of his talk with Mr. Ruiz and with Paul. Will freaked out, unable to conceive how Ruiz and then Paul had found out about so many details of his few experiments with The Tube. Logan explained the connection to Matti's father. Will was more freaked out.

"They knew, the bastards knew all along where to look."

Logan nodded, "It's been the plan all along, obviously. We just don't know who the puppet-master is."

Will went on a campaign to rid his lab of cameras and other gear that could be spying on him. There was nothing he liked less than to have people stealing intellectual property. Will's worst fear was having a colleague publish a paper or a company copy or reproduce a product that he was working on.

Will, Matti, and Logan all felt it was time to move on to continue The Tube research. The potential to develop a new, radical form of transportation was tantalizing. But they all fell back into their busy schedules. It was easy to cling to the status quo and not take action even when they knew they should take the leap and leave. Upending your life takes courage.

* * *

*Code RED. Code RED, Block 12, KIRA.* Logan and Matti's communication bracelets flashed together even though they worked in their separate station areas. Each reacted immediately. There was an emergency related to Kira. They ran through the station to Block 12, the emergency room in the health section, and arrived at the same time, breathless. A nurse met them and explained.

"Your daughter is in surgery for an eye injury. She was practicing with her cat in Weightless Training Room 5, where someone left tools unsecured. She should be out in a couple of hours. I'll have the doctor meet you here."

Matti asked if they could go in, but the nurse said they could not yet. They were doing all they could. Logan and Matti sat down in shock. How could this happen? Who left tools in the practice room? They were horrified and had plenty of time waiting to start wondering if perhaps it was unsafe to raise a family at the station. They went through all the pros and cons before they came up but ultimately decided it was just as safe as any American city in this day and age. But was it? Had they made the right decision?

Logan tried to track down the maintenance chief to ask why tools were left in the training room. He received an apology but no explanation. The chief was going to follow up with who had been in the room.

Three hours later, the head surgeon, Dr. Hamilton, came out. "Well, we've stabilized the injury, but..."

Logan and Matti looked at one another.

"But what?"

"She lost her right eye." Both Logan and Matti gasped and supported each other. Logan was weak in the knees. Doctor Hamilton continued. "I'm authorizing an emergency med-evac transport to Chicago where you'll be able to meet with bionic eye specialists. They've come a long way in the last twenty years, and there is no reason why Kira won't be able to see again on that side, albeit with an artificial eye. I'm sorry for her loss, but there is good cause for hope."

Logan recovered, "Thank you, doctor, I know you did all you could. Have you explained this to her?"

Hamilton checked his watch. "I've told her about Chicago. You will need to talk to specialists there to make a decision. Give her three hours recovery, then I'll have her transported to deck five for evac. You can see her now, but she is asleep."

Both Logan and Matti followed the doctor. They held each other tight as they went to Kira's side and held her hand.

After an hour, they made their way numbly back to their apartment and started to pack. Logan packed a few of Kira's favorite toys and stuffed animals. He then thought about The Tube. Will had given it back to him. His main thought was about Kira, but…this was a great opportunity. He stuffed it into their overnight bags.

They turned the apartment status to *away* without an end date then walked rapidly down to the transport deck. It was almost time. Major Sandy Pulaski met them at the transport.

"Major, I hadn't expected you to take this flight," Logan said, surprised.

"I heard about the accident, and you know I'd do anything for you both and Kira. I'll make sure your squadron is aware of the problem and that you'll be away for a while."

"Thank you. I appreciate it."

A door opened, and Kira was wheeled in. She was awake.

"Oh, honey," Matti soothed. "How are you? You're so brave."

Logan smiled and held Kira's hand. She tried to smile but couldn't. She managed, "I'm sorry. I didn't mean to."

Matti looked horrified.

"Oh no honey, it's not your fault, don't blame yourself. It was an accident. The doctor said we're going to get you a new eye that will be as good as new. Please don't blame yourself."

At that point, the attending nurse asked for everyone to get inside. They all took their places. The craft backed away from the station and started to change orbits to track to Chicago on an emergency vector.

\* \* \*

Logan and Matti entered Kira's private hospital room. For the last two weeks, it had been where they spent the majority of their time watching over Kira as she recovered. A whole different Kira was looking back at them.

The eye implant was installed successfully, and Kira was trained in how to use her new eye.

"Hey, cyborg," Logan teased.

Matti frowned. "Don't call her that!"

But Kira laughed. "Yeah, besides the whole horror of losing the eye and all, it's going to be pretty cool. I'll be the only one in my class with zoom capability. Did you know I looked out the window a few minutes ago, and I can read a sign a mile away?"

Logan and Matti were vaguely aware of what bionic eyes

could do but were unaware they were capable of things like that.

"Wow, honey, we're going to have to use you to spy on our neighbors from now on," Logan enthused.

Again, Matti rolled her eyes, but she was so happy to hear Kira laugh. There were tears in her eyes. The worry that Kira would never see correctly again had been all-consuming.

\* \* \*

Mr. Ruiz stood in his home office in Karavomylos, Greece. He was currently on a conference call with others in the Fuerte Group.

"We have a unique opportunity," he was telling them, "The Conover's are in Chicago due to a tragic circumstance related to their daughter. It may be an ideal time to make our offer."

Others on the call all agreed. Ruiz made a call to an associate. "Ruiz here. Yes, they agreed we should proceed. You can contact them and make the offer. If they accept, make sure they can get their friend Mr. Bonalado to accompany them. He must come along. The lab in Karavomylos is ready whenever you can get them there."

The Fuerte Group purchased one-thousand acres around Karavomylos, which included the world-famous Melissani cave. Construction equipment was already arriving to start building an underground city. It could support one-hundred-fifty thousand people, or up to one million people for shorter periods when completed in two years. Fourteen more sites were being developed around the globe. They utilized caves for protection. In Vietnam, they built around Hang Son Doong, the largest cave in the world. The Fuerte Group's fifteen-billion-dollar investment was going to do a lot more in a shorter time than the trillions being spent in space if the Group's plan worked out. Time would tell.

\* \* \*

Logan and Matti were in the Colectivo coffee shop, having breakfast. Logan took a deep breath, "We're going to have to start thinking about when, and if, we're going to get back up to the station."

Matti wasn't feeling any hurry.

"I'm happy we were able to be together. It has healed more than Kira. We were just so flat out busy, you know?"

Logan nodded. He felt the same but also felt guilty as he thought about abandoning the ESS station. Which was silly, as his family was clearly the first priority. But was the station still his second priority?

"You know, ever since I met with Ruiz in Florida, my heart really hasn't been into my work at the station. I just feel there might be a better way, and we're the only ones who know it."

Matti jumped in, "I want to leave just based on that video of my dad, so I'm in, but The Tube seems like a long-shot. It seems like a fantasy. Can you really believe it might work?"

The waitress gave them their check. A small note was on the same plate.

Logan looked down to pay the bill and picked up the note in a small envelope. He opened it.

'The Bean, four o'clock. Ruiz.'

"Wow, speaking of which…" Logan handed the note to Matti, who read it and stuffed it in her purse.

"OK, I guess everyone knows where we are."

They paid the bill and went to check in on Kira.

At four o'clock, Logan and Matti were standing next to the Bean, Chicago's famous work of art that reflected back all of the buildings and the park around it in a curved shape—looking like a colossal, shiny bean. Ruiz's associate walked up to them at precisely four.

"Hi, Mr. and Mrs. Conover. Glad to meet you. Mr. Ruiz sent me."

Logan was suspicious.

"Ruiz couldn't come himself?"

"No, he is out of the country, but he wanted me to express his gladness at hearing that your daughter will make a full recovery."

"What does Ruiz want?"

"Mr. Ruiz is prepared to offer you both, and your friend, Mr. Bonalado, a position as principal researchers in his lab in Greece. All expenses paid and comfortable home will be provided."

Logan and Matti looked at each other in surprise. Ruiz's associate continued.

"And you have The Tube with you?" Logan looked more surprised. The young man smiled, "We thought you would have brought it."

Matti looked over at Logan, and Logan nodded.

"Please give our offer serious consideration. If you need to talk to Ruiz, he can be reached at this number. Please just make sure you're in a secure area." The young man handed Logan a slip of paper with a contact number. "Just call that number with your reply. If you decide to join us, be ready in four days. And have Will join you. He is critical to the project as well."

The young man paused and then looked very earnest. "It would mean the world to us, Mr. and Mrs. Conover, if you would join our team. We need you and what you can bring desperately. Many feel this may be their only hope. This is a real cause worth working for. Even if it only has a forty percent chance of success, isn't forty percent worth it if so many can be helped?"

Logan was surprised by the young man's earnest appeal.

"Of course, we'll consider it, thank you," he replied.

With that, the young man nodded, then blended back into the tourists around them and walked away down Millennium Park. Matti was thoughtful.

"Wow. Just like that, we're supposed to leave our careers and chase a dream in Greece?"

Logan looked over at Matti and smiled. "Greece is a romantic location. Consider it a second extended honeymoon!"

Matti was amazed, "you look like you're considering it seriously! You really do believe in this Tube artifact, don't you?"

Logan turned more serious. "You know I didn't know for a while, but the what-ifs have caught up with me. I don't think I can put those thoughts away."

Oh boy, here we go, Matti thought. She knew Logan was always the adventurous type, but this was even bigger than joining Space Industries.

She gave him a kiss and whispered, "I hope we know what we're doing. You can call Will and tell him we desperately need his support."

Logan was happy. "I don't think we'll regret it. Even if things don't work out, we'll feel good we tried."

Matti wasn't so optimistic but didn't say anything. There

was no chance of changing Logan's mind now. She thought it was time to move Kira back to earth and back into a regular home. At least Matti would have accomplished that if the project didn't work out. Maybe she could also get closure about her father.

Logan and Matti told Kira about their desire to take the jobs in Greece, so they could settle down and have a quieter and safer time as a family. Kira wasn't buying it. Her response was immediate and upset, "But Mom, all my friends, are on the station. And Greece? Why Greece? I don't have any friends in Greece. How am I supposed to make them when *I don't even know how to speak Greek?*"

Matti was left to deal with the fallout of their decision while Logan went to O'Hare to pick up Will, who was coming in on a Cape Canaveral flight. Will hadn't blinked twice when Logan called him, suspecting something like this would come up after Logan told him about his conversation with Ruiz. "We need you down here, buddy. We could really use the help."

Will knew immediately something was up. He favored going in with Ruiz, probably because it represented a huge new challenge for him. One with an incredible technical achievement if they could figure it out.

He packed everything he owned on the chance that he wouldn't be coming back and was on a flight in twenty-four hours. When Will stepped off the plane and saw Logan's smirk, he knew he was right, "Ruiz?"

"Yep," Logan replied. That was all that needed to be said. They walked to the Blue Line to go back to their hotel downtown.

Three days later, the four of them, Logan, Matti, Will, and

Kira, all sat down at the Berghoff Café at O'Hare. Their flight to Athens was in two hours. Their plan was to escape as fast as possible and let the fallout from Space Industries just happen. Earlier that morning, they submitted their resignations via email to Space Industries. They ordered breakfast, then Logan received a call from Paul.

"What the hell Logan? You told me you guys were on board. I need you. What the hell are you, Will, and Matti pulling?"

Logan was sympathetic but determined.

"That was before the accident with Kira, that really threw us both for a loop. We decided we just can't continue, for Kira's sake," Logan added.

Kira rolled her eyes and whispered to her mom, "Why is it always the kid's fault?"

Matti smiled and patted her daughter's back.

Will smiled a huge smile; he had wanted to tell Paul to jump off a bridge for a long time.

Logan got off the call in a minute. "Well, he isn't too happy. Quite a shock, I imagine. Wait until he hears we're going to Greece."

Matti's concern was soberer. Wait until he hears we have The Tube, she thought. Then all heck was going to break loose.

\* \* \*

After landing in Athens, it was another short flight to Kefalonia island. Ruiz scheduled a car to meet them at the airport and settled them into their new home on the coast after the short ride. It was beautiful, with the Mediterranean's sparkling blue spreading out in the distance beyond their villa.

"See, a good start!" Ruiz gestured with open arms when they all entered the home. The housekeeper then entered the room. "Here is Mrs. Pateroglou; she will take care of anything you need. Here," Ruiz handed a map to Will, "is the way to your lab. I'm sure you'll want to come over as soon as you've settled in."

Will was staying with Logan and Matti until Carol could come down and find their own place. "How about if I meet you there tomorrow at noon. We'll have lunch, and I'll show you around?"

Ruiz then turned to Logan, Matti, and Kira. "I want to thank you all for coming. It took a lot of courage to leave the space station and take a leap of faith in us. We truly appreciate it." Then he added with an extra twinkle in his eye. "You won't regret it. We're going to do amazing things here. There is just fantastic momentum. We'll need to talk in-depth; your role is different than the research that is needed." Ruiz then left on that note shouting behind him, "Don't worry about the guys with guns outside. They are your security."

Logan and Matti didn't know whether to feel relieved or frightened by that comment. It was definitely going to be a new world.

The smell of cooking bacon and eggs woke Kira in the morning. The sun was streaming in the window of her new bedroom. The scent of honeysuckle wafted into her room. She bounded to the window and inhaled deeply. Maybe it wouldn't be as bad as she thought to leave the space station. Over the last several years, she had forgotten how beautiful Earth was. She could still 3D-text her friends at the station. They all thought she was on an exotic vacation.

"Kira, breakfast!" her mom called from the kitchen. Kira

threw on clothes and ran downstairs. Their two-story villa was beautiful, just like she imagined a house on a Greek island would be. Rustic and smelling old but at the same time fresh and full of adventure.

Matti smiled when Kira bounded into the room. "You look so refreshed and happy!" Mrs. Pateroglou served Kira a full breakfast that even included cooked tomatoes and local toasted sourdough bread dripping with butter.

"Wow, real food!" Kira exclaimed and started into her breakfast. "Yum!" she concluded after a bite of eggs and tomato.

Matti was pleased. Kira seemed to be taking the move better than expected. Matti was pretty happy to be back on Earth and have a home to themselves again. Living on a space station was like being in a dorm room with hundreds of others. She forgot how nice it was to have personal space and a home of their own.

After drying his hair from his shower, Logan came downstairs and smiled at his two girls having a wonderful time in the kitchen.

"How are my two favorite women in the whole world?"

"Great!" Kira said between bites.

"Smells great. Wow, real tomatoes!" Logan took a seat. Mrs. Pateroglou served him and Matti a full breakfast as well.

"I'm determined to tackle the strategic aspects of this whole new adventure and see if I can't bring sanity to what we're doing," Matti said to Logan. Matti was determined to use her strategic organization skills as she did on the space station. It was a new challenge, and she was raring to dive in and bring the same planning and effort to bear on this project.

Matti loved her family. They were the first priority, but she was also talented at creating purposeful organizations that worked well. She was excited by the challenge of what lay ahead. She knew she was also an excellent counter-balance to Logan and Will. They were great at dreaming and creating but strategic planning, pffft, not a chance. She was determined to keep them safe from themselves.

They arrived at the research facility at 11:30 am, hoping to wander around and explore. Ruiz met them in the foyer, all smiles as usual.

"Here are my favorite new celebrities!" he announced. "You have no idea how excited we are to have you here. We just completed this facility six days ago. I think you'll be impressed."

Ruiz led them on a path that emerged by the huge Kefalonia cave opening.

"The Melissani Cave used to be a tourist spot until we bought it," Ruiz added. "Come this way around. There is a new path to the more open areas underground."

Ruiz led them for a few minutes through the fantastic opening in the earth that was the cave entrance. A lake of beautiful blue-green water lay twenty feet below the space, and sunlight shown through to the sea, its long rays making the scene one of magical beauty.

Kira's face lit up with wonder as if she was in a new world. She couldn't wait to explore it all and go swimming in the refreshing blue pool of water directly under the cave opening.

"Is it safe to swim in?" she asked Mr. Ruiz politely.

"Perfectly! It has been a draw for tourists for years."

They went down a staircase and a hall and were led to a large opening underground. Ruiz tapped on an app on his comm device, and, behind the open area of the lake, a substantial underground room came to life as the lights came on.

"This is what we bought the cave for, two hundred acres of buildable space from between one hundred and five hundred feet underground. If the world heats up, the temperature down here will stay the same fifty-eight degrees Fahrenheit all the time."

Logan noticed there was already equipment in the space.

"You're building facilities already?"

"We have incorporated the Sheltered Refugee non-profit. Original plans call for large apartments and living facilities within this area."

"Enough to hold the world's refugees during the worst periods of the Global Burn?" Matti asked.

"We don't think any facility will be that big. I've left you our research you can read later. Our projections are that there will be hundreds of millions of refugees in as little as ten years. Our network of fourteen caves, similar to this one, will hold many more than prior facilities. Still, it will only be a drop in the bucket for the massive upheaval hitting many countries in a few years. We estimate we can build enough to support forty million."

"Still, an impressive amount," Matti remarked, starting to do the numbers of all the supporting staff and supply networks it would take to feed forty million.

Ruiz turned off the lights and led them back to the smaller office complex.

"Kira?"

Kira was surprised she was being addressed.

"Yes, sir?"

Ruiz smiled, "There are several young ladies that would like to meet you! They are in the cafeteria waiting for you. They are kids of the scientists and staff we have coming here to work."

Kira was surprised and excited.

"Wow, thank you, which way to the cafeteria?"

She then turned toward her parents with an inquisitive look.

Matti smiled at Kira. "Of course, go along. We'll catch up with you this afternoon."

Ruiz motioned down the main hall.

"Five doors down to the right, the big doors with the art in front." Kira bounded off down the hall. Ruiz continued. "The kids all just discovered the new pool and other recreational facilities. They usually hang out together after school. It's fine to bring kids to work. "

Matti was impressed already.

Ruiz led them through the facility. When they opened the door to the lab, Will was spellbound. He was polite during the tour, but the laboratory was why he was here. He immediately immersed himself in the lab, introducing himself to the technicians there.

"Will in his element," Logan commented. He gave Will The Tube earlier that morning. Will sealed it in a special container. Will was currently enlisting all of the technicians in depositing it into a unique analysis machine that could apply fifty different materials tests to discover what it was made of. Contrary to appearances, The Tube wasn't really transparent. It looked like glass, and you could see the ball fall through it, but there was a layer of circuitry around the entire surface. Will was trying to decode its structure.

"I don't think we'll see Will for another month or two," Logan concluded. Ruiz couldn't be happier. He had worked tirelessly for months to get Will right where he was now.

Matti and Logan followed Ruiz to the command center in the facility. Logan came to life, "Wow, what is this all for?" He asked Ruiz as he walked around the bank of screens and desks, all oriented around a central command console.

"I'm hoping it will be Matti's new office," Ruiz stated. He turned to both of them and, with a measure of gravity, said, "Right, no more mysteries for you two. You know the general nature of our challenge, but let me tell you how you fit into the grand plan. There aren't many of us at Fuerte. We tend to run our operations lean. So, you'll be interested to know that I've appointed both of you co-directors of this facility."

Logan and Matti were shocked.

"Yes, surprised? Well, you shouldn't be," Ruiz told them. "Logan, you've become famous and well known because of the artifact you found on Anteros. Matti, well, you may not be as well known in the media, but within strategic management circles, you have impressed many, including all of my bosses. They said to tell you directly that they respect your leadership and thinking and what you accomplished getting ESS One operational. They hope you will feel free to start integrating with all of the Sheltered Refugee locations we are building around the world. In a short time, they will be looking to you for leadership on a wide array of topics on our project."

Matti couldn't be more excited; she hoped to be heavily involved, but this was more than expected. Logan was smiling ear-to-ear, just looking at her response. On the space station, most of Matti's ideas went through five layers of red tape. It seemed that perhaps this organization was able to move more decisively.

Logan was still trying to figure out his role, as clearly there weren't any spaceships to pilot here. Ruiz turned to him.

"As I was saying, Logan, you are very well known, even in the developing world. That will be useful because we envision great things from you. You see, we need a face for all this, a leader to inspire everyone to buy into our approach, our plan. You have the reputation and vision to inspire them."

Logan was confused.

"You mean the few thousand people in this organization?"

Ruiz smiled, "No, no, Logan. This organization is relatively small. Matti and others can help keep it focused and effective. What we need is someone to lead our people home, a modern-day Moses, you could say."

Logan was still trying to grasp the big picture.

"Our people?" he asked.

"Yes. The billions of people we hope to save from the coming climate onslaught. The people that your Space Industries has left behind."

Suddenly the goal of the project seemed big indeed. Logan didn't know if he was up for it.

Matti turned to Ruiz. "But no pressure, right?"

Ruiz widened his hands, "It sounds big, historic, but if Will can come through and replicate and expand your artifact, then isn't that the natural conclusion you came up with? To just walk to another world instead of spending trillions and only saving the privileged few? We live in revolutionary times. But all that will take time and lots of work, yes? We have much to do. We'll have lunch now, and then we can spend this afternoon and the rest of the week getting to know your new co-workers and start your planning. I think you'll be impressed!"

With that, Logan and Matti started their work on Sheltered Refugee.

# Build-out

*Six months later, Cephalonia, Greece*

*Year: 2047 + 3.6°F*
   *Earth Population: 10,393,736,733*
   *Population off-earth in Solar System: 42,044*
   *Yearly population decrease due to Global Burn: 1,025,092*

Krishna Singh shouted back to Matti and Logan, who were in the back of the ATV. They were driving through the chaotic construction site, "These are the steel beams, just delivered, that will form the frame of the main residential block." Krishna pointed to a stack of hundreds of forty-foot long steel I-beams. "Work should begin in a week once we get all of the construction workers housed in a nearby village."

The front of the Melissani cave was kept intact with its beautiful lake and opening to the outside. The back of the cave was enormous, a mile in length. It had all been cleared and leveled, ready for the multi-story apartment complex that would be the shelter for up to a million refugees.

Krishna was Sheltered Refugees' new construction foreman. He was a graduate of the Indian Institute of Engineering Science and Technology in Shibpur, India, had several successful stints on large high-tech construction projects, then went on to get his MBA from Harvard. Krishna was in charge of the new underground shelters they were building, and he was giving Matti and Logan his weekly tour of the worksite.

"We've got parallel efforts going on at all fourteen cave sites around the world. Your plan, Matti, of using the same build-out plans for the facilities worldwide is a big help keeping all of the sites in sync. We're all working off of the same specs."

Krishna stopped the ATV, and Logan and Matti jumped out. Matti spoke to Krishna, "Thanks for the tour. It's progressing even better than we envisioned." Krishna smiled at the compliment and bowed his head slightly, welcoming the praise. He was working with Matti twelve-hour days and flying worldwide to hire all of the key personnel needed.

In purchasing the caves, the Fuerte Group originally planned on building substantial underground cities to act as shelters to mitigate the *Global Burn's* most severe effects. So, when a natural disaster or drought hit a specific area, they could migrate hundreds of thousands of the most affected people into underground shelters. They would provide food and necessities such as education and primary employment until those areas were deemed safe to return to.

Lacy Daughs, their public relations director, met Logan and Matti at the ATV after Krishna left them off. "Hi, we've got a publicity shot in twenty minutes. Can both of you come this way to get made up?"

On the public relations front, they brought in a corporate PR professional, Lacy. She could speak five languages and knew how to present initiatives like Sheltered Refugee to the world in a positive light. Lacy's job was to turn Logan from an alien artifact hero to humanitarian and leader of a worldwide movement to combat climate change using alien technology.

"Ok, you read the talking points?" she asked Logan as he was sitting down at the makeup artist's chair. She left nothing to chance.

"Yes. Communicate how we're building these sites for refugees around the world. We're not building camps like everyone else but facilities that can house refugees and give them the tools to be productive and find permanent new homes and work as soon as possible."

"And, that we've established onsite schools and training centers," Lucy reminded Logan.

"Right. We are also producing new desalination equipment based on the quantum power generators' technology to provide power and water at all facilities for a fraction of the cost. After testing, we're planning on making the equipment available to other countries that have freshwater shortages, which is basically every country."

Logan loved the effort to provide desalination equipment based on the power cubes. It was an economical way to start giving water to the four-billion people experiencing water shortages during the year. It was the number one issue climate change was causing. Developed nations were doing little to help developing nations with the issue. Logan advocated for new clean water supplies for countries such as India that were running out of water.

Will had applied his understanding of the alien-power generators to build a new generation of power cubes. Space Industries was suing them for copyright infringement. Fuerte had many lawyers and had defended the suit in the international court, claiming that they had done nothing more than Space Industries in building the power technology on publicly available technology. The ownership of the alien artifacts was still in court, and Fuerte had won several recent cases. The case for the artifacts being international property was being supported, so far, in the international and UN courts.

The plan was to manufacture the power cubes to run extremely efficient water desalination and carbon sequestration plants, sold at significantly discounted rates to thousands of locations worldwide. In this way, they could help developing nations reduce the impact of the *Global Burn*. After all, Ruiz argued in court, developing nations were taking the brunt of the effects of environmental disasters, so they should have at least as much access to alien technology as western countries.

Lacy had Logan join no less than ten non-profit boards whose goals supported mitigating climate change impact. He was just back from giving an address at the UN as their newly appointed special ambassador for climate change, a position Ruiz had helped secure.

While Logan was busy flying around the world, Matti focused like a laser on the fourteen cave-based facilities with Krishna. They were spearheading the initial build-out of the initial Sheltered Refugee living accommodations.

Matti and her strategic design group, which included managers of each of the fourteen cave-based facilities, developed several layers of plans— "plans within plans" as Krishna teased Matti when she would add another layer of backup or contingency. From her experience with space station development, Matti knew that a plan without contingencies and revision and testing was no plan but merely a dream, which she didn't consider worth the paper it was put on.

Every entrepreneur knew that a vision must be prototyped, tested, and refined to become practical. That is what made useful products that were efficient and effective. So, Matti's design team didn't just produce plans but were actively testing their living facilities and approaches to process and manage large groups of people through the cave-cities with test families.

The 'plan within a plan' supported migrating pioneers to a new world via quantum gates. If Will Bonalado and his team of scientists could build the quantum gate, these cave-cities would become the migration centers that would help train and prepare those who wished to migrate to the new world.

Sheltered Refugee was the frontman for the project they were now calling Quantum Pioneer. This would keep their ultimate plan protected as they feared resistance from the space program, where most of the world's money was currently being spent. Matti and others feared more competition for resources once world conditions became more severe.

They hoped the space groups would continue to ignore the bottom billions in developing countries and what Sheltered Refugee was doing to help migrate them to a new world, but they weren't naïve enough to think that would last. Thus, the additional plan within the plan was born. The caves that were the Sheltered Refugee organization would provide an excellent transition to their ultimate goal. In time they hoped to become the most significant planetwide migration that nobody knew about.

*Masdar, Abu Dubai*

Logan and Matti flew their Quantum Pioneer core design team, which consisted of thirty engineers, scientists, and architects, to Abu Dubai's ground-breaking sustainable city,

Masdar. They all met in a beautiful enclosed garden after settling into their accommodations.

Matti opened up the meeting, "Welcome to Masdar, everyone! As you know, the number one goal of any new colony will be to be self-sustaining. It *has* to be because there is no one to help them.

"To that end, I'm excited to announce a new member of the team, Tarik Al-Fassi." Tarik stood up from the group.

Logan did the introduction, "Folks, this is Tarik Al-Fassi, who was the lead designer for this wonderful city. He has agreed to head up our core new world colony design that needs to be completely resilient to withstand the new world's rigors with no support from Earth. I'll hand the meeting over to Tarik, and then this afternoon, we will meet in our new design studio to start our agile team designs!"

Tarik stood and greeted the teams, "I am thrilled to meet you all! Krishna and Logan have brought me up to speed on the nature of your project. I am in total awe of the opportunity before us! Rest assured, if Will and his scientists can get the gates built, we will do everything in our power to design a perfect sustainable city that you can replicate many, many times. A dream of mine is to design cities properly from the beginning. Ones that can last a millennium. Let me start with a demonstration."

Tarik tapped his computer, and a simulation of a medium-sized city appeared within a wooded landscape. A lake was on one side. "This is a modest city of fifty-thousand people running in my City Simulator. The software simulates all activity of the people in this city and their resource use. It uses today's approaches, commuting, city water, gas-fired power plants, and farms for food. Basically, how we've built cities for a hundred years now. The numbers on the right measure water, energy, CO2, and all other core resources used by the city and provided by or taken from the surrounding environment. Let me set a time-sequence of one second to be equal to one week and run it for twenty-five years."

The simulation ran. The city was healthy, every indicator was green, but the surrounding environment supplied most of the resources. Nothing was renewed or reused.

"Now, let me run the simulation so that the city has grown to two million people, then I'll set the environmental parameters to their natural limits." The simulation ran again, and the environment turned yellow, then red, and then the simulation stopped with the message "Fail." The date showed the simulation ran for seventeen years. "This is the challenge of Earth right now. For the last ten thousand years, we have designed assuming Earth was big enough to provide all of our critical resources such as energy, water, and air. We never designed with a top-limit population in mind because the environment seemed to be relatively unlimited. Now, we get to design sustainably. At Masdar, we were able to keep the city sustainable for eighty-five years in the simulation! Quite an accomplishment."

Everyone in the crowd was nodding and couldn't wait to get their hands on the cool simulation tools, which would immensely help their task.

"So that is our design task! In Masdar, we developed technologies and systems to address most parameters, such as water, transportation, energy, and waste and made them efficient. We'll be able to build on these learnings.

For Proxima communities, we'll need to have local food production and an ability to build-out the city rapidly since we expect tremendous growth from migration over the first twenty years. Also, we will have to produce all of the household and industrial items we need locally. We have to assume we can't just order widgets from Earth if Earth's systems break down. This will require extensive additive manufacturing capability that we didn't have in Masdar.

"A huge task that I can't wait to start with you all! I invited my design staff to join this team. Five of them accepted and have joined us today." Tarik introduced his core team, and everyone welcomed them.

Matti stood up, "Thanks, Tarik! I feel like you've taken us at least half-way to our goal. I know everyone's super excited to have the opportunity to accomplish what mankind never has before, a city that can grow and scale in total harmony with the environment it is placed within.

"We should also introduce several team members from the ESS One station design team that I led five years ago. As you know, the ESS One design is very sustainable and efficient, being sixty miles above the Earth, although we did assume Earth could provide many supplies. Food and waste are all managed locally. This gives us two great examples of sustainable cities that we'll be drawing from." Matti then introduced her team members as well.

Matti continued after everyone introduced themselves, "Let's have lunch, then Tarik and his team will spend the rest of today taking us on tour. We've set up training sessions for the rest of the week to learn the water, energy, food, and waste techniques they've used at Masdar and that we used on ESS One. We'll then head back to Greece to take the design forward. Our goal is to design a fully sustainable city and be able to test it in Tarik's sustainability simulator to the point where the fail message never appears!"

\* \* \*

All of Sheltered Refugee's plans hinged on Will and his group's ability to produce a quantum gate.

Starting in the late 20th century, many television shows featured quantum gates. Stargate, Quantum Leap, Star Trek, and other shows always depicted a murky, pulsating portal, almost made of water, that you would dive or walkthrough. So the concept wasn't new, but no one had thought they were actually possible until now.

If Will were right and could expand his experiment of sending a small robotic camera through The Tube, it would open a doorway to another world. On one side would be Earth, and on the other, a new world. The thousands of light-years of space between would be bridged over through the magic of quantum physics.

He hoped they could drive trucks and other equipment right through a gate that would be hundreds of feet wide.

Of course, all of this was conjecture, but Will's first small experiment of sending a robot to the new world was repeated in his new lab many times. They started to put together a picture of what was on the other side, even creating an atmospheric sampling robot that returned with atmospheric samples from the different world. This was utterly mind-blowing, but the most significant task was to duplicate the portal. Will spent ninety-nine percent of his time on that primary goal.

They had made progress, but no breakthroughs.

Their source of inspiration was that they knew the gate was

possible. Will believed in this source of inspiration so much that he hosted a 'drive-thru' showing The Tube each week. He insisted people see it with their own eyes, not just view a recording or simulation.

Marcos Arula swatted at Angela's back, "You're taking up all the room."

Angela Chin smirked back and moved to block more of Marcos' view, which elicited a heavy sigh. Marcos walked around the other side of The Tube's transparent case. A large environment-controlled Perspex case surrounded The Tube. It was mounted on a single bracket that was fitted with a slew of monitoring devices. At the top of The Tube, a specialized robot was positioned. It was the same size as the original marble that Logan dropped through it the first time.

The researchers found nothing special about the glass-like marble, so they replaced it with a robot of the same proportion and mass, a miniature mobile research platform. They also found that if they kept The Tube horizontal and moved the robot to the exact center, they could extend the time the robot was in the other world indefinitely.

Will started the demonstration, and it became quiet. Some were present for the first time, while others the tenth time. No one grew tired of the demonstrations.

"I am moving the robot into position just before the transition," Will narrated. The robot moved to the center of The Tube. "I will put the robot on automatic and move it one millimeter forward."

Suddenly the camera view mounted on the screen blanked out. "The robot and its camera have now traveled four-point-two light-years!" Whoops from the audience. "We found this out by triangulating the position of the planet from the data the robot collected while away. The planet is Proxima Centauri b, an Earth-like planet that orbits Proxima Centauri four-point-two light-years away." Thirty tense seconds passed, then the robot and its camera view reappeared.

Will then said the magic words, "I will replay the digital recording the robot just shot. It moved a few inches onto Proxima, filmed for thirty seconds, and then returned to its starting point here in the lab."

The recording played, and for thirty seconds, everyone was enthralled. These were images from another planet. Unbelievable! The photos showed a plain with dust and shrubs blowing. Small hills were in the background. A star shone in the sky, which was a dull red color.

"We have measured the gravity as one-point-one times that of Earth. The surprising thing is that it has an atmosphere that is similar in density and composition to ours. Measurements of the planet from early Earth-based telescopes thought that it might not have an atmosphere, but, apparently, that was wrong. We'll now have a status update from teams. Marcus?" Will prompted.

Marcus ran the high-energy physics team that was responsible for gate power requirements. "We have analyzed the power usage during transit and, as suspected, it is off the charts. It is ten times that of a first-generation quantum power generator created from The Object. We have precise readings and are trying to get a smaller object to transit to compare readings. We want to get a per ounce estimate when we scale up to transfer larger objects.

"We feel immense power is the key to take us into this new world of quantum transfer. Power for our own gates should be possible using new generations of quantum generators.

The breakthroughs made by Will and his team that developed the generators should work for this device—we just have to scale up the power transfer for gates significantly."

The word 'just' was always a loaded word. In the team's vocabulary, 'just' usually meant a significantly herculean effort but one that the scientists would gladly devote themselves to without a second thought.

Will asked Angela to give the materials report as she headed that group. "We have exciting news. We know the exact atomic composition of The Tube and are working on reproducing the constructed material. But reproducing the material and getting it to exhibit the quantum effects are two different things. We haven't made much progress on that front. Also, the circuitry hasn't been replicated."

Will took over from there to talk about the quantum effects, "We are using what we learned from the quantum power generator project about how to reproduce the particular quantum effect needed for matter transfer. The Tube is more sophisticated than The Object, contrary to its size.

Will summarized, "We see the transfer happen, know where it is happening, can see the power used, and can even analyze the quantum material. But how that material is tuned to its quantum equal is unknown. At this point, we are hoping that we can reproduce the quantum material at the exact 'frequency' of the current tube but in a larger area. We hope that the receiving quantum material on the other planet is more extensive than The Tube or can adapt to a more significant quantum 'plate' on our end."

Will then ended the meeting by saying, "Great progress, let's not be discouraged. We are playing with the sciences of the gods."

To emphasize the point, he replayed the thirty-second clip from Proxima Centauri b.

\* \* \*

Matti's comm unit awakened her at one in the morning with a flashing red alert. It was the Mt. Kenya cave complex. "Oh, my." Matti breathed.

"What is it?" Logan asked. He was waking too, his comm unit flashing red.

"Explosion and cave-in at the Mt. Kenya facility."

They were scrambling now to get dressed as fast as possible. "How bad?"

"Really bad. They are trying to get to those under the collapse now. Ten percent of the new structure collapsed. Luckily, they hadn't moved anyone in yet, but workers are trapped."

Logan was on the comm with the airport, "They will have a plane ready by the time we get there. A rescue team will be aboard too."

When they landed in Nairobi, Kenya, they were picked up by a helicopter. It was crowded, as expected. The company's rescue team was on the same chopper with their full equipment.

When they landed at the facility twenty minutes later at the Panga ya Saidi cave complex, they couldn't believe the destruction. A lot of the top layer over the cave complex collapsed. They were triaging the survivors by the entrance, and many helicopters and emergency vehicles were on-site.

Matti ran over to where it looked like a command center was set up and started working with the lead rescue officers.

Logan ran over to the facility's entrance and down the stairs, asking where he could help. He ended up putting on a gas mask and air tank and ran with other rescuers to the scene of the disaster. They were using a forklift to lift beams to get to survivors. Logan slid into another forklift and started helping carefully removing beams as other rescuers helped check debris. After saving five trapped workers, a rescuer signaled Logan he was needed topside.

Logan gave his seat to someone else and made his way back up, carrying the front end of a stretcher. Matti waved him over when she saw him. "We need you to talk with the reporters. Lacy is over there." Before Logan went to Lacy, he stopped to talk to the chief of the fire and rescue team.

"Logan Conover, I lead Sheltered Refugee; what can you tell me about the extent of the damage, and do you have any causes?"

"The ceiling of floor three in Unit D collapsed. We don't know the cause yet. Twenty-four people were trapped, and we have gotten twenty out."

Logan then made his way over to Lacy, who talked with a reporter, and she pulled him over.

The reporter recognized him and asked him, "Mr. Conover, you have just been down to the cave-in?"

"Yes, I was helping move debris. The rescue team is working hard to save the few people that are still trapped."

"Thank you, sir; any official comment on behalf of Sheltered Refugee?"

"We will work with the families of any injured to make sure they have everything they need. We take care of our employees, and we believe in this facility's value in helping refugees. This is a temporary tragic setback, but we will rebuild and continue to provide a shelter for those in need."

It took another month to get the facility back on track. They changed their contractor as it appeared from the investigation that faulty cement was used in one portion of the building and was not inspected properly. Matti and her team had insisted the construction crews check all of the rest of the facilities to make sure they were built correctly. They especially made sure to test the cement before they started rebuilding the entire collapsed housing unit.

Matti and Logan returned to Greece weary but glad they had met the emergency with a proper response. The Kenyan facility was back on track. They also made arrangements to tour all other facilities and Proxima buildings to ensure all regulations were followed. They rearranged their schedules and for the next two months toured facilities with structural engineers. They might have an intense schedule for getting Proxima ready for new pioneers, but any more accidents would derail their progress on all fronts.

\* \* \*

Two years passed, and the team accomplished an immense amount of planning and preparation at Greece's facility. Kira was fifteen and could speak fluent Greek. She was heavily involved with her own plan on how to save animals. She was familiar with the plan within the plan and was involved in the scientific research needed to see what animals could survive in a world with one-point-one times Earth's gravity. Would dogs and cats adapt? What about farm animals and wild animals, too? She helped biologists on the team to prepare farm animals to live on Proxima.

Most importantly, from Matti's and Logan's point-of-view, Kira thrived in her new environment, convincing them that they made the right decision to come.

Matti was at an important meeting with her top construction contractor executives in Malta. They had just finished lunch, and she launched into business, "We have just one more thing I'd like to discuss." None of the companies knew her plan within a plan, but she was about to take them into her confidence. Matti's Quantum Pioneer design team had just finished their designs, and it was time to start bringing the world's leading construction companies in to build the world's largest 3-D printer. The plan called for printing all of their buildings, a radical approach that would allow them to automate and rapidly build entire cities in the new world.

Rans Larsen, CEO of Bech Corporation, Chester Hayes of BritCon, and Lai Ling from Beijing Construction all turned to her in surprise. They had just finished approving the final contracts for the cities they had almost finished for Sheltered Refugee in the fourteen underground sites. They didn't like surprises.

Matti smiled, "I appreciate all of your professionalism and cooperation in wrapping up the Sheltered Refugee building phase. But there is another phase of a somewhat larger scope that I would like to offer you."

Rans recovered soonest. "Really? I'm intrigued. Please proceed!" All of the executives settled back in their chairs, curious by the potential new offer.

"We want you to help us build out entirely new cities whose primary purpose is to achieve self-sustaining expansion—cities that build themselves bigger." This alone got their interest, then Matti dropped the bombshell. "And we need them to withstand one-point-one gravities and be built on the new world of Proxima Centauri b."

They were all stunned.

Ling was the first to recover, "You're joking."

Matti lifted her hands in a shrug, "No, I'm not. Let me take you through the history of this and why I'm presenting this now. Consider your Top-Secret security clause of our contracts invoked."

Matti took a deep breath, "You all know of my husband's proclivity to find alien artifacts?" All of the executives nodded. Logan's reputation was well known. "Well, he has found another artifact. Welcome to Quantum Pioneer, our phase II project that will save one billion of earth's poorest people from the hardest-hit areas of the *Global Burn*."

Matti called in her top Quantum Pioneer designers, and they proceeded to outline their work with The Tube and the city build-out design for construction of a colony on the new world. "The centerpiece is to construct a city for three-hundred-thousand people from each of our underground facilities. But these cities will have the ability to keep expanding themselves. Over ten years, each city splits and creates four additional cities of just over ten million people, for a total of a billion new pioneers. All this will be kick-started by an initial set of massive 3D building printers and automated mineral extraction facilities we would like your help constructing.

"When complete, the cities will enable the most significant human diaspora in history, dwarfing the previously most massive migration when twenty-million people were displaced in 1947 with India's Partition. That displacement created the Muslim countries of Pakistan and Bangladesh."

When Matti was finished with the presentation, there was silence for a full forty-five seconds, which Ran broke, "Well, that's damn ambitious. I assume you've worked out how to get to this new world safely and within our lifetimes?"

Matti then proceeded to show them the video from Proxima Centauri b. They were duly impressed. Even shocked. Once they learned that they could just drive over equipment and people without years of travel, they became excited that the work was more than a fairy tale project.

After Proxima's introductory video, Ran modified his question, "Do you know how to get there at scale? Bigger than a marble-sized robot?"

Matti confided that that ability was not yet working but wanted to proceed from a design and logistics point of view, assuming Will and his team would make the breakthrough they needed.

"Clearly, this plan will necessitate an entirely new approach to staging materials. It will add new meaning to the term *working remotely*," she stated. "But consider this, we calculate that using a ground-based approach will be one hundred times cheaper than building in space and transporting everyone up the space elevator."

Everyone nodded at this and knew that this was, at least on the surface of it, a better plan than trying to put a billion people in space. There were limits to what they could accomplish with even the latest human technology. Basing the strategy on proven technology for the built-out made sense to them, assuming the gates could be built.

Matti brought in Mr. Ruiz, and he talked about the financing of any potential project, "After the initial build-out, we anticipate a self-contained economy. We very much take the word *pioneer* to heart—on a project of this scale, we can only provide seed-money for making our pioneers self-sustaining. We can finance the first seven million, the first twenty-four cities, but after that, it has to be self-sustaining. Please operate from that point-of-view and not a contract to build the entire facilities on this new world—we are building cities that can build themselves, not building it all—that would require the trillion-dollar budgets of our space friends." He couldn't resist the jibe.

The fact that the bottom billion were already used to austere conditions and were perfectly happy without one-thousand-plus square foot per person living space as those in the Western world were used to was a huge emotional and financial advantage. Developing nations' thinking was much more adapted to migrations than first-world citizens in many critical ways.

After the meeting, executives spent a lively three weeks with their home offices, taking into confidence their key engineers. They met again in Greece and agreed to proceed, which generated a great new sense of energy for the Quantum Pioneer team.

\* \* \*

While Matti was convincing the world's largest construction companies to take on the Quantum Pioneer effort, Logan and Will were having heart-to-heart meetings about the quantum transfer research. Will's team had made further progress by creating a three-foot-wide prototype gate, but they could only see through it. Passing material through the bridge eluded them. While it was genuinely fantastic progress, it lacked the critical and all-important ingredient needed to succeed, actual transfer.

Logan and Will were in Logan's office, with its broad, expansive view of the Mediterranean, when Mr. Ruiz entered the office to join them.

Logan waited until Will stopped intensely talking to greet Ruiz, "Great, you're here! Here is the problem in a nutshell," he started. "We need more information on this alien artifact. Will's team has done wonders, but they are hitting conceptual walls, and we feel we need to expand our efforts to get more information to work from. Ideas?"

Ruiz smiled and seemed incredibly proud of himself. "I was wondering if this was going to happen, so I took the precaution of having our intelligence wing plant someone on the UN's alien research team that is still going over your last find on Anteros."

Space Industries and the UN continued their joint sharing agreement in the research they did and maintained a small team on the Anteros asteroid.

"Perfect! That will be really helpful." He then put on a more serious expression. "But we were feeling that it's going to be critical that we visit the original site on Anteros."

Ruiz lost his smile, "Oh."

"Exactly," Logan continued. "We feel there must be more artifacts related to The Tube and that the current research team is missing key evidence we need. I just stumbled upon The Tube, but there may be more alien artifacts still there. Maybe even an instruction manual," Logan joked.

Will perked up. "You joke, but they may have left something like that. I mean, if you were an alien, you wouldn't just scatter technology like that around. They must have placed it with intentionality. They must be used to working with alien species enough to know education is required. I keep feeling we have a slice and not the whole picture. We have to have the whole picture. And soon," Will added.

Logan gave Ruiz a 'there you go' look.

Ruiz frowned. "Do both of you need to be there, or can we send someone else?"

Logan thought about it. "Both of us. I know where I found The Tube, and Will is the world expert on the artifacts' technology."

Ruiz nodded. "OK, wow. I'll let you know when I figure something out."

Logan called, "Thanks, boss!" as Ruiz was on his way out. Ruiz grimaced.

# Tipping Point

*Year:2049 +4°F*

*Earth Population: 10,893,736,733*

*Population off-earth in Solar System: 124,044*

*Population in other Star Systems: 1 Robot*

*Yearly population decrease due to Global Burn: 30,225,092*

In the calm of the Pacific in June of 2049, typhoon Huko started as a tropical storm. It was erratic for longer than most and stayed in the mid-pacific for over three weeks. On July 11th, it gained speed, turning into a monster category seven typhoon with winds exceeding 265 miles per hour. It roared directly toward Taiwan.

Taiwan was six hours away from what appeared to be total destruction. They evacuated as many as possible to mainland China as even China took pity on what they viewed as their errant province's doomed residents. Only two million of the twenty-five million on the island escaped before the devastation began. Huge waves rolled over the island, the winds alone destroying most buildings. Social media transmitted the horrific scenes of death and destruction as it was happening. When it was over, there was nothing left of Taiwan except the mangled buildings of a once-great nation.

Three days later, a massive fire rolled through southern California's dry grasses directly toward Los Angeles. The fire moved at an incredible thirty miles per hour, leaving everyone scrambling to get out of its way. It cut a one-mile-wide gash through Los Angeles, destroying nearly one hundred thousand homes and causing one trillion dollars in damage.

Five days after the fire, a heatwave hit central and eastern Europe with temperatures reaching one-hundred-fifteen degrees Fahrenheit for over four weeks. One-hundred-thousand people perished, unable to endure or find refuge from the intense heat.

While the heatwave was rolling across Europe, a massive chunk of the Antarctic, the size of Texas, broke free. This represented a complete collapse of the West Antarctic Ice Sheet. Rapid melting was predicted to raise sea levels by one meter in less than four years. This more rapid than expected rise of water would overwhelm many cities worldwide and put most of southern Florida under threat.

If all of these disasters weren't enough, the strain of ten billion people and the lack of rain-water in many areas of the world were causing local water wars. The worst of these was the war between Egypt and Ethiopia over the life-giving waters of the Nile.

Sugiyama Matsuko was a journalist that was covering the war for BNN. She was reporting from a dam built on the Nile in Ethiopia, "The devastation you see behind me is the latest act in the water war escalation between Egypt and Ethiopia. Egypt is reported to have bombed the Eddel dam that was recently completed by Ethiopia. The dam was intended to control eighty-five percent of the upper Nile water. Egypt has argued that it was an act of war for Ethiopia to try and capture and stop the flow of water downstream to Egypt since that water is critical for Egyptian life and agriculture."

Sugiyama's cameraman panned out over the entire dam. It was a mess of bombed concrete and water spray where the dam was breached. "Officials are evacuating the entire downstream residents of the dam as they fear the entire dam will give way soon due to the damage."

General Moray Mosa was originally from Tanzania and was appointed by the United Nations to form a humanitarian and military force. He had a stocky build and moved and spoke with clarity and determination. Unlike previous military forces at the UN, Moray was working to put teeth in his. Currently, he deployed his troops to block Ethiopian and Egyptian forces from clashing after the dam was attacked.

He was on a call with the Secretary-General, Dr. Sabine Olsen. General Mosa nodded, "Yes, I can hold them here as long as you start negotiations. We have to give them a path to resolution, or I fear I won't be able to contain them."

"Perfect, we will resolve this quickly, or neither will end up with water. Let's keep in touch daily." Sabine turned to her staff and spent the next hour, putting together a plan to meet with the Egyptian and Ethiopian ambassadors. She would even sweeten the deal with access to Sheltered Refugees' new desalination technology. Logan and his group gave the UN the ability to leverage the latest technology where it was needed most, which she was very grateful for.

Dr. Olsen was doing wonders at the UN. Their strategy was working across the world. They sent enough firepower to maintain a ceasefire and then simultaneously forced both sides to the negotiation table and made sure both sides received enough help to make it easier to cooperate than to fight.

Sabine believed the UN should be a revenue generator to support its own expenses and not be dependent on countries for assistance. For instance, they were receiving billions off of the quantum power generator licenses they sold. Since they jointly held the patents with Space Industries, they received revenue from the sale of generators worldwide. It was this strategy to finance the UN that gave it renewed life and influence on the world stage.

It was past eleven at night when Sabine finished talking with the Egyptian and Ethiopian ambassadors. Both agreed to the outline of a peace accord. She stood in a room adjoining her office that she had set up as a personal command center. On one entire wall was a digital image of the world, color-coded to show all of the events, metrics, and UN resource deployments that were occurring. She had the world's pulse and was making plans to bring the UN's resources to bear to alleviate as much hardship as possible.

Even with all her efforts Sabine still shook her head. A metric in the lower right of her screen kept going up by millions every day. It was the projection of the number of refugees in five years, and it was already at two-hundred-fifty million or over two percent of the world population. The number below it was in red and showed the number of deaths due to climate change. It was thirty-million for this year alone.

\* \* \*

Matti and Logan were overwhelmed with the surge in activity for Sheltered Refugee. Logistics for their organization, UNICEF, and many others were consolidated into the World

Relief Organization, which maintained the best infrastructure already in place to coordinate world relief efforts. The number of climate refugees was already four times the number of people displaced by non-climate causes such as war. Droughts, floods, ocean-level rise, famines, fires; the list was endless now, and they all forced people to flee their homes.

Matti activated their underground shelters two months ahead of schedule to respond to the immense need and hardship occurring in the world. Matti and Logan were glad they possessed a tremendous capacity to permanently shelter refugees rather than just provide the usual standard the world had adopted for refugees: tent camps. The many tent camps that did exist across the globe were over-burdened and unhealthy. Those classic and rapidly built above-ground camps did not have the water and resource infrastructure that Matti and her planning group designed into their cave-cities.

The World Relief Organization liked Matti's model so much they were copying it around the world. Displacement was the new normal, and they needed more permanent facilities to respond to the need.

Matti and her team were on an emergency footing, bringing thousands of volunteers and temporary workers to meet the refugee population's rapid scaling at their new facilities. Their refugee population went from an experimental thirty thousand to over four million in two weeks. An additional four million were planned over the next six months as they brought all of the facilities online.

Sheltered Refugee also received additional funding from the UN and Fuerte Group to double the size of their facilities, adding another ten underground cities, bringing the number of sites to twenty-four.

Almost every significant cave in the world was being developed by the organization as a refuge for climate refugees. The Sheltered Refugee logo became recognized worldwide as a source of shelter and hope. Matti specialized in branding and applied it to marketing refugee centers as much as any commercial product. She also knew a positive brand image would be critical when they needed to have the world's trust to support their Proxima migration plans.

\* \* \*

Chi Pham held onto his two daughters' hands while looking back to see if his wife was keeping up. They carried large backpacks and had left their home in Ho Chi Minh city in the middle of the night. A new typhoon was headed straight for the heart of the population center.

Chi's father and mother were killed in a flash flood the previous month. Chi wasn't taking any chances. He heard of the Sheltered Refugee city built in the Son Doong cave in the north. They took a train for eight hours to get there. Many other refugees were also headed to the cave, hoping it would provide shelter. The cave was near the coast, but he assumed, being underground, it would be protected. An hour later, after a special Son Doong bus picked them up, they arrived at the cave entrance. The cave entrance was impressive and beautiful, but it took them another three hours to register.

Being the largest cave in the world at over two-hundred meters high, Son Doong was a real wonder. Both his daughters looked through sleepy eyes, which grew wide when they reached the entrance. They excitedly talked about the beautiful colors of the cave and water. The moss and greenery inside the cave's opening showed bright, with shafts of early morning light coming through the open top. The reflections off the water at the base made the entrance appear like a magical adventure, quite unlike how Chi felt. Still, it bolstered his spirits to be going through such a beautiful spot. Maybe it is a sign of good things to come, he thought with a glint of hope.

In Ho Chi Minh, Chi earned his Ph.D. in civil engineering and specialized in robotics and 3D printing construction. A year ago, he almost took a position with Space Industries working on the new ESS space stations but chose to work in a lab on experimental methods to optimize ground-based building because of his family. But that was all gone now, and he was happy to have kept his family safe.

"Transfer document, please," an agent at the registration desk asked.

"Here it is. We certified it in Ho Chi Minh," Chi said as he handed over the one piece of paper that represented his family's future. The agent smiled up at him and his wife, which was surprising considering all customs agents he ever dealt with usually bore a frown and looked at everyone suspiciously.

"You are all set, Mr. and Mrs. Pham; enjoy your time at the Son Doong facility."

Hang gave a slight bow. "Bạn thật là tử tế," that is very kind of you.

Hundreds of other families were also checking in. Amidst the chaotic atmosphere, Chi and Hang were able to go down at least fifteen floors in an elevator and find their assigned apartment. They shared a balcony to a large courtyard that was brightened by a distinctive skylight that funneled light from far above.

The complex was large, with at least five hundred other units in their courtyard. Their apartment was spacious and nicely furnished. Both were pleasant surprises. There were two rooms, the main room with a kitchen, and a back bedroom with a small bathroom. All in all, they felt relieved. Chi had envisioned a smelly rat-infested refugee camp, so this was practically heaven.

In the morning, Chi and Hang took their two daughters for a tour of the city then spent the rest of the day at the employment office. Everyone in the community was required to sign up for service of one form or another. Hang signed up for daycare duty. She was excited that she would work so close to her daughters as they were still too young, at three and five, to go to school. Sachi, her eldest, could soon sign up for the kindergarten that was provided. She looked forward to that.

When Chi went up to the agent in charge at the employment center, it took longer.

After ten minutes of questions, the agent raised his eyebrows, "We need to have you come this way to meet with our manager. We are in great need of your skills."

Chi was encouraged by this news but wary of who *we* was; who in a refugee site could need 3D printing skills?

The manager was courteous and interviewed Chi for ten minutes, then came to a decision, "Mr. Pham, it turns out your construction skills are critical to us right now. We are willing to move you and your family to a larger apartment in another complex. We can also provide you special privileges and a salary of ten million Dong per month if you would be willing to work in our construction team to help build our facilities. Is that acceptable?"

Chi was thrilled.

"Yes, very much I would like that job. I was not expecting my skills to be useful, and I am happy to accept. Would we still have access to the daycare facility my wife will be working at?"

The manager said, yes. It was near, so no change in her job would be required.

Chi came out and told his wife. Tears filled her eyes. So much good was happening to them here. It was more than she could have wished for. Chi and Hang moved that day into their new apartment, which was even more beautiful than the last. It contained two bedrooms and plenty of space for their entire family to be comfortable. Hang ordered takeout food to celebrate. Chi couldn't wait to start his new position the next day.

\* \* \*

Logan was busy with a massive surge in demand for the products his non-profit companies manufactured to help mitigate the effects of the Global Burn. Desalination equipment saw a five-hundred-percent increase in sales over the last year. The useful devices were in especially great demand at refugee centers to convert seawater into drinkable water. They provided the equipment at cost for humanitarian centers.

Logan wrapped up a worldwide conference call with his supply chain vendors for the desalination equipment. He was ensuring they could handle the increased demand. He then received a call from Ruiz.

"You and Will need to drop everything and be in Singapore at three in the afternoon tomorrow. You are part of a *scientific* expedition that was just approved to go up to ESS One."

He emphasized the word scientific enough that Logan picked up on the idea this was not an ordinary request.

Logan replied, "Should we be prepared for space-based EVAs?"

"Yes, and more," Ruiz responded. "And good luck. You'll be traveling with my best people. Meet them at our space readiness facility in Singapore as soon as you can."

Logan spent the next few hours making arrangements. Will knew immediately what was going on when Logan mentioned Singapore since the space elevator was located there. He was thrilled! If they could get back to Anteros, maybe they could uncover the additional clues they needed to help them solve the mystery of how quantum transfer could be achieved.

When Logan got home, he woke Matti and explained the situation while she helped him pack. They opened their cache of space equipment they were sent when they resigned from Space Industries.

"Are you sure you will be able to find what you are looking for?" Matti asked, clearly worried.

Logan took her hands and looked at her.

"My intuition hasn't steered me wrong yet, and I really feel there is a lot still up there. It's a nagging feeling I've had since I was on the site the first time. I feel an alien civilization intentionally left this technology. We just have to put all the pieces together. And I don't think the research teams to date have been thinking broadly enough! They see it as an ancient dig site they are excavating. I see it as a priceless puzzle with all the clues we need to recreate the technology for our own use. I think the difference in perspective will be key."

Matti could see he was determined to go through with the

trip. "Do you have military protection? It could get dicey up there."

Logan thought about it and called Ruiz back and talked for a couple of minutes. "He said he has two retired Space Seals that are going to be on the 'scientific' team with us."

Logan kissed Matti and held her for a minute. He wasn't a commando, and he knew it. The little hand-to-hand training he received in the military wasn't the real deal. He thought of calling his brother, who was a Commander in the newly christened space force. Logan didn't want to compromise him, though. So instead, he left him a text telling his brother about the expedition he was going on and then drove off to catch his flight that was leaving from the private airstrip at their compound.

Will met him at the airstrip, and several company employees began loading their gear. The jet would fly them to Singapore in ten hours, so there was just enough time to get ready to go up the space elevator to ESS One. How they would be received at the space station would be another issue, but it was the only way to get to Anteros. It felt like they were walking into a trap. He hoped he was wrong. Will and Logan climbed aboard the plane, found their seats, and didn't even feel it take off. They were both fast asleep.

# Back to Anteros

It took another day to get to ESS One after they arrived in Singapore. True to his word, Ruiz provided two agents, and three scientists were heading up to the artifact site on Anteros as well.

Ruiz's team provided a disguise and false identity for Logan and Will, but Logan wasn't sure it would be enough. Face recognition software was flawless these days. Logan knew it was all worth it if they could make a breakthrough. And he knew they would make that breakthrough if they could just make it back to the discovery site on Anteros.

The ESS trip was uneventful, and they were ushered into a shuttle that was to take them to the dig site where there were accommodations for the investigation team. Logan was surprised at how well the whole expedition was proceeding. Just a day later, they made it to Anteros, which was now peacefully orbiting the moon. They took a Loadstar over to the dig site, settled into the nearby facilities, and prepared to go out for their first walk.

* * *

Back at ESS One, Colonel Alexander Tibbets walked into Paul

Manning's office and waited patiently while Paul finished a conference call. Things weren't going well at ESS. Highly placed Earthside trustees of Space Industries and government officials were putting enormous pressure on them to start taking on residents into the several ESS stations under construction. ESS One was almost at capacity, but it mainly held construction and technical personnel responsible for building the other ESS stations. ESS Two and ESS Three were located at the same altitude and spaced evenly in a circle around the earth with ESS One. The other ESS stations' construction schedules would be extended two to three years if they opened them to residents before being finished.

Their plea for patience was falling on deaf ears. There was little patience Earth-side after the numerous disasters. Many wealthy stockholders were afraid that the next catastrophe would take out *their* city, and they wanted to escape to the stations. Colonel Tibbetts briefly wondered, as he heard the last part of the latest conversation, whether there was any formal approach to choosing who would get to come up. He wryly suspected it would be those with the best connections and not those with the best credentials.

Paul finished the call and looked up, weariness in his eyes.

"Are you sure it's him?" he asked.

The Colonel nodded, "Absolutely. Logan thought he could get through security with his simple disguise, but we immediately tagged him and Will. We then let them through to the site to give them false hope."

Paul finished the thought by adding, "and to see what the heck they are up to."

The Colonel asked, "When should we bring them in? I assume you'll want to question them?"

Paul wanted to string them up by their thumbs and lock them away forever. But he was intrigued by what they were doing on Anteros. He thought they were up to something before they left the ESS station four years ago, but he was too busy at the time to pursue his concern. He turned back to the Colonel.

"No. Let them have the week and see what they find. As they prepare to leave, send in the troops and grab them and confiscate what they find."

The Colonel smiled. "Gladly, I never liked how those two left us and started their own organization. We'll get down to the bottom of what they are doing and what they know."

The tenser the situation on earth, the more the Colonel tightened up security on the station. He didn't like loose ends.

\* \* \*

Logan was walking slowly around the Anteros artifact site. Gravity was minimal on asteroids, so the suits he and the investigators wore were configured with special weights in them so they could walk without floating off into space. This was a much better solution than grappling hooks like Logan used when he was on Anteros.

Being back woke disturbing memories from the last time there. He felt the stillness again. Not being panicked this time, he found he possessed an ability to look at the site with fresh eyes.

Two excavations were underway, and each was formally staked out like every archeological dig he'd ever seen. Each area had perfect vertical walls and was dug from three to five feet down, formed into perfect squares. A real feat on an asteroid. But he noticed the researchers focused on the fifty feet or so around where The Object was found. He found The Tube twenty meters from there, off to the side. He mentioned this to Will, who was looking over the site as well.

Will looked up then toggled their pre-arranged private comm channel. "You go ahead and move over to where you want to explore. I'll keep the rest busy here with questions."

Logan left the area taped out and walked thirty paces to where he had found The Tube. By the looks of the ground, the research crew had not excavated this area. It looked exactly the same. He remembered the rock formations like it was yesterday. How he had bent down to pick up The Tube where it was lying half-submerged in the gritty dirt.

He set his empty artifact case down to the side and took a small shovel from the backpack he carried. He kneeled down slowly, the only speed of movement one ever dared on an asteroid with so little gravity. He started to brush away the loose sand and loosened about twenty spades of soil, six inches deep when he hit something solid. He cleared away the additional ground until he exposed a two-foot by two-foot lid.

"Found something," he remarked to Will on their private channel. "Can you believe it even has handles? Looks a lot like the box we found The Object in."

Will radioed back, "How are we going to get that out of here without anyone noticing?"

Logan was too excited to care when he talked to the agents Ruiz sent later. Surely, they would have a plan to conceal what they found on this trip. He did, however, kick himself for not talking to the agents before they went out. Whatever they did would be difficult to hide as Space Industries, and the UN would instantly file a legal claim to any findings on the site. Then his thoughts turned more belligerent. He was trying to save millions of people. They could take their legal games, and… he never finished the thought as his spade hit another object.

He spent another hour uncovering the boxes. He found two, along with a shallow one and a smaller square box. He lightly covered the boxes to find them again quickly, then walked back to the research base.

When he finished getting through the airlock, he motioned to the two agents. They followed him to his room. When the door was closed, Vicky motioned for silence then tapped a few buttons on her watch.

"There, that should secure the room," she informed the others. Logan related what he found, and Vicky finished his thought with, "and you want to know how we are going to conceal your findings, right?"

"Exactly," Logan responded.

"We came prepared for that. We have another agent on security at ESS One who will be flying the last shuttle here. That is when we think Paul and his folks will make their move."

"You think Paul knows I'm here?" Logan was surprised.

Finn, the other agent, smiled. "Not only does he know you're here, he probably hopes to learn about and confiscate everything you find. We've anticipated that, and our double-agent will help get us all out of here when the time comes."

Finn saw Logan's surprised look and continued, "Sir, ever since you and Will first left ESS One, we've been working to divert any attempts of governments or Space Industries to figure out what you took. We've been working in the background for a while to give them false leads and misinformation. That's our job."

Logan was impressed. He didn't keep up much with this aspect of the job but knew Ruiz had put in place extensive security. It was how Ruiz found out about The Tube in the first place and how a relatively large team could keep their Quantum Pioneer efforts from hitting public notice for so long.

"OK, what about the other scientists?" Logan waved his hand back in the direction of the other rooms where the scientists were.

Finn answered. "They've been briefed by their superiors to give you space and not to look too closely at what you find. Believe it or not, they know who you are. You're pretty famous on Earth, you know. They are sympathetic to the cause. They also told us they expected you to share any findings with the UN."

They all left the compartment and went to the galley for dinner. Tonight, as every night, dinner consisted of two tubes of purple and green paste each. *Ah, to be back in space again*, Logan thought. He didn't miss the food in space.

By day three, Logan enlisted the help of Will and the two agents. They uncovered the two containers that were buried. The square box contained five more Tubes, a fantastic discovery with huge implications. The other box contained several other small devices similar in size to The Tubes. The two agents took the two containers back to the base to hide them and left Logan and Will at the site.

Shortly after they left, Logan saw a hazy shimmer in the light from the direction of a large boulder a few feet away. He walked in that direction.

Will was behind Logan about fifty feet and suddenly saw

him disappear. Will ran over to the spot Logan disappeared and then stopped short. He thought better of running after Logan and, instead, radioed the other agents who hurried back out to the site.

Logan was walking toward a blurry, shining area he saw by one rock. He cocked his head to the side. When he got to the place, he hesitated, then walked forward slowly with his hand out. Suddenly, he was in a completely different space. Startled, he looked around. It wasn't another planet; it was more of a neutral space, neither light nor dark and endless in all directions. The ground was gravelly and brown, but there were no hills or obstructions in any direction. Logan was excited.

"Where am I?" Logan shouted. A slew of images and diagrams filled his vision that he couldn't comprehend.

He breathed a deep breath to calm himself. "What can you tell us about the tube?" As he said it, he mentally formed a picture of the Tube they had found. An image of the Tube was displayed in front of him, and then it started growing until it was a full gate. The image showed a shadow of a person walking through it, and then the person was in another world. The images were time-lapsed and showed a small colony being built. Wow, Logan thought. This is it. They really gave us this discovery to go to other worlds and live. He was so excited. Now all he had to do was get back and get Will in here.

Logan formulated a picture of an exit sign.

"How do I get back? Exit?"

This time a single image of a light leading back behind him appeared. He turned around and followed it for several steps. His final step was onto Anteros. He was back. Will and two shocked agents were facing him.

"Whoa!" Finn yelled when he reappeared.

Logan exclaimed to Will, "This is what we were looking for, a device that will answer our questions. You have to go in there! It must be a training device. It's all empty, but it inundates you with visual information when you mentally ask a specific question. I couldn't begin to comprehend all that it was trying to show me. Will, you've got to go over there. You'll know what to ask and hopefully how to understand it."

Will was still in shock. "You want me to go to God knows where? Where were you exactly? Are you crazy?"

Logan smiled and saw from Will's point-of-view. "Look, I came back, right? Getting back was easy. I just asked how to Exit, and a big Exit light came on behind me. This is the only way we're going to figure out how The Tube works, I'm sure of it."

Will regained his composure and saw Logan's point. But he didn't know if his intellectual curiosity was as intense as his sense of self-preservation. Like when he was on a boy-scout trip as a kid, this seemed awful, and everyone was jumping into a big pond from a fifty-foot cliff. To him, they were plum nuts, and he was not going to jump. Could he jump now? Logan was staring at him expectantly, and he reasoned this was the key they were looking for, something to explain the technology.

"OK, but if I die, I'll never forgive you, and may you feel bad about doing me in your whole life," he stated.

Will edged forward and then suddenly disappeared.

He was gone for two hours. Logan started getting worried and was thinking of stepping in after him. He really didn't want to have to tell Will's wife, Carol, 'sorry, but I lost your husband in another dimension.' Just as Logan was about to step through the space, Will finally came back. He had a big grin on his face.

"That was amazing!" Will exclaimed. "Oh my gosh, that was unbelievable. I don't understand everything, but oh my gosh, I have a good idea of what we're doing wrong. I'm starting to get it. Oh my gosh."

Logan was relieved. Not only was Will back in one piece, but they had been right about coming back to the site.

The agents onsite suddenly looked up and looked concerned. "Sirs, there is an incoming unscheduled craft approaching the site."

Logan and Will looked up suddenly with concern. Logan looked at the others, "OK, we have to hold them off until we can find out how this Instructor system is hooked up. It's still active, and it's critical to take with us."

Will and Logan worked quickly to find what was powering and running the Instructor system. Meanwhile, Finn and Vicky ran back to the facility and reemerged a second later with rifles and... grenades?

Wow, Logan thought. They came prepared. He hoped it wouldn't come to an all-out war.

They could see the shuttle now, but it would still be a few minutes before it could land. Why now? They were so close.

Will finished figuring out the Instructor device. It consisted of a power device like the original Object and another box that must be what passed for a computer, mental projector, or whatever they had walked into. The fact they disappeared still baffled Logan. They also found a long strip of material similar to The Tube laying in the ground between two rocks. It was three feet long. That would prove interesting to try to reverse engineer. They carefully picked up all three devices once Will

161

detached the power source. It was possible since it was similar to the power Object they had understood for several years. They stowed the three devices in another artifact case, and both Logan and Will carried it back to the facility.

Finn and Tracy were waving them on to hurry as the shuttle was just about to land. Logan and Will lugged the case into the facility just as the shuttle was landing. They struggled to get it stowed in the wall that held all the artifact cases they collected. It was amazing how much they found; Logan would hate to lose it all now. He possessed zero faith that Space Industries would use the new finds the way they should be used. Logan knew that they would lock them up in research for years, whereas Logan and the Quantum Pioneer program could use them immediately for all they were worth. They needed to get these artifacts back to Greece as soon as possible.

Logan went back outside. Two security guards and Colonel Tibbets came out of the shuttle and were walking over. They didn't look like they were here to help. They had as much weaponry on them as Ruiz's agents did. When they were fifty feet away, the Colonel spoke up over the comm.

"I don't know who you two are," the Colonel pointed to the two agents, "but you are trespassing on private territory under false pretenses and in a heap of trouble. There is no back-up out here. Stand down now, and we won't press charges. And you," he pointed to Logan, "have a whole lot of explaining to do."

Tracy looked over to Logan and signaled to him to stall. Logan didn't know what she was plotting but played along. Tibbets had nerve talking to him that way.

Logan stepped forward, "Listen, Tibbets," he started, "You do a great job running security, but you have no idea what is going on here and how important it is for Earth. ESS One is one solution but not the most important one. This is bigger than your space program. Do you think these artifacts weren't placed here on purpose? We need to use them now, not put them in a lab for the next decade."

The colonel wasn't having it.

"Save it for court, Logan. I'm the one with the law on my side, and whatever you've stolen from Space Industries is going to be returned. I thought better of you. Now I know you're just a cheap thief."

Hah, Logan thought, now I've got him. I can stall for at least another few minutes. He hoped Tracy and Finn were hatching a plan. He waved his arms around dramatically and shouted back at Tibbets, "Cheap thief, huh? And you're still just Paul's guard dog, what do you know? While I've been out trying to save more than the high and mighty, you've been following orders like a good soldier boy."

That might have gone too far, he thought, after saying it.

Colonel Tibbets didn't respond. Instead, he waved his arm back at his shuttle. In a minute, three more soldiers came out with massive guns. Uh oh.

Suddenly, Logan saw another light coming nearer from above the horizon. Tibbets saw it too and looked confused. He put his hand to his ear, clearly communicating with someone. Suddenly he threw his arms up and waved for his soldiers to retreat. Just then, a third shuttle flew overhead. It let loose a missile that hit Tibbets shuttle and exploded. Tibbets and his soldiers started running toward Logan and the agents.

The agents laid down covering fire, and everyone hit the ground.

Tracy shouted at Logan, "You and Will get your cases out

and over to the third shuttle. Get out of here! We'll hold these guys down."

Logan noticed that the third shuttle started to set down behind the research facility. A soldier jumped out of it and was loping over in their direction.

Logan headed inside the facility. He and Will emerged as quickly as they could from the back carrying the Instructor case they found. They were met half-way by a giant soldier who took the case by himself and took it back to the waiting shuttle. Logan and Will went back inside and started grabbing the other Tube case box and the other small case that held other artifacts. They hurried out the back and out to the waiting shuttle.

Tracy and Finn were still in a firefight with Tibbets and his team. As much as Logan didn't want to think of leaving them behind, he moved up into the shuttle and was shocked momentarily when he saw who was in the cockpit. Major Sandy Pulaski! She waved for him to get strapped in, then flew the shuttle back over the facility. She laid down fire at Tibbets' team, then swooped low and hovered. Tracy, then Finn, and finally the giant soldier that came with Major Pulaski jumped up and through the open door.

"Go, go!" they shouted, and Sandy immediately pulled the shuttle back up and out from the facility, gaining distance rapidly away from Anteros.

Will was disheveled and in shock. Logan unstrapped and ran over to Tracy and Finn. Finn was bleeding from the leg, which also showed signs of decompression. Tracy was helping him stand up and took him over to the shuttle's small medical area.

Logan headed up front to the cockpit. "It sure is good to see you, Major!" Logan enthused to Sandy. "I didn't know you'd come over to our side."

Sandy smiled over at him from the cockpit controls.

"Welcome aboard, sir. I was always on your and Matti's side. Space Industries has its place, but I couldn't stand by and see your effort fail."

Logan smiled back.

"I'm glad you did, Sandy. You may have single-handedly saved our cause. We found what we came for, but we have to get back to Greece as soon as possible. Is it possible for you to get us there in this?"

"It just so happens I can. Not normally for this kind of shuttle, but we have fitted this one for atmospheric re-entry. We thought we may have to bypass ESS One," Sandy explained. "The real issue is whether ESS and the military will be waiting for us if Tibbets gets a message back to the space station."

Logan thought about that while Sandy continued.

"There is another agent in ESS One. Lieutenant Biam Dressler. She works in communications, and her job was to support us. Hopefully, she was able to keep a lid on my little act of defiance without getting caught herself."

Ruiz had told Logan there would be a lot of support, that his intelligence network was extensive. If there was ever a time to use their assets, this was it. Finn and Vicky came up from the back. Finn talked to Sandy for a minute, and Sandy gave him a headset. He then started talking to his team on Earth, letting them know they had retrieved what they came to get, but they needed support as they entered Earth orbit.

When they were within five-thousand miles of Earth, they received a communication from Biam at ESS One, picked up by the Major. Sandy turned around to address the rest.

"Biam says she delayed as much as she could, but ESS now has the alert from Tibbets, and ESS support craft are on their way to intercept us. I have picked up three scout ships approaching from ESS One. They will be able to intercept before we can enter the atmosphere. Ideas?"

Finn was back on his headset, talking to his people.

Within five minutes, the ESS ships pulled up on either side of their shuttle and broadcast, "Shuttle 9822, this is Space Industries security Commander Descartes, you are in violation of numerous laws including the destruction of Space Industries property. You must accompany us to ESS One, or you will be fired upon."

Sandy remarked, "Well, he has his shorts all bunched up."

The three scout vessels pulled up to box their shuttle in. At this point, one of the scouts pulled back from the others, and they heard, "ESS Scouts 1 and 33, be advised that I have you in my sights, do not fire, or you will be fired upon. Major Mike Fitz, out."

Sandy was astounded. Mike commandeered the third shuttle. "Well, that was unexpected."

Logan let out a whoop, "Alright, Mike!"

He and Mike stayed in touch since Logan left ESS One. He wondered if his old partner might be able to help, but he just hadn't taken the risk to contact him.

Just when it couldn't get more complicated, Sandy held up a finger for silence and listened to someone speaking on her headset. She flipped a switch, and the communication came out on the speaker.

"This is UN Cruiser Abernathy. Everyone and I do mean everyone, stand down and enter a standard orbit at the following coordinates. We will be sending boarding parties."

Sandy listened and raised her eyebrows. "The commander of the vessel is Mark *Conover*, any relation?"

Logan smiled, "As a matter of fact…"

Sandy smiled and turned back to her console, "Shuttle 9822 entering prescribed orbit and standing by per instructions, Commander."

Logan thought if they were forced to go public, he would rather the UN step in. After all, the ownership of the original artifacts was in the UN's hands. Space Industries was making a bundle off of the power systems. Still, the courts had designated the artifacts' owner to be 'all mankind' rather than a specific company. This would give all companies access to the foundational information and technology that Logan and Will collected. Logan was okay with that. It was better than Space Industries spending years commercializing the technology in dribbles and only when they deemed it was in their interests. Also, Logan was already doing other work for the UN, and he believed he would get a much fairer hearing.

The UN Cruiser boarded the shuttle and confiscated all the artifacts. Everyone was taken into custody, including the Space Industries pilots. They were all flown down on a UN shuttle to UN headquarters for questioning. Logan was amused that a lot of the UN personal knew Logan and greeted him cordially. He had spent a lot of time with the UN over the last several years and had a good relationship with their personnel. That relationship was paying off now.

After three weeks of legal arguments and hearings, the UN recognized the potentially priceless value of the recently acquired artifacts and put them under UN jurisdiction following a recent ruling on the previous artifacts that also put The Object under UN jurisdiction. The technology would be open

167

for study and use by both Space Industries and Logan's non-profit, Sheltered Refugee, jointly. The one stipulation was that they would be kept in New York City in a UN lab and vault and could not be moved.

They were all released without charges after Fuerte agreed to pay twenty-five million dollars in restitution to Space Industries for the destroyed shuttle, a small price to pay for access to the priceless artifacts.

Logan was just exiting the UN compound after receiving his comm device and other personal property back after their detainment. His phone rang, and it was Mark. "Hey Logan, sorry I couldn't contact you sooner. You ok?"

Logan was overjoyed to hear from Mark, "I'm doing great now. I can't thank you enough for showing up when you did. I thought we were going to disappear into ESS One and never be heard from again."

"No problem, little brother, I'm just glad you and your team got released relativity quickly. I think there must be others on your side at UN headquarters. Listen, I know you want to get home, but can you, Matti, and Kira come to New York and visit after you settle? We'd love to see you all."

"Of course, we'd love to! And, I'm sorry we haven't stayed in touch much. Events have carried us away for too long."

Mark nodded, "I feel the same. I'll be in touch, take care." Mark closed the comm device and smiled. He realized how distant Logan and he had become over the years and was glad things were changing. He missed his brother.

Back at their Greece headquarters, Logan welcomed Mike and Sandy into their tight-knit community. Mike's family was given a cold-shouldered exit off of ESS One within a week of the incident and joined Mike in a new apartment close to where Logan, Matti, and Kira lived. Mike's son, Sam, was a year younger than Kira. They knew each other when they were younger on ESS One and immediately re-bonded. Kira was thrilled to take Sam around and show him all the cool spots in their compound.

*Three Weeks Later*

The Boeing 797 jumbo jet with four hundred and twelve passengers landed with a bump and a puff from its wheels at Newark airport in New York City after flying eight hours from Athens. Will and five of his key staff were on board. They caught the flight the day after the UN officially opened the Anteros alien archives for research.

Will's assistant, Marcos, had scheduled an electric self-driving car to pick them up when they left the Newark terminal. To everyone's surprise, Will was nervous about the plan.

Apparently, Will had been in a self-driving car in the past that had been hacked. Everyone assured him the taxi was secure and would get him to the hotel safely. Will wasn't so sure. He would rather research a world-changing quantum transfer gate than ride in a car with no driver. They finally convinced Will it would be ok and they climbed into the car.

Marcos took out his Flexi-tablet. He accessed the information he'd compiled to date and shared it with everyone else's devices. "Hey Will, you know what the UN is making available since you used the Instructor device on Anteros. Can you tell us about it and how you want us to proceed?"

Will took a deep breath, "Right, when I stepped into its 'zone,' a kind of empty expanse, it reacted to my thoughts.

169

I formed an image of The Tube and the concept of how it worked, and it started sharing pictures and inner views of the device. It seemed to be trying to teach me the principles of the devices. I only started getting into it, but we have to fully understand the principles behind the power, materials, and programming of the tools to have a chance of building our own.

"Marcos, you use the Instructor device first. Then, Angela, you schedule a rotation of use of the Instructor with Marcos. Two-hour shifts. And believe me, after two hours, your head will be spinning with the new physics the Instructor reveals. Both of you will need to hand off experiments to Vin and Sophie to validate what we learn. We will not leave until we have a design that works in our simulators!"

He nodded toward Vin and Sophie. "You both know your job, to work side-by-side Marcos and Angela to develop computer experiments and simulation models of the core components needed to build a working gate. These models will then be turned into engineering designs of actual devices to be built and tested when we get back to Greece."

"We're ready," Vin enthused. Vin was having the time of his life, building physics experiments way beyond what he did in graduate school at MIT the year before. He couldn't believe his luck in getting this position with Will and the team.

Sophie smiled too. "I have the Cantos materials simulation ready for whatever new twists you can come up with. I'm so excited. This is going to take our knowledge way beyond where we are at today."

Sophie's enthusiasm was catchy. Will found himself smiling too. "Yes! When I spent time with the Instructor, the images I saw adapted to my level of understanding. It would display a short simulation, an animation of a component working. I would puzzle on it, and it would replay the same sequence in different angles, about five times until I understood what it was trying to teach me. Then a new video was presented. The whole process was like I was back in graduate school, uncovering the secrets of high-energy physics at Fermilab."

They pulled up at their hotel and took a nap and a bite to eat before taking another taxi over to the UN, where they spent three hours filling out all the paperwork needed to start their research. *Red-tape never goes away*, Will thought to himself as they showed all their credentials to the officer at the vault.

When they were finally ushered into the room with the Instructor and Tubes, they thought they were entering a museum rather than a lab. All of the objects were safely stored in individual containers. A technician went through the procedure they were to comply with to ensure the objects were handled correctly. Of course, no one knew how to handle alien artifacts, but the UN was trying to preserve the global treasure.

Will noted the UN technician's excitement the moment the group walked in. He talked briefly to the technician, Manny Silvers, about what they wanted to do. He finished with, "Thank you so much for your dedication to these priceless treasures and helping us to unlock their mysteries."

"The UN supports your efforts, sir. In fact, all of us in the UN Tech-corps are super-excited about these artifacts and what we can learn. Anything your group needs, please ask."

Marcos joined the conversation, "Well, now that you mention it," he started, then proceeded to discuss the need for a room to set the Instructor up in as well as power requirements and an area for Vin and Sophie to run simulations. In a short while, The UN artifact corridor was transformed into an applied physics lab. Manny ended up pulling in two more technicians from the Tech-core just to provide all that they needed. They were supplied with additional computing resources and time on the cutting-edge computer network the UN maintained.

Will noticed they were going beyond what they usually provided. Clearly, they were excited about what his team might discover. Manny might even make a promising recruit for the team in Greece. Will thought if things worked out, he could make Manny an offer to work with them in Greece a few weeks after they were done. He wasn't above pilfering good assistants.

After two weeks of progress with the Instructor, Will started tackling the new set of Tubes that they found on Anteros. There were five in total, and Will knew enough about them from the first one found that he could decode the individual frequencies and parameters that made each Tube unique. It turned out each Tube they found was keyed to a different frequency. This frequency tuned the gate to match a different gate somewhere in the universe. Each of the five was a potential new world, an entirely new home for mankind.

The implications stunned him. For some reason, he thought all the tubes might be the same. Having five new worlds available to them was more than he could fathom.

Will was walking from the parking lot to the hotel with Marcos. He stopped Marcos to speak privately to him.

"Marcos, tomorrow we're going to start decoding The Tube frequencies. I want you to get all the parameters from each Tube, store it in multiple ways securely, and then go immediately back to the hotel and use our secure communications-link to transmit the information to our lab. Also, copy Logan, Matti, myself, and Ruiz. Do you understand?"

Marcos understood perfectly and nodded to Will that he did.

"Yes, sir, you can count on me." Marcos understood that each of the alien Tubes represented a potential new planet. If they succeeded in creating the gates, this would represent a priceless resource. His team represented fifty-percent of the people in the world that knew what those Tubes were. Gate research was the most protected activity at Sheltered Refugee, and Ruiz's groups' intelligence personnel, more than once, let them all know the importance of secrecy.

Marco's team focused on getting a gate to Proxima, but the potential for opening up travel to multiple worlds was mind-blowing. Each new world could change the course of mankind forever. Marcos marveled that entire futures on other worlds might hinge on recording the access frequencies from each Tube. Will could see Marcos suddenly turn pale and figured he had dumped a pretty hefty responsibility on him. But then, Will had lived that way for several years now, ever since Logan brought him The Tube the first time, and he saw the potential in it. He'd survived the stress by focusing on the day-to-day. Overthinking about what-ifs always got him in trouble.

"Every day is a big deal in gate science, but just remember to take it one day at a time. Thinking about the future is too overwhelming. Focus on today." Will reassured Marcos.

"Yes, sir, that helps, thanks," Marcos nodded.

The team spent an entire month at the UN, learning more in a month than they had in the previous two years back in the lab in Greece.

Every two days, Will would hear the team shout in excitement about what they just discovered or a successful simulation result. The simulations and model-building were vital to the work they would do in the lab in Greece, where they would turn all the theory into building real component prototypes.

After dinner a night before they left New York City, Sophia leaned over to talk to Vin, "Can you believe the things we've been learning? Our team must be a thousand years ahead of the rest of the world in quantum displacement."

Vin smirked. "Yeah, can you imagine our CVs when we get done with this? 'Alien quantum gate expert.' Pretty cool."

Sophie remarked back, "Vin when we get done with this, we're going to be working on another planet."

Vin's eyes grew big as what Sophie said sunk in.

They spent the last day securing all of their data and caught the red-eye flight back to Athens, ready to finally build the world's first quantum gateway to Proxima b.

# New Ground

*One year later, Cephalonia, Greece.*

*Year: 2050 +4.3°F*
  *Earth Population: 10,893,736,733*
  *Population off-earth in Solar System: 240,044*
  *Population in other Star Systems: 1 robot*
  *Yearly population decrease due to Global Burn: 24,524,552*

Will's team returned from New York and immediately became more successful. They were amazed at how much they had learned about quantum transfer from the Instructor device. Their new prototypes started working immediately, and it wasn't long before the first full-size gate test came.

Will and his team were in the lab with lots of onlookers, including Logan crowding into the back. Will checked the readings on his instruments and felt upbeat. Everything was ready. Their gate sat in the middle of the room, a large steel tunnel about three-feet in length with cameras and instruments surrounding it. Large cables fed power into twenty connections spaced around the device, which drank power like a thirsty runner after a race.

Something about momentous moments in life, Will thought.

They always were uplifting, extraordinary. You could tell your life wouldn't be the same after. That's how this moment was. The room's energy came as much from the anticipation from all those present as it did from the quantum power generators.

Marcos was coordinating, "OK, I have set the power level to the coefficients calculated by Waters' last full simulation."

They now understood that the transfer of anything more than light particles took a tremendous amount of energy and frequency accuracy. They would apply ten-thousand times as much power as was used by the sample Tube. Without the new third-generation quantum power generators Marcos' team had just finished, they wouldn't have a chance to succeed.

It took a while, but Will's team had transformed their thinking about power usage. Where they started with 20,000 volts, now they used one-hundred megawatts for a single device. All of a sudden, at those very high levels, quantum physics was possible.

No wonder, Will thought, humanity hadn't developed these technologies before. They couldn't generate and use this kind of power before. Now they could, and it took them to a whole new level. He was excited by the many different possibilities this new level of physics enabled.

Marcos continued going over the team's preparations, "We have calculated the parameters for the destination down to twenty decimals."

Setting up a gate to a frequency was a delicate procedure, but the alien race revealed how to make the whole process possible through the Instructor. Will was appreciative that thousands of years of development must have gone into the technology, and it was given to humanity for free. So much for the movies about aliens waiting out in space to destroy or enslave humankind. The alien race that left this technology for humanity seemed only to want to help the civilizations they discovered save themselves.

They assumed the alien race went to great lengths to set up the matching quantum pairs on different planets so that races could find planets with atmospheres they could live in and worlds they could expand to. Without the aliens seeding quantum gates on planets, they would have to send physical ships out to deliver these gates, an impossible task for mankind with their current technology level.

"We are recording from all angles and are ready to proceed," Marcus announced.

"Start the test!" Will declared.

A small spherical robot two-feet in diameter rolled forward into the gate and disappeared. All of the scientists and engineers in the room looked at each other in shock.

Marcus was the first to speak. "Oh, my God! It worked. The darn thing worked."

Shouts of hysteria were heard through-out the room, and others came running in from other labs. Will was pretty impressed but wanted to see if the robot was still intact when it returned before celebrating. Retrieving the device in one piece was the most crucial part of the experiment. They all looked at the countdown timer. Nine, eight. The robot was programmed to roll forward ten feet, pause for twenty seconds, and then roll back through the gate, a total of a one-minute trip. The minute was almost up. Three, two, one, zero.

The robot rolled back into the room, fully intact. Data from the robot started scrolling again on their monitors.

Marcus started screaming again, "Oh my God! It worked. I

told you it worked!"

Will smiled. OK, he thought, I guess it worked.

Everyone was high-fiving and even crying. How many years had they worked for this one proof-of-concept? They built their own working gate! They examined the robot, and it still functioned. They displayed the robot's recording, and it was similar to the scene from the smaller robot using The Tube. They could see the same dry sandy soil and red sun high in the sky.

This larger robot performed the additional task of taking a soil and air sample with a small built-in sampling shovel and nozzle. Back in their lab, they now securely transferred the samples from the robot and put them in full quarantine until technicians could test them for any harmful elements. They also wanted to run a comprehensive analysis of the composition.

In the back of the lab, separated by a glass wall, was a small auditorium where Logan, Matti, and Kira were celebrating. School was off today, and workers across the facility were given a few hours off to view the test.

Will turned to Logan, and their eyes met. Logan nodded to his friend and pressed the speaker button to the lab, "Congratulations, everyone, this day is the happiest of my last few years."

They undid the container holding the sample and poured it out on a sample tray with cameras rolling. They ran the analyzer, and it started detailing the soil and mineral content.

The geologist running that experiment commented, "this is definitely exo-terra soil."

Everyone was smiling. Soil from another planet. Wow.

At dinner that night, the Quantum Pioneer team gathered

in the dining hall.

Will summarized the team's findings and the new plan, "OK, congratulations to the gate team!" Everyone hooted for two minutes, and Will continued, "It's a whole new ballgame. Our goal, as soon as feasible, is to turn our experimental platform into a production system. The exploration team needs a ten-foot by twenty-foot gate. That is our next goal."

Those who knew the tremendous power requirements groaned.

Will continued, "Yes, I know, it's a tall order. We need to build fourth-generation generators. The power team will come through, right?" The power team hooted from the back. "Once we have those gates, we'll shift focus to the deployment of our explorers who will verify that we can survive on this new planet. Then we proceed to construction infrastructure. The construction team wants four *forty-foot* wide gates to work simultaneously, twenty-four hours a day. Then, if that isn't enough, we prepare for actual colonists. But that's all in the future. Tonight, we celebrate!"

And with that pronouncement, the chefs rolled out a gigantic cake for the occasion. The party was on.

Kira was at a table with her own friends. "I bet I could," she was telling them.

Kira proposed sneaking down to the lab and seeing if she could put a cat into the new world. "Andromeda," Kira's cat, "would make it back. She is good at coming if I call her."

Kira's friends, Sam and a few others in their group, didn't think it was a good idea. "Yeah, but you would get in sooo much trouble, especially if you lost the cat or broke the gate or something."

Kira was sure of herself. "That wouldn't happen. The robot

came back just fine."

Her friends weren't buying it. Kira backed down, "OK, maybe not right now when we just got the gate working, but in a month or so. Wouldn't it be so cool to have the first pet that walked on another planet?"

Her friends were glad she backed down and were really excited by the idea sometime in the future.

Sam spoke up, "Maybe by then. We could get permission to do a research project in the other world for school, wouldn't that be cool? It would beat the socks off of any lab class here in Greece."

Everyone started talking about how cool that would be and started thinking about what clothes they would have to pack. They even speculated if there would be any animals in the new world.

Logan and Matti walked over to Kira's table and were happy to see her getting along so well with her group. Even more, the kids had already shifted to a new perspective that assumed they would be living in the new world soon. Wow, Logan thought, this is their moment. Their future would be on a new planet. It was a happy day.

Logan turned to Matti. "We celebrated the big break-through, but your team deserves just as much credit for keeping this whole organization going, especially in the political environment we're in."

Matti smiled and was glad Logan appreciated her and her management team's efforts. Indeed, everything that happened at the headquarters in Greece and the other twenty-three sites was her team's planning and smooth management of their resources. "Maybe you could tell that to our team soon."

Logan nodded, "I will."

She asked Logan, "Just how long do you think it will be before we can send our first real pioneers over?"

Logan thought for a minute. "Well, we would need five years if it was a normal project, but given the state of the world, I'd be surprised if we have two years."

Matti nodded. "Or maybe only one. Once we open the gates...let me just say that my group has been planning on being able to process thousands of new pioneers per day at each facility."

They calculated the numbers a thousand times. Growing cities at a five-hundred percent growth rate per year across twenty-four facilities would still take many years to process and successfully house a billion people. It was a herculean task that could never have been accomplished with the space program.

"It will take fifteen years to transfer a billion people through twenty-four facilities, each running all year and processing eight-thousand people a day. The question is, do we think the world has fifteen years?"

\* \* \*

Chi was the happiest he had ever been in his life. His family was safe, his kids were getting an outstanding education, and he was promoted to manager of the 3D printing division, with twenty employees under him. The Director of the Quantum Pioneer build-out on Proxima, Sana Osterwalder, realized Chi was more experienced in additive manufacturing than anyone else they hired so she kept giving Chi more responsibility.

Based on his experience building in space and on Earth, Chi built an excellent Quantum Pioneer infrastructure that could scale rapidly and operate with minimal additional resources. "Just add water" was Chi's joke to his team.

He was one of the few people who was made privy to the fantastic goal that Quantum Pioneer would travel to an entirely new world and that his group would be building the first colony there. When he was first told, it blew him away, but he started feeling a great deal of pride in his role. He focused that pride on building the best system he knew how.

"We need to test these again using our new test suite," Chi was talking with his design engineer for the core 3D printer they would be manufacturing shortly. The prototypes were working well.

His engineer responded, "OK, but they passed at 99.7 percent, which was more than any other component. Why do we need to rerun the test?"

Chi couldn't explain the real reason, so he used a default excuse, "Because your and my names are on this design, and I want it to be the best in the world. These systems are going to build entire cities. Do you want to be responsible for even one of them causing a structural failure?"

It was a good argument even if they weren't going to be sent four-point-two light-years from Earth.

"OK, yes, I agree. I'll do it, but it will take an additional two weeks to go over the numbers. What is this requirement, 'System must be able to withstand four gee work environments.' Where are we going that we'll need to sustain four gee forces?"

Chi responded with a very plausible answer, "We experienced gee forces like that at ESS One. If a printer is put on any moving object and changes direction rapidly for over a few seconds, you get at least two to five gee forces. We have to ensure it will not mess up what it is printing if it is mounted on a moving surface in extreme conditions."

His supervisor was nodding now. "Got it."

Chi knew the exploration team had gotten to Proxima b, and he looked forward to the day he could start working in their new world and share the secret with the rest of his team. It wouldn't be long now.

\* \* \*

All the team members working on Quantum Pioneer were on hand for the first human crossing. The team's soil and atmospheric samples from the previous robot crossing determined that the air was breathable, so it was time to test the transfer with humans. They also confirmed the radiation levels from Proxima b's red dwarf sun were higher than Earth but low enough for the planet to be amenable to human colonization if they built to minimize the radiation's effect.

Two people made the first human crossing, Matthew Rosetta, a civil engineer, and Sugiyama Matsuko, a well-known Japanese journalist that Ruiz knew. Sugiyama covered the recent Nile water wars between Egypt and Ethiopia. She was so happy to have been hired by the Quantum Pioneer team for this fantastic assignment because it was a message of hope, a possible solution to the many issues facing the world. She was even happier she was away from the climate war zones.

Both Matthew and Sugiyama were chosen for the crossing. Sugiyama was in a ready room, giving a pre-crossing report into her portable camera rig.

"This is Sugiyama Matsuko, and I'm in Greece at the headquarters of the non-profit Sheltered Refugee, the worldwide humanitarian organization that has helped millions of refugees from the recent climate-related disasters around the world. What you might not know about Sheltered Refugee is that its founders are Logan and Matti Conover, the same Logan that is famous for discovering Anteros' alien artifacts."

Sugi stopped to change her background to show the busy work of the team behind her. "I am here today to share a historic event! Behind me are the technicians that run the world's first quantum crossing gate to another planet. Yes, you heard me right. Logan Conover, the same Logan that found the first alien artifacts, has done it again! He and his research team found more artifacts, including a sample transportation device. His team has unlocked its mysteries, and if their gate works today, it will allow humans to cross to another planet in our galaxy. The hope is to open up a new land free from today's climate disasters, a land that new pioneers can call home. It's a few hours until we cross. With luck, I will talk to you next from the soil of a new world!"

As her friends called her, Sugi knew her report wouldn't be broadcast to the world yet, but she hoped they would release it as soon as they started building the first colony and were ready to make the general announcement to the world about the discoveries.

Matthew was checking their equipment one last time. They would cross in a lightweight electric all-terrain vehicle modified to withstand heavier gravity. The ATV contained water, air tanks, and scientific systems that would measure twenty different atmospheric properties. Cameras were mounted on the front and rear. They would be recording the whole time they were away. Matthew even packed a rifle in case there were any unfriendly creatures on the other side. This, of course, was a classic debate that went on for hours during the planning of the trip. Many argued we really couldn't test for intelligence before shooting, and perhaps we would be causing a chain of events we couldn't control. Those that argued that defense was critical to the success of the mission won in the end.

Matthew and Sugiyama would cross two times, the first time for just five minutes to make sure they could live without any mishaps. In other words, to make sure they were still alive. The second crossing was planned for two hours. During the first short trip, they would gain critical information about how big the gate was on the other side, samples of the atmosphere, and a general survey of the area within a one-mile radius of the gate.

Much work went into determining how deep the gate needed to be. If the gate were too thin, an object would end up being in two worlds at once, with disastrous results. They tried a narrow gate with a rod of steel during the testing of original gate designs, and the rod was severed into two pieces. Not a good result. Driving the robot and timing the distance from when it disappeared from one world and appeared in the next, the team determined that the gate depth could be changed depending on the width of the gate used and the power applied. They worked out precise formulas with these parameters to control the gate's depth depending on who or what was crossing.

It was noon, their scheduled departure time. Matthew drove the buggy forward amidst cheers from the team. Sugi was narrating continuously. She stopped to put on her air mask. The buggy crossed into the 'no man's zone' or depth of the gate. No one really knew where this zone existed, but it took a short time to traverse.

"We are driving through the gate. It is exceptionally spooky as there is no light, no sound, no anything while we are in the gate's 'no man's zone,' but I can feel the movement of our ATV, and, oh gosh, we just crossed over! I can see the night sky in Proxima Centauri b. There are stars! So many stars! What, Matthew?" Sugi stopped her narrative to listen to whatever Matthew was saying. "Yes, Matthew, I feel fine, are you OK? We both are leaving our air masks on for this trip, and we are doing fine. We haven't felt any adverse effects from the crossing. Matthew is going to stop here."

Matthew busied himself with his instruments, checking air quality and other vital measurements. He stopped the buggy twenty feet from the gate. Sugi pointed her camera at Matthew and was silent as he performed his checks. Sugi continued when Matthew put the buggy in reverse.

"OK, all looks positive. We're going to back up now through the gate and return to Earth." They slowly backed into the dead zone of the gate and then reemerged into the lab. "I can't wrap my head around this, one minute we're 4.2 light-years away, and now we're back in the lab. But, whoo, I am so disoriented."

Both Sugi and Matthew saw all of the cheering around them. Matthew held his hand up for silence. The crowd immediately quieted. Sugi and Matthew were shaking their heads like they were waking up. The medical team ran over and started checking on them.

The lead medical team member raised a thumbs up, "All vital signs are positive. Perhaps their disorientation is just a physiological reaction to the sudden change of location."

After fifteen minutes Sugi and Matthew said they could

think clearly again. They were led away to a side room where they were both given a complete physical. It took them two hours to finally readjust, but they were fine after that.

The team waited until the next day to resume their exploration after a full debriefing. Meanwhile, their instrument readings were analyzed.

The atmosphere was completely breathable. It contained a few higher levels of several inert gases, such as argon and xenon, but they wouldn't cause any harm at the levels recorded. They planned to have two more explorers on the next trip, a geologist to take core samples, and a physician to study radiation and other potential health issues more thoroughly.

Logan watched the first crossing the previous day and was there for the start of the second. He felt a distinct sense of satisfaction that they had achieved the space program's ultimate goal to get people to another world. They accomplished the leap for pennies on the dollar compared to the space program. And they could save people directly from Earth. It was a wholly logical and practical way of exploring and expanding into the universe.

Matti was standing next to him on the next crossing and saw he was contemplative. "What are you dreaming up now?"

Matti was worried when Logan looked absent, as it meant Logan was creating yet another strategy that might cost too much money or risk his life.

Logan looked over, "Did you ever wonder if man was really made to go into and live in space? The thought would have been heresy at ESS One, but everything now points to quantum gates being the way man will expand into the universe, not expensive rockets or warp drives and so on. Perhaps, all along, humanity hasn't found too much evidence of space flight by other worlds because there isn't much—everyone connects worlds through quantum gates and just drives around the galaxy."

Listening to Logan, Matti imagined a funny mental image, "Hey mom, let's drive to

Betelgeuse planet three today, I hear they have an awesome waterslide. Something like that?"

Logan laughed along with Matti. "Kind of blows your mind doesn't it?" he offered.

Matti shook her head, "No, I think it is exactly what humanity really needs right now. We've all been waiting for the lightening to strike and find a way to save ourselves from the mess we've made of our planet. This is it, and I'm thrilled we figured it out."

Logan smiled, "Me too. I can't tell you how many nights I've been up wondering if we were on a crazy, expensive wild goose hunt. But it all makes sense now; it was all worth it."

The explorers finished their second trip through the gate. This time they spent eight hours on Proxima and were not disoriented when they came back. They also devised a small robot they could send back after their transit to let everyone know they made it. 'Hey mom, I made it OK. You don't have to worry anymore.'

Logan and Matti said their goodbyes then headed out of the lab. Everyone was in good spirits, feeling victorious. They couldn't have asked for more.

On their way out, they stopped to see Kira, who was in the lab. She was finishing her school project, a documentary of the lab workers during the first transit. Her fifteen students' class was hoping their video would be picked up by BNN or another news organization once they could release news of the quantum crossing. It probably would. They were working their hearts out for the last three months on the project.

The Quantum Pioneer team heard about the students' project and couldn't wait to see it. Team members were so focused on their own area of the project that they were excited to get a bigger view of the whole project. Besides, they were the stars. The premier was going to be in four weeks after the class edited it.

Logan made a mental note to make popcorn at the screening and to announce the payment of the ten percent bonus that they had promised everyone when they reached this critical milestone. The film premier would be a great team event, especially after the intense work over the last ten months since Logan, Will, Mike, and Sandy brought back The Instructor and the other Tubes.

* * *

"Everyone on the alpha team, comm check. Lu?" Marty commed the exploration team. Marty Mechum was second-in-command on the first Proxima exploration team. He was going down a checklist while Lu, the team leader, talked for a few minutes with Logan before departing for Proxima.

"Reading you with a signal strength of 1.4," Lu responded.

"Suzanna?"

"Check," Suzanna grunted as she lifted the last piece of equipment onto their buggy. They were taking a modified dune buggy usually used in deserts, and she was the communication officer, also responsible for all recordings and data collection as they progressed.

"Rafael?"

"Onboard, sir!" Rafael Vera was only five feet three inches tall but packed a punch. He was a prize-fighter before joining the US marines and had fought in every continent of the world. He lifted his M4 and checked his ammo clips. He was there to protect the team from all possible animals or other hostiles.

Logan hired a professional exploration team after the initial first trip to Proxima. The four-member team's goal was to prove if they could live safely on Proxima and survey the land for the construction team to determine where to start building. It was a tall order.

Lu, the team lead, was an experienced explorer. He led scientists on explorations through untamed and unmapped jungles, rivers, and mountains. He was trained as an engineer but turned hunter and explorer once he found he was talented in navigation and tracking. He couldn't imagine why Sheltered Refugee hired him until they showed him the video of Proxima. It blew him away. It was a dream come true, to explore an entirely new world. He had been looking forward to the moment of crossing-over to Proxima for the past three months.

Lu spoke out, "OK, we're all set. Close helmets. Marty, take us over." They all closed their helmets on their environment suits, which were close to space suits but more oriented to protecting against radiation.

Marty engaged the drive. Logan saw them disappear as they crossed the gate. They had a hell of a job ahead. Everything Logan worked for to this point hinged on their success. He hoped the new world the aliens programmed into The Tube was habitable. So far, it looked like it was, but now the exploration team would find out, one way or the other.

It drove him crazy he couldn't go with them, but, as Matti

pointed out correctly, they were more qualified for initial exploration than he was. "Let the experts do their job," he recalled her saying. He headed to the command center to monitor their progress. The command center sent over a communication robot to the Proxima side that would roll over to Earth every minute to transmit data and then roll back to Proxima. The robot was affectionately named "Huey" after a drone from the old movie *Silent Running*.

Logan spoke to Matti when he arrived at the command center, "Did Huey pick them up? All well?"

Matti smiled at Logan; boy, was he nervous. But so was she. This was their first real look at the planet. In response to Logan's question, she tapped a switch that changed the main screen to the exploration team's near-real-time images. It showed the readings of fifteen meteorological instruments at the bottom of a video of their progress. Distance traveled, radiation level, temperature, pressure, wind speed, time on the planet, and pertinent information.

Lu and Marty were in the front of the buggy. Suzanna and Rafael were in the back. Marty inched the ATV forward once they crossed.

Lu commed, "Good idea, take it slow. Let's stop over there," indicating the top of a low rise, "so we can get a good look around."

From the small hill, the land was revealed for several miles before a haze took over. The planet was dry with scrub and low vegetation. There were many rolling hills and mountains in the distance, but there were no lakes, creeks, or other bodies of water in evidence. The planet reminded Lu of Arizona, dry and barren but with enough vegetation to sustain some wildlife. Lu's first goal was to verify if the environment had water, perhaps buried just underground.

Lu believed the aliens had given them this world intentionally and that it would support life for humans. Many people didn't believe that theory. They felt the artifacts were just random junk, left by careless aliens passing through. Standing on Proxima, breathing the air, Lu couldn't disagree more. There was nothing accidental about him and his team standing on and exploring this new world.

Before the exploration team launched, Greece's Quantum Pioneer team had brought a small satellite over to Proxima and launched it. The initial satellite scan had shown several small water bodies on the planet but no oceans or other significant features that would indicate an active water circulation system such as Earth's.

"This gravity is pretty oppressive at first, but I'm getting more used to it now," Suzanne commented. The others nodded in agreement. Suzanne continued speaking for the Quantum Pioneer team listening in, "At first, moving and breathing are more labor-intensive like you were wearing a heavy backpack. But after one hour, the team is getting used to the extra ten-percent of gravity. The exercise regime works well." In preparation for the exploration, they all spent three hours a day exercising in the gym.

"Looks like Arizona scrub." Rafael spent a lot of time in New Mexico and Arizona in the United States. "Dryer if that is possible. But the air is breathable. Here are our instrument readings for air quality." Rafael then transmitted his current data over to his and the Quantum Pioneer teams.

Over the next couple of minutes, they all took off their helmets. The air seemed healthy, a slight scent of dried grass. The only sound was that of a wisp of wind blowing through the grasses. They all walked around for a few minutes, experiencing the fantastic feeling of walking on and breathing the air of a new world. Suzanne even did a little dance.

"Hard to get used to the dimmer light," Suzanna commented. Proxima's red dwarf star wasn't nearly as bright as the sun, and so everything seemed in perpetual dusk with only fifty-percent of the light they were used to on Earth.

Lu pointed out to Marty the location they needed to head to set up their first camp. Based on satellite images, they had selected a base camp located on the highest ground around. Marty changed course and commented, "We are en route to our first base camp. ETA two hours." The buggy rolled on over the scrub.

They arrived at the base camp location right on time, and everyone started unloading equipment. Lu began to give directions, "Marty and Suzanne, can you get the drill set up? Rafael and I will go scout the site for wildlife or anything that might be dangerous."

Rafael grabbed his M4 and Lu his shotgun. They walked for two miles in a big arc around their campsite and only stopped once when a small groundhog-like rodent popped his head up.

"Curious fella." Rafael commented, "looks like a bearhog."

Lu laughed, "a bearhog, good name." The critter did look like a small bear, probably due to the more massive gravity. It was about a foot high with four solid little legs. It slowly came out of its hole, approaching the explorers walking on its four feet. Rafael raised his rifle. Lu laughed, "Really?"

"Can't be too careful," Rafael protested. The little bearhog came up close, hissed, and stomped its tiny feet. Rafael lowered his rifle, won over by the adorable creature. "I think he likes me."

They continued exploring around the base camp, the bearhog walking behind them. When they arrived back at camp, Suzanne was surprised to see the small bear-like animal following them. "You got a pet, Rafe?"

"Yeah, I've named him Berti."

Suzanne laughed, "You realize you just found the first example of other life in the universe, right? That's our first alien."

Rafael's eyes widened, "Quick, take pictures of Berti and me. We're famous space alien buds!"

Suzanne started making an astronomical position sighting. Marty needed help starting the drill. "Are you guys finished goofing around? Can you help me test this drill?" Marty shouted over to Rafael.

Rafael came over and checked a few numbers on the drill, as Marty called them out to him. "Looks all set; you ready?"

Marty locked the drill down to the ground, setting its feet firmly in the soil. "Start it." The drill made a thrumming noise but otherwise went pretty smoothly into the soil. "Pretty soft once you get about six feet down."

In thirty minutes, Marty yelled to the group, "We've struck water! Or at least some kind of liquid." A thick yellow goop came up out of the drill pump hose into a holding tank.

Marty reached a test tube down and scooped up some of the liquid, then inserted it into their portable chem lab, a small machine that would test for two-hundred types of chemicals and minerals.

Lu was on the radio to the gate robot. He was relaying his initial report back to Logan and the Quantum Pioneer team back on Earth. The Quantum Pioneer team received them loud and clear and had appreciated all the teams' work so far. They were excited. Lu was still in a wait and see attitude. He had never been to a new location without hidden surprises, but he was satisfied with the teams' progress. He walked over to the others surrounding the drill. "What have you got?"

Marty, being the biochemist of the group, gave the report. "Well, quite a mix in the liquid. We had to go five-hundred feet down, which is deeper than what we expected we'd have to go. There is H2O but also a lot of sulfur and a bunch of other metals. The soil is mineral-rich, and the liquid is similar."

Lu cut to the chase, "Can we filter the water, and will it be drinkable?"

"Yes, sir, it will." Marty nodded confidently. "We just need to set up a treatment plant like what we use for waste systems back home. But we should drill more holes further out, preferably in a ring, to determine the extent of the liquid and if the depth changes. Unlikely, but we may have just been lucky."

Lu agreed, and the team started drilling again. It was going to be a long day.

* * *

The team woke early and had a tasty breakfast of oatmeal and juice. Suzanna stretched, feeling the effects of the extra gravity. She started checking over the recent radar scans. They hadn't seen anything all night, but Suzanna wanted to check again before they moved out for the day's work. Her eyes grew wide as she looked at the last five-minute scan. "Marty, Lu, come take a look at this radar scan!" Suzanna yelled out as she fine-tuned their radar and took a look at the active scan.

Lu ran over. He looked over her shoulder. "Uh, oh." His eyes widened when the dot on the screen split into four. "Incoming!" he shouted to the team who was just packing up their gear from the previous night. They had stayed on the top of a mesa overlooking the barren landscape below. They only saw one sign of life so far, the small *bearhogs* that liked hanging around the camp. Several more had come out and hung around since Rafael had brought back Berti. They were not aggressive and hid a lot, usually only coming out when someone was eating.

"What've you got?" Marty shouted as he threw the gear into the back of the buggy and ran over.

"Four bogies, approaching fast. They are moving over thirty kilometers per hour."

Marty looked through his binoculars to try to get a visual. They were coming in from the West. He could just make out something on the horizon. At the rate they were moving, he calculated they would be arriving in two minutes.

"Everyone, get aboard, Marty take us to that cave," Lu shouted to the team, pointing to a cave he had scouted out the night before. It looked like they had to go in if they wanted to avoid contact with the incoming threats.

Marty estimated they wouldn't make it to the cave before the objects overtook them.

Suzanna saw them first. "They look like huge versions of Berti!" she shouted as she watched unbelievably agile and large muscles move the creatures forward at an astonishing speed.

Marty drove as fast as he could, but the mammoth bearhogs caught up to them. They arrived with a cloud of dust and surrounded the vehicle. Marty stopped.

"The creatures must be fifteen feet in length and weigh two tons," Marty surmised to the group. The creatures were making a loud keening noise, which set Marty's neck's hair on end. "That is downright chilling. They will also be a lot stronger than your average bear since the gravity is stronger."

Rafael pointed his M4 in the direction of the largest animal. He began to wish they had brought missiles. He wasn't sure the automatic rifle and a few grenades would bring down what was, essentially, a tank in the flesh.

Lu grabbed his shotgun and spoke to Suzanne, "Any chance of communicating with them?"

Suzanne tried simple sounds and radio signals at many frequencies; nothing provoked any response. "Not yet, sir, I'm trying." She continued to work to communicate with the animals who were circling from twenty yards and then stopped.

Lu commented, "That doesn't bode well. Rafael, if they charge, open up on those two, and I'll target the two on my side." Just as he said it, the creatures charged, barking loudly.

Rafael opened up with his M4. The two creatures in front stopped, but when the dust cleared, he could see they weren't hurt. They resumed their charge. He switched to grenades, and the concussion of the close-in explosions rocked the buggy. Marty moved out toward one of the creatures on Lu's side. The grenades brought down the two animals on Rafael's side, but when they cleared their heads from the explosion, they saw one animal reaching down for Marty. He tried to dodge, but the bearhog swiped him with a claw, and it ripped through him.

"No!" Lu shouted. He and Rafael filled the last bearhog with ammunition until it dropped. Thirty empty shells from their rounds lay on the ground.

Running over to Marty, they found the injuries were fatal. Suzanne and Rafael wrapped him in a blanket and carried him back to the buggy.

Suzanne didn't have any encouraging thoughts, "Our initial satellite images didn't detect any life. Perhaps they go underground and don't come out often. I'll recheck the satellite logs and see if there are any more signs of them on the planet." She put on her virtual reality glasses and started scanning the satellite logs, programming the scanner to look for movement based on the size and speed of the animals they saw. Instantly the scanner beeped. "Looks like the system flagged them as 'atmospheric effect,' sir, the system got it wrong."

Lu shook his head; people trusted machines too much. "Reprogram the system to map all such findings, especially in the hundred-mile radius from where we are. And see if you can get a live feed. We need to know what we're dealing with."

When he saw the first delayed video of the attack, Logan notified the rescue back-up team to get moving. He then took a buggy over immediately with a communications technician. He commed Lu now live from the Proxima side of the gate, "Lu, the backup team will be there in twenty-minutes. Please rendezvous with them and return to the gate." Logan drew in a breath, "Let's get back across the gate and regroup."

During the beginning of the construction phase of Sheltered Refugee, several workers died in accidents, now this death. He had friends who were killed in space. It was different knowing he authorized and organized this mission. He set up the exploration parameters, and he had not given enough protection to the first exploration team. He saw that now. He should have sent two buggies, one with troops.

There was a formal ceremony for Marty back in Greece. Logan, Lu, and the whole team was there and said their farewells to their brave companion.

Two weeks later, the Quantum Pioneer team had prepared both sonic and heavy ammunition defenses for the bearhogs.

The exploration continued when the original team and a large security escort went back to Proxima. The large bearhogs showed up, and they found that the sonic defense was effective. Logan and the team were relieved. They would be able to protect pioneers against the creatures. When an inaudible high-pitched sound was broadcast, the animals turned aside and ran away. Logan and the teams intended to install the sonic systems on all buildings in the future.

The exploration teams made substantial progress on the second trip and provided critical data to Greece's teams who were planning the new world's communities. Extra radiation shielding was added to the building designs, and special filters were installed in the air systems. They had explored an area one-hundred miles around the gate and had found several deep but extensive sources of water that contained a high content of sulfur but could be treated to produce drinkable water, a huge win.

*Three months later, Proxima b*

Chi broke away from his computer screen and sighed, putting his head in his hands. Adjusting a hundred-foot wide 3D printer that weighed twenty tons and resting on the soil of Proxima Centauri b was no easy task. The monster machine ate rocks and minerals for breakfast and built an entire building by dinner. Doing what had never been done before was exhausting.

Chi worked fourteen-hour days, six days a week. His family was happy with the new living arrangements and schools back in the Greece Sheltered Refugee facility, which he was very grateful for. But he knew he was working too much.

"Marcos, are the gates holding up with our needs?" Chi asked Marcos, who had come over from Will's team to help coordinate and fine-tune gate usage for the construction and research teams going back and forth to Proxima. Having a steady, perfectly balanced stream of raw materials was the key to a perfect building printout.

"We're going to need to add a few more power generators; you folks are ramping up even faster than we anticipated," Marcos replied.

Chi nodded. He wasn't surprised. They had spent several years getting the machines and supply chains set up to build on Proxima, so the ramp-up was rapid.

Chi next spoke to his chief engineer, "Amanda, do you have the results for our test building we printed yesterday?"

"All set! Here they are," Amanda confirmed, sending Chi the test results over their comm system.

Chi took a moment to look over the results and nodded. Everything looked on target. They had printed a small security installation as a test building. They couldn't proceed tomorrow without knowing where they needed to make adjustments. They were already using twice as much oil as anticipated. The gravity on Proxima was making everything work harder.

Even though he was so busy and couldn't remember the

last time he saw his two girls, he was as happy as a clam as he looked over the new planet's horizon. They had mapped out the city to the last beam and wire back on Earth and executed their plan. It felt good!

Two weeks later, Logan made his way over to Chi's office, a small command center for the construction engineers. "You look as happy as I feel to get this community underway finally."

Chi smiled back, "Yes, sir. It was frustrating waiting for those forty-foot gates and fourth-generation quantum power generators to be brought online, but now? Buildings are going up according to plan."

Logan smiled. He loved Chi's enthusiasm and professionalism. He could also see Chi was exhausted. He met Chi six months ago when Chi had been promoted to director of 3D building printing. Logan liked him immediately. He possessed an enthusiastic attitude sorely needed on the project amidst all the challenges.

"Are you getting what you need? The supply chain from Earth has been hard to get started but should ramp up quickly." Logan referred to the hundreds of suppliers contracted to deliver all of the electronic and necessary raw materials needed to start building on Proxima. Eventually, they would mine and manufacture what they required from Proxima itself, but they would need to ship materials over through the gates—an expensive endeavor for the first year.

Chi answered, keeping his eye on critical read-outs from the 3D printers and automated mining drills. "Well, drill rig alpha1 is over there," he motioned behind him, "one mile away and has started to dig our mine. Once we can mine our own resources from Proxima, we can make real progress. Relying on Earth for material for the initial core infrastructure is slow.

So, whatever you can do to make the deliveries consistent and help keep our mining capability on track, that is the critical path for us so we don't hit delays."

"You got it," Logan promised, "let me know if I can make any more calls. You're our number one priority right now."

Logan bid Chi goodbye and got out of his way so he could make progress. He thought, number one priority along with our two other number one priorities. Before leaving, he scanned the worksite. The planet's gravity took a lot of getting used to. It felt like you were continually exercising. Matti commented on how bulked up he was looking, though, so there were side benefits.

Many events moved Logan over the last few years. His appreciation for his fellow workers was the source of his increased determination and joy in the project. Everyone was so committed. He felt such a great sense of purpose, more than at any other time in his life. The purpose fed his soul. He looked out over the beginning of the colony construction and mentally took a snapshot of the sight before him. He wanted to remember it forever.

*Washington, D.C.*

Senator Barrister finished reading an intelligence report from the Boieng Corporation lobbyist. His friend Neal Morrison, the CEO of Boeing, had written a note on the front of the report, *We need to get on top of this. They are more of a threat than we suspected.*

The Senator tapped his pencil a few times on the report, contemplating his next action. Few people still used pencils, but he was old fashioned that way. He still liked writing on paper, still loved the smell of a legal pad of paper on his desk.

Congress was located in Philadelphia for only a couple of years after Ida flooded the buildings, and they were now able to move back to Washington. Senators moved back into the old Russell or Hart Senate office buildings. These were a couple of the first buildings cleaned, along with the Capital itself. The newly polished marble on the floor was somehow reassuring that at least some things didn't change.

The Senator reached over and pushed the button on his intercom that connected to his assistant. "Hello Tom, please get the team in here. We need to strategize. And have Paul Manning give me a call as soon as he can. Yes, Paul at ESS One."

His key staff filed into his office ten minutes later.

"What's up, sir?" Karen Nightly, his chief-of-staff, spoke up as they were all settling into the old leather chairs that circled the bosses' desk.

"Our space strategy is being threatened; that's what. An upstart pilot who used to be on ESS One, the one that found those alien artifacts?"

"Logan Conover," Karen supplied.

"Yeah, him, he started a group named Sheltered Refugee. They do a lot of good work for refugees. The organization bought a lot of underground caves and have built bunkers, cities really. Anyway, something else is going on, too, bigger than hiding underground. Here, read this."

Barrister handed the intelligence report to Karen. She scanned through it then passed it onto her aide, Idora, who read through the report as well. Ten times the amount of construction material was being shipped into the Greek and other facilities than should be needed to support their refugee operations. An enormous amount of material for an underground city. There was also a Sheltered Refugee team that spent over a month at the UN headquarters researching the new artifacts.

"Should we make sure we have eyes inside?" Karen asked.

Senator Barrister looked directly into her eyes, "Yes, and more than that. Call this number. Set up a face-to-face meeting with their director and myself."

Karen looked at the slip of paper. *Black River*. She knew the outfit. They were involved in the mop-up of the China Sea war. They were a mercenary military outfit for hire with powerful sponsors. She tucked the paper away in her folder, then picked up her phone and spoke for a few moments to Paul's assistant. "Paul will call in here in two minutes," she relayed to Barrister, who nodded. Karen and the team left the room to give the Senator his privacy.

The computer rang. Paul's face appeared on the screen. "Sir, what can I do for you?" Paul seemed surprised at the call. He hadn't heard from Bannister since the last funding approval for the ESS One extensions.

"A friend of yours, Logan Conover, just came on my radar. I'm forwarding an intelligence report to you. You should have contacted me sooner about his hunting trip up to Anteros. He must have found what he needed because he is building something big underground at many facilities on Earth under the cover of an organization named Sheltered Refugee. He is using way too many resources to just house refugees."

Paul was taken aback and angry. He had hired a private investigator to tail Logan after the incident in space. It looked like Logan was just working with Sheltered Refugee. "I guess your sources are better than mine, sir. We assumed he was just trying to build better power generators for his operations."

"It's more than that. Much more if my sources are correct. I need to have you work with a group I know to protect our assets and interests."

"We have good security at ESS One," Paul began.

Barrister raised an eyebrow.

"Ok, so we couldn't stop Logan at Anteros. He somehow received help from inside ESS One, and then the UN stepped in."

"Exactly, you need to work with my group. They will post operatives on ESS One to work with your people. Then they'll be working down here too. Interestingly, they have military resources as you'd suspect, but their real strength is top-notch social media experts that can provide a hell of a spin for us. You haven't been selling the ESS project enough to the general public. You know the proverb, 'you have to win hearts and minds' in any endeavor. People have to get excited about humanity's salvation, worth every penny of the trillions we're spending on it. We don't need Logan providing an alternate approach."

"I'm on it. We'll figure out what Logan's up to." Barrister left the call. Paul sat, steaming inside. He was trying to build something great. Logan was doing who knows what to subvert it. He had been too naive about Logan. Logan must have found something at that alien artifact site, and he needed to get this Black River group to find out what they were up to that could threaten ESS One and its mission. Logan was now enemy number one. Or two or three, Paul was starting to get a long list.

# The Proxima Trail

*Cephalonia, Greece and Sheltered Refugee sites around the world*

*Year: 2052 +4.6°F*
  *Earth Population: 11,100,755,113*
  *Population off-earth in solar system: 260,044*
  *Population in other star systems: 4,542*
  *Yearly population decrease due to Global Burn: 55,524,552*

"Welcome, Sheltered Refugees! Thank you for joining this special broadcast meeting of all refugees in the Sheltered Refugee program. We have a special opportunity to announce to you today that will entail job opportunities for everyone in the program."

Matti was just starting her announcement of the Quantum Pioneer program and was so excited. It was like Christmas, being able to offer a path of hope to those who were subjected to the worst of the *Global Burn* consequences. This is what she had worked so long for, and looking out on all the refugees' faces filled her with great joy.

"Today, we offer you a personal choice. One with far-reaching consequences for you and your families. A good choice! But first, before presenting you with your choice, let me give you some history."

Matti then proceeded to show a short video her team produced explaining how the Quantum Pioneer gate research developed over the last six years. It was a fantastic story.

When the video was over, there was an excited buzz from the group. She continued, "This research has been successful! We now can walk to a brand-new world. One that is still challenging but doesn't have killer hurricanes. Let me show you."

Matti then showed everyone the Proxima video with its red sun, vast expanses and hills, and a view of the new colony they were building.

"So, here is the choice. You all can choose to move to and be employed in this new world. There is no fee or charge for you to do this. It is a gift. All we ask is that you be sincere in your effort to establish yourselves and thrive in this new world." Now there was a lot of talking amongst the refugees. Surprised faces and expressions of wonderment and fear as well.

"This is a lot to take in, but know that we have worked for years to provide this promising new path for mankind, and you are the first we are offering it to."

"I won't lie. It is a hard choice. It will be a big change, but we hope you will agree that Proxima provides the best long-term safe solution and future opportunity for you and your families. You all will be getting a link that you can use to explore the new colony's video tours and a detailed list of the types of jobs that will be available. Look it over, think about it and within the next three weeks, if you wish to interview for a position in our new community, contact this link. We will work with you to transition. The first settlers in the new colony will be going over in exactly one month. We expect there to be a large and rapid increase in the migration after that."

*One Month Later*

Thousands were living on Proxima, but they were the construction crews. On April 21, 2051, Idi and Fatou Camara, from Gambia, had the distinction of being the first official permanent Quantum Pioneers to cross over to Proxima Centauri b. They were training with a group of twenty-thousand pioneers who would be the first to inhabit the cities whose section A buildings were finished. Section A was the first twenty residential buildings. They were built with self-contained power, water, and other necessities for starting a community, including educational facilities.

Idi trained to be a plumber and Fatou to be a daycare worker. Their three children were five, eight, and eleven years old and would be enrolled in a school and after-school daycare.

Idi smiled over to Fatou and engaged the buggy's drive. Pioneers were driving light-weight electric buggies that could be driven across and then driven back for more pioneers. The entire trip would be two miles, but they would be four-point-two light-years from Earth when their day was finished.

When they crossed the gate and found themselves in a new world with a dimmer red sun and much stronger gravity, they were quiet. Their excitement was palpable, but they realized just how different life would be in this new world.

A welcome agent met them on the Proxima side. "Hello, my name is Marissa. Welcome to Proxima. I'm sure this is all exciting but also a lot to take in. I'm going to drive with you over to your new home, and then after you settle in, there is an orientation for the next couple of days for your whole family."

The Quantum Pioneer team had created a training program on Earth and orientation once families got to Proxima. They wanted to make the transition as smooth as possible since this would be the second massive change for the refugees last year. The first was having to escape environmental disaster on Earth when they came to the Sheltered Refugee facility. So they wanted the resettlement in Proxima to be a forward and prosperous step of hope, not another anxious time for the pioneers.

Marissa climbed into the buggy with the Camara's and headed out. Essa, their eight-year-old, spoke up when she saw the ten-story apartment building they were approaching.

"Is that where we're going to live, mama? It's pretty and all new!"

Fatou was happy that Essa liked their new community, but what was more exciting was when young Isa saw the playground. The colony architects planned well and built extensive playgrounds and green space in the apartment buildings' courtyards. Proxima itself only had a small amount of native shrubbery, but the builders experimented with hundreds of types of grass and shrubs and found several that thrived in the sandy and iron-rich soil.

When they arrived at their building, Marissa led their family up to their small two-room apartment. Fatou and Idi were wide-eyed at all the new furniture. There were even toys in the bedroom! Food was in the refrigerator. Marissa made sure they were comfortable and then told them she would see them with other new families in the morning.

When Marissa left, Fatou said to their three kids, "Anyone

want to go out to the playground?" Everyone did. It was an excellent start to their new life.

Thousands of others followed them to the new world, and the path to the small city forming on Proxima started being called the Proxima Trail. Like many other pioneer trails before, it was a big step to take, but it led to a better future.

* * *

Once word traveled back from the first refugees that the new colony on Proxima was not only livable, but a peaceful and modern city that was safe and thriving, ninety percent of the refugees signed up to become pioneers in the new colony. The training classes became packed, and construction proceeded as well as could be expected, given the constant disruptions from interruptions in their supply chain. Even so, they had already built enough housing for the second wave of fifty-thousand migrants. The first ten-thousand were settling in well, and the migration was picking up pace.

Meanwhile, Matti found the basis of the Fuerte group's concerns and why they wanted to ramp up pioneers' transfer rate to the new world. Research by Dr. Itu Izakowa had estimated the Global Burn's effect on the world's supply chain, and it wasn't positive. He had created a simulation that showed a breaking point in the world's supply chain's resilience due to disruption to logistics from natural disasters. It turned out they were close to this breaking point, if not past it, ever since the intensity of disasters reached the current relentless cadence.

More than an academic exercise, this disruption raised prices on most goods a hundred percent. It would rapidly make logistics uneconomical—in other words, the world would soon no longer be able to viably ship goods globally.

Once Matti understood the issue, she started putting a plan into place for Sheltered Refugee to own their own mines close to each cave in their network. Her plan slowly migrated eighty percent of their needs to local suppliers. But the other twenty percent couldn't be sourced locally and was at risk. It would someday dry up entirely. Even with stock-piling, there would come a day when they simply couldn't get certain critical parts and materials.

Matti worked with her team to make sure that the colony would be mining and building all the material it needed from Proxima itself by the time this happened. They would be self-sufficient. In fact, it was the only way to accomplish the feat of building cities for a billion people. But getting the colony to be self-sufficient and scaled up before Earth's systems broke down would be a race against time.

On a relatively warm May day, Matti was planning with her staff and running over their ideas for the benefit of new staff members. "Our plan is for one city of five million residents to be built with direct involvement from Earth at each cave-site. From each of these self-sufficient cities, ten more of equal size will be built; thus, two-hundred cities, each with a capacity for five million people, will spread over Proxima in a several thousand-mile-wide area on the main continent. A massive plan to migrate and house one billion people."

One of the staff asked Jet Yan, "Are the twenty-four facility sites' gates not transferring to the same gate on Proxima?"

Matti answered, "Great question. We have been able to vary the parameters very slightly, and each gate transfers to a spot two hundred and fifty miles apart from each other. Oddly, we don't know why, but the entire Proxima planet seems to receive transfers from our gates to it. There doesn't seem to be anyone receiving quantum gate. The whole planet's surface can act as a 'tuned' quantum gate. Our aliens were superb scientists."

Another perceptive question was asked by Maggie O'Donald, recently in from Dublin. "I'm still getting used to all of this magic, or that is how it seems. How much time do we have to get our initial colonies sustainable so that they can expand independently? There must be a ton of requirements to be self-sufficient and tons of different manufacturing needs."

"Good segue Maggie, this is my number one mission right now, and I am passionate about it for obvious reasons. Please, everyone, review Chapter Five – Requirements and Schedule for Colony Sustainability tonight." Matti told all of the new employees. "I will be assigning tasks from this chapter of the plan tomorrow because this is the number one priority of this group. Make no mistake, without achieving self-sufficiency within our rather small window of time will lead to the entire project's failure. Our colonies will not survive if we cannot supply everything they need locally. We cannot afford to supply everything the colonies will need from Earth, nor can we rely on Earth's supply chains forever."

Everyone nodded thoughtfully and looked determined to do their part.

"Thanks, everyone. See you tomorrow at 8 am," Matti said, closing the meeting.

As Matti was wrapping up, she overheard Maggie's comment to the others around her, "You have to wonder why there wasn't a Chapter Five Sustainability Plan for Earth." Another commented, "Apparently, there was something like that back around 2020, but hardly anyone followed it; they were too fat and happy with the ways things were. Total denial."

Maggie shook her head as she walked out of the room, "And our generation is paying the ultimate price."

\* \* \*

Logan stood on Faraway Hill on Proxima with Matti. The hill was on the crest of a high valley full of wild grasses, transplanted from Earth. The spot was idyllic, like the Nebraska Sandhills back in the United States. Kira was running with friends of hers from school around the hills, exploring if any wildlife had spread to the hills. Kira's friend, Sam, Mike's and Marisa's son, was a biology major and was already helping with the translocation of animals and plants to Proxima.

Surprisingly, many species adapted to the new gravity after an initial few month adjustment period. As long as the animals could find a source of water and food, they adapted quickly.

Logan and Matti took the weekend to be with Kira before starting college at the new Proxima University. It was Kira's idea to come to the hill and have a cookout. The waft of the cooking burgers made Logan smile. "Boy, it sure feels like old times," he commented to Matti.

Matti set out a picnic blanket on top of the hill. "It sure does, the best of times," Matti smiled over at Logan. She cherished every moment they were together as a family.

"Kira!" Matti shouted across the fields. Kira and her friends stopped and looked back toward Matti. "Time for the picnic!"

Matti set out the food. Logan and Matti's coworkers all worked a miracle to get picnic supplies fabricated. The fabrication machines were dedicated full time to necessary items for the colony, but the staff knew how little time Logan, Matti, and Kira could spend as a family and found a way to get them the supplies.

The sun was setting when they finished dinner, and they sat around talking. Kira and Sam spoke for a couple of hours about how the animals were doing in the new colony. Logan and Matti were happy to listen to the fantastic work the students were doing.

They were so proud of how amazingly Kira and all her peers adapted to coming to a new planet. Who would have guessed that Kira would go to college on Proxima Centauri b? Even though the colony was small, one of their priorities was to start a college. And the college curriculum sounded really exciting. The students would go to classes part of the time but spend even more time getting practical, hands-on experience by helping out in the colony.

Kira sometimes joked, "Mom, I'm in Pioneering 101."

To which Matti responded, "Honey, you're ready to teach Pioneering 101!"

It was going to be Kira and her peers' world... they all knew it.

*Two months later, Andermatt, Switzerland*

Logan and Matti checked into the Grand Suite of the Chedi resort in Andermatt with trepidation. The suite was gorgeous. They were given one of the best rooms in the hotel. But the meetings over the next couple of days worried them. Ruiz told them to come prepared to the gills as this was a critical meeting of the entire Fuerte Group. They were going to brief their program sponsors, who were the most influential people in the developing world.

Ruiz told them two days ago, "I need you both in Switzerland for a full board meeting, and, yes, I know you have never met directly with the board, but this is a critical meeting. The board has to decide on critical changes. Quantum Pioneer is in the middle of it all."

They ordered room service and together pulled several parts of many presentations to be prepared for anything tomorrow. Matti offered a brilliant idea to cut the presentation down to two critical slides for each main topic area and have lots of video evidence. From their experience in briefings with executives, they rarely clicked past the first slide before the room submerged itself in multiple simultaneous discussions. It was essential to keep any slides concise. Some groups they met with even insisted they present without any visual aids and preferred discussion instead. Still, they thought videos of the new world and their progress were critical to demonstrate.

The next morning, a Feurte assistant named Ms. Chandler came to escort them to the meeting room. "I hope everything is to your satisfaction, and you are having a pleasant visit?"

Matti gestured around the room, "Oh, this has been wonderful!"

Ms. Chandler led the way past impressive displays of flowers and fountains to an ornate room looking out over the Alps.

They were introduced briefly to each board member then the meeting began with Chairman Dr. Chandrama Panikkar opening the conference. "My friends, welcome. We have much to discuss and put in motion, but it all seems to revolve around the Pioneer project, so we have invited our friends from Greece, Logan, and Matti Conover, to give us a briefing."

Dr. Panikkar looked over at Logan and Matti, "Please if you will, could you give us a sense of your breakthrough and how you are proceeding on our new planet? We are particularly interested in expansion timing."

Matti started the discussion with the short video of Proxima Centauri b. The footage showed the current infrastructure built and then used animation to envision the city they planned to build. A date display was at the bottom of the screen showing each phase's completion date as it progressed in the animated build-out. All of the members nodded, happy with the significant progress and plans.

When the video was finished, Matti summarized the finances and timing. Chandrama asked a single question, "What would we need to do to start processing pioneers into the colony in six months at a rate of sixteen-thousand people per day per facility." Matti raised her eyebrows. Their current plan was to get to four-thousand per day. This would quadruple their goal. Chandrama raised his hands, "Yes, I know that is asking a lot, but we are in desperate times, Ms. Conover. We are prepared to invest considerable resources if we can achieve a faster schedule. Put the question in the context of an emergency plan."

Matti and Logan asked to have a fifteen-minute break. They spent it on a conference call with several lead directors on the project back in Greece.

When they reconvened, Logan took the floor and put up one slide with five numbers, "This is an immediate plan to achieve your goal. In short, we would need to double our staff and quadruple the number of gates and 3D printers we have on-site currently. We would need six months. Then we could start achieving the rates you are talking about. But…"

Dr. Panikkar smiled and said, "We were waiting for the 'but.' Please proceed."

Matti took over, "But, our supply chain is constrained by many variables, supplier capacities, country regulations, and so on. We can't see how we can quadruple the flow of needed material into Proxima in that timeframe. It is just too complex."

Dr. Panikkar nodded and asked Mr. Nadu to enter. He introduced him. "We anticipated this problem, and we have asked an associate, Mr. Karam Nadu, who runs the operations of Hindustan, the largest and most successful construction company in India. We would like you to work with Karam on the issue you mentioned and then report back through Mr. Ruiz as soon as possible. Suffice it to say if we can solve this problem, we will likely want to implement your proposal. You see, our economies are stressed beyond the maximum. Everything is deteriorating rather rapidly. From our vantage points as industry leaders, we see it coming as do many corporate leaders in the Western world."

Matti asked, "One question, your rate assumption, what overall timeframe do you have in mind to accomplish the transfer of people to Proxima b?"

"The year I am about to give you is highly confidential. If made public, it would cause a panic."

Matti nodded, she understood, and Dr. Panikkar continued, "Our projections indicate we have ten years, Ms. Conover. We forecast by 2062 it will be challenging to get any organized worldwide effort to be successful. We think at that time the world will split into many disconnected regions, each of which will struggle for basic services and even basic survival."

On that grim note, the meeting ended.

Later, Logan and Matti met with Karam and a small staff of his. They conferenced in their key supply chain staff from Greece. After a quick rundown of their current progress, Karam was impressed and mentioned several ways to create a new but similar supply chain by cannibalizing a few billion-dollar companies. At the mention of this, Logan and Matti looked at each other and whistled. Clearly, they were working at a whole new level.

Karam looked surprised. "It's OK. These are failing companies and require dissolving; their business models lacked any staying power. Especially given our new timeline, I think even if they were important companies, we would still do it."

They agreed that Karam would come back with them to Greece and make his office there. They promised to touch base daily and then decided when they could report progress to Ruiz. All of them felt a renewed sense of pressure given the doomsday scenario that the Board laid out. They were in no doubt that 2062 was the high end of the estimate based on news reports they saw lately. Eleven years. It wasn't long.

Logan and Matti worked in their room to talk via video with their teams to get a new team set up that would handle the plan. They needed to create a parallel effort so as not to disrupt their current teams and projects.

Matti smiled. "A plan within a plan," she offered.

Logan laughed and finished "within yet another plan."

They met Ruiz in a lovely lounge that had both hot and cold water flowing in a small stream between the chairs. You were supposed to dip your hands in while you talked. One hand in hot and the other in the cold. It was an exciting sensation.

Ruiz joined them, and Logan took the lead, "We wanted to

talk about how we were going to announce to the world the Quantum Pioneer project."

Ruiz nodded and thought for a moment.

"We're not," he stated. Logan raised his eyebrows. Ruiz continued with a question.

"Do you think we would have enough good candidates for the migration if we offered the trip to the refugees we have in the facility now and others that might come?"

Matti took that one, "If the same ratio of highly educated refugees stays the same as it is now, probably. But won't we start getting just about everyone?"

Ruiz smiled. "When we start processing, let me know if it's an issue. I'll think you'll find there are already many qualified individuals from the areas we're drawing from. The notion of people in developing nations being full of illiterate people is a horrible myth. The reality was in 1960, the world literacy rate was forty-two percent, but by 2015 it was eighty-six percent. Today, in 2051, it is at ninety-six percent. With the opportunity you are giving them, a fresh start in a new world, they will thrive and prosper. They are motivated to keep their families alive. They will be the best representatives this world has ever seen."

Logan was still worried, "You don't think the world has a right to know of our breakthrough?"

Ruiz shook his head. "It will probably leak sooner or later, but given the timeframe we're up against, I think the stir and publicity we would get would derail our effort at this point. Besides, the task is difficult enough to pull off as it is. Let's get more established."

Matti and Logan both thought about it for a minute then said they would rather not have the public microscope if they could avoid it. Logan and Matti wrapped up and were driven to their private plane. They were back at their offices in Greece a few hours later.

\* \* \*

Logan, Will, and Matti were managing the entire Quantum Pioneer program and knew they couldn't take on this new initiative as well. Matti and her team had built a solid business foundation and managed the twenty-four cave-cities that were now home to six million refugees escaping the escalating global catastrophes. Matti knew she couldn't keep housing these refugees permanently, but her plan all along was to offer the refugees a place in the new world to become pioneers and colonists.

Meanwhile, Will had been running research, and Logan took on public relations and the construction program. The three of them were talking within a conference room.

"OK, we know to start this expanded Pioneer effort we're going to need to quadruple portals and printers and that the supply chain effort is where we need to focus," Logan summarized.

Matti and Logan managed the supply chain effort, but they knew they needed to bring on others now. Matti chimed in, "So who do we want to bring in?"

They thought for a moment, then Logan's eyes lit up.

"Sandy and Mike! They haven't directly worked in supply chain, but they were both involved in managing projects that had extreme conditions in space. And I trust them. I think they've earned the role, helping save the day on our trip back from Anteros. They are also going crazy, having been taken out of ESS One without much notice, and now they can't go back."

The idea grew with Matti and Will. Matti nodded and chimed in, "Their management experience and direct knowledge of space building technologies are hard to find. Building in space teaches you things you can't get anywhere else. They can work directly with Karam, who has tons of supply chain experience but not much experience working on 3D printer-based additive construction projects. I definitely want someone I know who has proven I can trust them if they join the executive team. Mike and Sandy have shown their loyalty beyond question."

"Let's do it right now. You good, Will?"

"I'm good," Will replied. "We need people we can work with that understand the broader political issues and have a historical viewpoint from before we started the Quantum program. They certainly fit the bill."

Matti called her assistant to call Mike and Sandy to join them. They were helping out with just about everything in the two city construction sites. They came ten minutes later.

Sandy smiled. "What do we owe the pleasure? This looks like a power meeting if I ever saw one."

Mike chimed in too. "Let me just say, when I first saw that you were building not just one city but two at the same time, I was blown away. And on Proxima? Wow, you guys have accomplished something that, well, I am in awe and disbelief." Matti motioned for Mike and Sandy to sit down with them, then let him continue raving, "I know you have a lot going on, but we want to be a part of it! You guys are about to make history. We want in. We'll scrub the floors!" he joked.

Sandy was nodding along on all points and chimed in, "I

hate to admit after all the work up in space, but this work you're doing is accomplishing more than the space program. It's a whole new level. It's based on alien technology, which is sure to get us ahead faster than our own tech. It also feels like the right approach because everyone I see is not only dedicated but happy. It's working. I'm impressed."

Logan took on a grim expression and let the silence linger. "Well, being in security and a pilot doesn't leave much room." Mike and Sandy started to get dejected looks. Logan continued. "So, we thought you could help by being our new supply chain co-directors for our new Phase II plan."

Mike and Sandy had looked ready for the worst, and when Logan mentioned the positions, they squinted their eyes, and Sandy laughed, "You always were a tease!"

They all laughed, and Mike was the first to jump in. "Now that's what I'm talking about! You can count on us."

Matti smiled, "We know we can." She then outlined their idea to have Mike and Sandy start a parallel. Still, separate supply chain and construction effort—to create a whole new project timeline that would allow them to scale the entire program without upsetting existing plans. She further reviewed with them who the Fuerte Group was, and Mike and Sandy's head really started spinning.

Matti wrapped up the session, "So you guys still feel upbeat about this? You realize that we have to have a solid plan to present to the Fuerte Group in three months, including secure contract options with suppliers. Also, you'll be working with Mr. Karam Nadu, a real supply chain heavyweight from India."

Mike summarized his feelings. "Wow, you have been busy. This whole operation is amazing. You can count on us; we are all in with you, even if I don't come up for air in the next three months."

Sandy took on a look of firm determination. "Absolutely; this is where we need to be. And thank you for your trust."

With that, Mike and Sandy joined the core team that was expanding their Quantum Pioneer goals to transfer, house, and employ one billion people within the next ten-year timeframe. At the end of the day, Logan shared one final thought with the group.

"You know, some would say we're desperate, and everything might just fall apart, but I see this differently. I see this as an opportunity to be our best, the moment we expand beyond the cradle. This is a natural solution. As crazy as this is, history will look back and see this as the right and only way to move humankind from one planet into the universe. The small short-term picture for us will be chaotic, but the big picture, what we achieve, is downright magnificent."

After a pause, Matti broke the spell, "So let's get some pizza!"

# Attacks

*Year: 2053 +5.2°F*

  *Earth Population: 11,040,755,113*

  *Population off-earth in Solar System: 320,044*

  *Population on Proxima: 185,000*

  *Yearly population decrease due to Global Burn: 65,524,552*

Karen Nightly was sitting in a café in Paris, waiting for her contact to arrive. She loved having the salted butter caramel sauce crepe. It was to die for. The shop, Crêperie du Cloître, was near the newly rebuilt Notre Dame Cathedral. The cafe was small but still managed to fit a dozen two-person tables in, an awning opening it to the busy street outside.

A man in a worn leather jacket entered the cafe, looked over to her, and then joined the line to get his food. He kept glancing over, and Karen knew it was her contact. Why were green recruits so bad at hiding their intentions? Black River recruited him once they found a list of who was on the construction team for Proxima. Finding out that Logan was building on Proxima was a shock. It took another six months to find the list of workers on their Proxima project since Sheltered Refugee hid construction workers for Proxima on the same teams that built the refugee apartments in their caves.

"Hi, I hear the coffee here is always served black?" the man asked after he got an order of pom frites and a hot dog and had come over to Karen's table. He was using the code words he was told to use. Karen nodded to the seat, and the man, Jeremy, sat down and started eating.

"Were you able to get information about Proxima? Is it real, are they really sending people to another planet?" she asked, cutting to the point of the meeting.

Jeremy looked nervous and took out a memory stick and placed it on the table. Karen covered it with her napkin. "Yes, these are pictures. It's amazing, really. They actually did it. They are sending people over to Proxima."

"Have you been over?"

"Yes, I'm on the construction team. A lot has been going on. Review the pictures."

"A few more questions. Is it safe?"

"Well, is exploring and developing any new world safe? Not really. There have been deaths."

"Really, can you get details?"

"Not without blowing my cover. I'm not a pro at this, you know."

Karen was tempted to say, *Really?* But instead just continued, "We need more on the problems going on. Do you think they'll make progress?"

"It might be dangerous, but the progress is unbelievable. You can just drive equipment and materials across and, poof, you're on the construction site. It's amazing. They're building faster than any site I've ever been on. They have these 3D printers that are amazing..."

Karen cut him off. She wasn't interested in engineering

details, just in what she could use to smear Logan and his group. "How many people have transferred over? Is it just workers so far?" She really didn't think they would have time to have any kind of population yet. It took the ESS project ten years to start bringing up regular residents.

"Are you kidding? They have thousands living there already, and they have thousands more in pioneer training classes. It's an efficient operation they're building."

Black River had undoubtedly done an excellent job recruiting. Jeremy was giving them a lot of information they hadn't heard before. The Senator was going to be livid.

Karen slid an envelope over to Jeremy with twenty-thousand dollars in cash. She didn't like carrying a lot of cash. No one used it much anymore, but it was still the best way to keep transactions untraceable.

"Thank you for your time, and please continue to collect information. You are helping your country." She put her finger on the bill to pay for it and left the restaurant.

Jeremy didn't know about helping his country. He thought Sheltered Refuge was doing amazing things, but he really liked having the extra money, so he took the envelope and walked out after he finished his fries.

\* \* \*

Karen was right. Senator Barrister was livid. "They what?!"

Karen briefed him on what Sheltered Refuge was doing on Proxima and showed him the pictures to back it up.

"And will you look at these numbers?" The senator was looking at an estimate Karen had put together based on the images Jeremy provided. The estimates of how many people would migrate over this year and next were high. "They're going to surpass ESS by two-hundred percent in two years? I can't believe they have this much of an operation this fast."

Karen's team worked with an analyst at Black River and put together a pretty good picture of what was happening on Proxima. Karen summarized, "Yes, our contact hit the nail on the head. It's a lot easier when you can just drive over to your construction site. Paul is going to flip when he sees Logan's broken through their research hurdles and now may have a more strategically viable program than ESS."

Senator Barrister wasn't so sure. He had a lot of time and money invested in the ESS program and couldn't let that go so quickly. "I'm skeptical. No one can open a new frontier this rapidly, keep on digging and see if you can get info on these deaths our contact mentioned. I think this still might be a big sham. Could you also place a call to Paul and brief him and give him these materials and pictures? Oh, and video record his response. I can't wait to see it," he cackled dryly.

Later that evening, the senator placed a call to his ace in the hole. The UN had made The Tubes and alien artifacts available to any serious researchers. Through his partner companies, the Senator was financing a research project that involved a particular quantum physics professor short on cash, Professor DeGraff, formerly of Cal Tech.

\* \* \*

Dr. Vonegutt DeGraff shouted over to his graduate assistant, "Turn off the generator, turn it off!"

DeGraff was the head of a secret team, sponsored by a North American and European consortium to build a gate of their own. They had not figured out the right power requirements and the critical step of creating a quantum envelope to travel through, so their portal did not have the proper depth to it. The results were horrific.

"Choi, go in there and clean that rat up," DeGraff shouted over to his lab assistant, who was beginning to think his Ph.D. in physics came down to scraping up the remains of dead lab rats. Their experimental gate cleanly and instantly cleft any object into at least two pieces. It just wasn't possible for part of an object to transfer to the end location with part of the object still in the original location. Messy.

DeGraff called his contact at the consortium.

"Mr. Smith." DeGraff couldn't believe his contact was named Mr. Smith, but he went along with it. "We are working hard. I assure you we are making progress. But we need more than the fifteen people allocated so far. This is the most advanced physics device ever conceived."

DeGraff listened for a while, "Yes, but we need to go to the UN again to get more information from this alien Instructor machine. And can I ask if our attempt to force the Sheltered Refugee group to share their research is successful yet?" Again, he listened. "OK, we will hire additional resources per your original rates and conditions. Thank you."

DeGraff hung up the phone feeling like he always did when his sponsor made demands but did little to work as a team to help tackle the real problems. At least he received permission to hire more staff that he could send over to the UN.

DeGraff found out Sheltered Refugee spent a month at the UN offices researching with apparent success. He went over to the UN and tried to replicate Sheltered Refugee's work, but he just didn't have the same help and equipment to do it right.

He was determined to follow in their footsteps and gain this incredible capability. Maybe he could even submit patents and articles before Sheltered Refugee did. He just wished his team was as dedicated a team as they had put together.

As he left the lab for the night, he heard Choi dump another dead rat in the waste bin. They smelled terrible.

* * *

The UN meeting was scheduled for nine o'clock on Friday morning. The timing on Friday to hit the news cycle before the weekend was not lost on Logan as he woke in his hotel room in New York City and showered, ready for a challenging session. He walked into his room from the shower and picked up the morning New York Times. His eyes grew bigger when he read the front-page headline, "Is Sheltered Refugee killing their refugees?" with a Paul Manning quote.

"Reports of thousands of missing refugees, with hundreds disappearing daily, must be investigated. I knew Logan Conover personally, and he is little more than a hot-shot pilot. It sounds like he is way over his head. Stories of Sheltered Refugee using a sort of cross-dimensional space-gate to beam people to another planet are sheer nonsense and clearly a cover for more nefarious actions."

The article continued with other derogatory quotes from Senator Bannister and others.

Logan shook his head; it was clearly a ploy to cover their space station delays and problems. But still, Logan was sad his former boss twisted the facts so much. He met up with Ruiz for breakfast before the UN hearing.

"We are going to respond, right?" he asked.

Ruiz was calm as usual. "They are just trying to bait us. Our activities are perfectly legal. But perhaps it is time for an official demonstration to let the world know there is a better solution than spending millions per person to house people in space."

They finished their meal talking about the more positive progress they were making and how excited new colonists were.

Ruiz and Logan entered the large UN meeting hall and took their seats up front at the witness table to testify. The UN International Court of Justice was holding the hearing, and an appropriate cast of hundreds was present, from country representatives to reporters from all major news outlets. The disinformation campaign against them was having an effect.

Kotov Leonidovich, the Russian Justice, opened the session with a provocative statement. "Gentleman, thank you for coming. There is a primary question to clear up. It is this: did your group achieve a breakthrough using UN supplied evidence, the alien artifacts returned from Anteros, and have not disclosed it as required by the UN policies, or," he paused for dramatic effect and looked at the cameras, "are you a bunch of murders and thieves that we should lock away?"

Since the question seemed rhetorical, the Italian judge Soccorso Tosti spoke up. "I purpose this body adjourns for three weeks to send scientific representatives of the Court to determine if indeed Sheltered Refugee and Mr. Conover can prove any success in their research with the artifacts. We need access and evidence, gentleman, to clear up all of these rumors and accusations. We need the truth."

There was a lot of talking in the audience and general commotion.

230

Mr. Ruiz leaned forward to the mike to be recognized. Justice Tosti nodded.

"I can assure the court that we can send people and material to another world," he stated. There was an uproar from the audience. Justice Leonidovich had to bang his gavel several times to restore order.

Ruiz held up his hand in a placating gesture and continued, "This capability is still in formative research stages. According to regulations, we are not required to disclose our findings yet. We are close to disclosing and simultaneously file patents related to the equipment we have developed. I can assure the court we are cooperating to the fullest."

"Then you agree with our verification request? You will accommodate our experts in your new world?" Tosti inquired with incredulity.

Ruiz nodded in the affirmative. Tosti concluded by banging down his gavel. "This case is adjourned. We will reconvene in three weeks when our technical experts can give testimony to the true status of Sheltered Refugees' claims and the safety of their operations."

The mob at the airport was unbelievable.

Ruiz leaned over. He shouted in Logan's ear, "Now, do you see why we delayed as long as we could?"

Logan nodded and forced his way through the crowd to get to their private jet. Soon they were in the air. Logan was already on the phone arranging the UN representatives' visit whom they had met briefly before leaving the UN.

There were four experts assigned to their case. They possessed backgrounds in astronomy, geology, physics, and engineering. They would be arriving at their Greek island labs in two days. Logan and Ruiz talked most of the way to

Greece about the details of the visit. They also discussed what they would need to do once the breakthroughs were known to the world. They anticipated a rush of new applications for pioneers from the world community and technology sharing requests. They were entering a new phase of the work.

Ruiz smiled after he got off the phone with his lawyers, "They're ready," he told Logan, "they've been working for a year now on the patents and contracts we're going to need for negotiating with the UN. But they are ready. We're going to be protected." Somehow, Logan wasn't reassured. The dam had broken, and he could feel the wave coming.

\* \* \*

The UN scientists were professional. They only took pictures of the labs that weren't designated as proprietary, but they insisted on seeing everything. They also requested lists of all refugees and of those that transferred to Proxima. They were shown the records. The scientists wrote down random names of people they wished to talk to when they visited the new world. Logan could see they were all skeptical that they would actually get to see a new world. Boy, were they in for a surprise!

After a few hours tour and a safety exercise, the scientists were surprised to be strapped into a buggy that joined the queue of carriages ready for transfer. As much as they were trying to be objective, their excitement was building. Will rode with the scientists. He described the experience in detail, but when asked detailed scientific questions always responded with the phrase Ruiz advised he use.

"I cannot comment at this time about that aspect of the

project due to research disclosure constraints."

The scientists nodded. They had heard that phrase before.

The moment of transfer. The scientists' buggy rolled forward. Two of them winced in anticipation of pain during the transfer. The others looked like they expected nothing to happen and that this was all a con-job. As they rolled out onto Proxima Centauri b, they changed their opinion quickly.

They looked around in awe. Logan smiled, "Welcome to Proxima." The UN observers were all stood up then sat down quickly, feeling the increased gravity. The transfer point was on a slight hill and allowed everyone in the buggy to see out over the new settlement, which expanded to the horizon.

They spent several minutes asking dozens of questions about what they were seeing, and then the astronomer, Dr. Carl Jacobson, asked Logan, "Where can we set up our instruments?" Logan had set up a spacious outdoor area for the group near the first community established and drove them there. They took an hour to set up their equipment.

"What does that do?" Logan asked, pointing to a large telescope with a computer keyboard attached at its base.

"That is the most important instrument we will be using," Dr. Jacobson explained. "It takes astronomical observations to establish that we are indeed where you say we are. Star locations will verify that we are in another world or not."

Other readings of soil, air, and so on were taken, but the most compelling evidence would be the star locations. They wouldn't lie. They would establish the veracity of Logan's claims or disprove them.

They waited until it was dark, and then Dr. Jacobson made his observations. When he finished, everyone on the UN team waited anxiously for his results.

Will and Logan transferred over to be at the site when the location verification was announced. They knew what they would find, but still, it was a pretty significant moment to have it verified by the UN. They had run the same experiments many times, always being astounded when they looked back at the Earth's sun and saw its faint light from four-point-two years in the past.

After several minutes, Carl looked up from his pad to report his findings to the group, "My God! There is no doubt. We are actually on Proxima Centauri b. I have checked three times, and the computer verifies. One hundred percent confirmation. Congratulations, gentlemen, and ladies! This is astounding." Carl directed the last comment to Will, Logan, and Matti. Logan smiled. Clearly, Carl was entirely skeptical up to the point of being convinced by the evidence.

The other scientists were eager to have Carl run through his findings step-by-step, and it took them all an hour to do so. They then proceeded to replicate his results until they were all convinced with their own measurements. Logan understood. Their careers hinged on being right. In the end, it was confirmed by all of them.

The head of the group, Dr. Marcella Darling, concluded for them all, "I think the world is going to be astounded. This is truly the biggest event in the history of science."

Will couldn't help but smile. Gone was the skepticism and hostility from the UN group. In its place was a childlike scientific wonder.

"Isn't it wonderful?" he said. "And all you have to do is walk on over."

Marcella nodded and continued, "I think our work here is almost done, gentleman." Clearly, the group couldn't wait to get back to Earth and announce and publish their fantastic findings.

The UN scientists spent time in the housing communities, gathering evidence of the community's mood and its residents' safety. They found that everyone was happy, and no one reported any serious safety issues, and minor ones were being addressed. There were plenty of unfinished projects and buildings. Clearly, this new community was still getting organized and settled, but it looked to be working.

What truly impressed the scientists was that each resident had a remarkable story of woe of their time back on Earth and was overjoyed to have been given a chance to migrate. Unlike many in the West, these people experienced the worst effects of the *Global Burn* firsthand. To a man, woman, and child, they were all genuinely grateful to be safe. Rekindled hope was evident in each of their responses and their faces.

Marcella mentioned afterward to Logan, "We, frankly, expected to see tents and people in extreme hardship, but this is amazing. You have already achieved an apparently sustainable community. No wonder your refugees are eager to come."

Logan smiled, "I'm so glad you were able to come over and see the truth. We hope you will take back a story of all the good we're starting to achieve." Marcella nodded. She was convinced.

*Two weeks later, UN Headquarters, New York City*

Back at the UN, there was a different buzz in the air than at the last hearing. The proceedings started with the judges calling for a report from the UN science team.

Dr. Darling took an hour and presented hard evidence and data to the group. She summarized at the end, "Your Honors, it is a rare pleasure for me to conclude that our team unanimously concurs the Sheltered Refugee organization, with the help of financial sponsors, can transfer humans to Proxima Centauri b. Further, they are well on their way to building a sustainable community for thousands of people, many of whom we interviewed and found grateful, healthy, and content. We have submitted all evidence for inspection."

Dr. Darling continued on a more personal note with a great smile on her face, "The investigation committee will also be formally submitting Dr. Will Bonolado for the Physics Nobel prize. We want to honor and bring attention to the great scientific achievement that our findings have verified."

This upbeat, and obviously unexpected announcement, brought a considerable amount of excitement to the hearing room. All of the reporters switched their attention to Logan and Ruiz, shouting questions. The judges restored order in the room. When it was quiet again, they proceeded.

"Hearing the unexpected and amazing conclusion from our science team, we are compelled to close this hearing with an admonition to the Sheltered Refugee organization that we expect timely and orderly submission of research findings per the UN articles of technology sharing. We would also encourage them to follow United States President Eisenhower's footsteps in 1953. After atomic energy was developed by the US, the technology was shared with the world, knowing this was the most peaceful way forward. This hearing is closed."

Ruiz and Logan had prepared remarks and a press release, including photos from Proxima showing healthy living conditions, which they gave out right after the hearing. They wanted to make sure people formed a positive view of Proxima before any influencers could spin a negative and incorrect narrative.

Outside of the UN hearing room, they took a couple of questions from the press. A reporter from BNN shouted out two questions, "How many people are you able to migrate? Is this a viable solution to the Global Burn?"

Logan took the questions, Ruiz preferring to blend into the background.

"Our mission has always been to find ways of maximizing help for refugees. We anticipate being able to migrate, house, and employ many millions of refugees and consider this a viable solution for those suffering from the Global Burn's direct effects. We are focusing on helping those suffering the most and not just those who can pay the most.

"I worked on the space station for years, and space was truly the new frontier. But I left when there was this hope, this glimmer of hope, that there was a more efficient way to help all of the world's peoples. We have been gifted a more humane and natural way for us to expand to the stars. You can literally walk to another world."

Ruiz stepped forward and said, "We've released a great press package. You'll love the photos from a planet with a red sun, the first photos from another planet. Please review that and the release of a press report video from internationally known reporter Sugiyama Matsuko who has traveled to Proxima. We will be talking and sharing more as we can. It's a wonderful day for humanity!"

With that, even though reporters kept shouting questions, he took Logan's arm and guided him from the room and let their media director, Lacy Daughs, hand out press releases and take more questions.

\* \* \*

Later that day, as Ruiz and Logan were packing to go and ignoring their phones, which had been buzzing non-stop, the Secretary-General of the UN called Ruiz through her official channels. They took that call.

"Good evening Ms. Secretary," Ruiz answered and listened for a minute. "Yes, I see. Of course, we want to do our part, but timing is delicate for us to succeed in our plans." He paused again to listen. "Yes, I understand you have emergency powers. Could we talk in person to discuss the details? Thank you, Ms. Secretary. We can be there in an hour."

Logan looked on while the conversation proceeded.

"Well, that didn't take long. We need to meet with Ms. Sabine Olsen, the Secretary-General, and talk about helping the world figure out how to use our technology. She has already gotten demands from many countries to share the technology immediately. Do you see why we tried to get as far as a head start as possible? I'll need you for a couple of days because they are bringing in many technical and high-level administrators. They are putting together an international UN team. They want to talk about setting up hundreds of transfer points and building colonies. They obviously trust their scientific team's report implicitly. This is moving faster than I even imagined."

Logan nodded, "Desperate times. Millions are demanding solutions to the problems of climate change. I just never thought humanity would migrate to the stars as an emergency evacuation. I had hoped we'd have at least twenty to a hundred years to expand."

Ruiz nodded, "I think they want to refocus from the space effort to this approach if it continues to pan out for them. We knew the world would reach a tipping point where they finally realized time was shorter than anyone thought. With millions dying every year, they see our solution as drowning men who just saw a life raft. I think they are finally ready to take action. So, we're going to help them if we can, but we can't risk the Sheltered Refugee sites."

Logan picked up the thought, "If we can help them with their own sites, then they won't try to take over our sites."

Ruiz nodded, paused, then looked into Logan's eyes, "Be careful, my friend. The space consortium and corporations earning trillions will not take this lightly. If we win, they lose, and they know it. You've already seen their first volley. Expect more."

Logan nodded. Ruiz moved on to more immediate concerns, "So, what do you think about getting Mike, Sandy, and Karam on this? They just went through the learning curve. I would rather the UN not touch our current program."

Logan thought for a moment. He thought of Mike, Sandy's, and Karam's efforts that were proceeding quickly. They had purchased five large sites, two in Asia, one in Africa, one in Europe, and one in Central America. Fuerte struggled to fund all of the new sites, so it made sense to have UN countries pay for the expanded effort.

"OK," he said. "Why not? If the UN can keep this from turning into a circus or worse, let's blow it open. Are you OK with opening up other worlds as well? I would rather keep Proxima for Quantum Pilgrims. Which means we need to

239

give them one or two of the other worlds."

Logan referred to their ace in the hole, the five other Tubes to other worlds, just sitting in the UN archives. They had taken the technical readings on each and could, theoretically, travel to any of them. Part of Mike, Sandy, and Karam's plan B was to open two new worlds.

Ruiz responded, "The genie is out of the bottle. Now, they'll figure it out soon enough on their own. Give them two more and save the other three. But don't give anyone any help on that front. Guarding the secret of The Tubes is the most important secret we can keep. We own our intellectual property, and we want to license the gate technology we've developed, not teach others. We should provide the technicians to set up and manage any new gate."

The next day Ruiz and Logan were driven in UN vehicles over to the Jacob K. Javits Convention Center, commandeered as the international effort's emergency headquarters. Mike, Sandy, and Karam met them there, just coming in on a UN helicopter.

There were many groups, each with their own command table. A placard with large letters announcing their group names. They were already organized into two main categories Transfer and Colony. Colony groups were 'Colony: Food Services,' 'Colony: Energy Resources', and many others stretching down an extended length of the conference room. The UN had called in their military and relief commanders to run the emergency effort. Logan hadn't ever seen a full UN operation startup before. It was impressive.

Logan and Ruiz huddled with Mike, Sandy, and Karam.

Logan briefed them, "We knew this was going to go public sometime, sorry to pull you in on such short notice."

Mike nodded and asked the most crucial question. "Are we sharing it all, working side-by-side now?"

Ruiz nodded. "I spoke with an emergency session of Fuerte last night, and they agreed that to protect our resources, this was the only way. In return for cooperation, we get full UN military protection of our Sheltered Refugee sites. Optimistically, which is unusual for me, they might cut through the usual bureaucracy and help save people if they are this organized. Heaven knows we can't do it all ourselves.

"So, it's a go. Open up each of your five sites under construction and two of the five reserve worlds. But we keep Proxima a Quantum Pioneer effort only. You three will be on the UN International Emergency Board, which will govern all operations and have thirty-two members. The members are one from each of the twenty-five host countries, you three, and three other counterparts that will shadow you until they get up to speed. The Secretary-General herself will be the chairwoman of the committee to, in her words, 'kick whatever butts need kicking.'"

Logan and Ruiz spent two hours with the Secretary-General and her team late the previous night, working out the details of the directorship of the new emergency effort. Sabine, the Secretary-General, was a princess from Denmark. She had come a long way from an acting career. Starting as the ambassador from Denmark to the UN, she had risen quickly in international circles until being elected to Secretary two years ago. She was the most effective Secretary-General in a long time.

Karam, Sandy, and Mike were escorted to the front of the room and introduced to the other board members. They went to have a two-hour lunch meeting. The Secretary-General went over to talk with Logan and Ruiz.

"I can't thank you two enough for trusting our process and opening your technology in such a short amount of time. I'm determined to make this the best UN effort ever undertaken. Given that it's the world's only real chance to save the bulk of our citizens, I have more than high hopes; I have a mandate. I'm going to hit everyone over the head with it."

Ruiz bowed, "Our pleasure Madam Secretary."

Logan gestured wide with his arms. "I am so impressed already. It took our group over a year to get so organized."

Ms. Olsen was complimentary, "You are the trailblazers. I can only hope everyone will put their egos away and follow your lead on construction and procedures." She narrowed her eyes, "In fact, I'm going to insist that that is exactly what we do. We don't have time to reinvent the wheel. Now, if you'll excuse me, I have to open the Board meeting."

Logan and Ruiz were ushered to a luncheon of their own with the heads of all the groups. They could take a few moments before the chaos started to get to know the group heads. When the Board finished their meeting, there was a cascade of other conferences where Ms. Olsen gave everyone their marching orders.

The next three days were long but organized, and to everyone's surprise, at the end of the three days, there was a three-hundred-page joint action plan complete with multi-billion-dollar funding commitments that all twenty-five host countries signed.

The only catch was that all of the countries wanted a six-month pilot project to verify the UN scientists' claims before committing to spending billions on colonies and to convince the general public that the new worlds were safe. That approach made perfect sense to Logan.

Over several years, the extended plan was to build gates ten times the size of what Sheltered Refugee was building, allowing sixty-million people per month to migrate. This broke down to two-hundred-thousand people processed per day through each of ten mega-facilities the twenty-five host countries would provide. This was the same number of passengers the London Heathrow airport in Britain processed each day, so airport managers were pulled into the task force to ensure smooth operations. The goals were ambitious but necessary. More importantly, since the technology and city building plans were proven by Sheltered Refugees' Quantum Pilgrim program running for two years, it was technically and socially tested.

All countries agreed to license the building designs, 3D printers, and transfer technology, so Sheltered Refugee was due to collect tens of billions of dollars in licensing revenue. Logan and Ruiz already planned to put these funds right back into their operations.

Each country needed to ratify the agreement individually. Still, it was a fantastic start at a ten-year emergency plan to evacuate humanity from Earth, under the banner of a noble migration to new worlds.

Logan never felt so much positive energy out of New York City, and once the press and the world citizens were briefed, the world received a rare but needed lift. The same spirit of individual good-will seen at disaster sites seemed to be spreading worldwide.

But Logan had noticed that every positive move forward they made was met with a negative counterforce from competing interests over the last several years. The more significant the progress, the harder the counterforce. This was a big step forward, so he was more apprehensive than ever.

\* \* \*

Space Industries was mostly on target to achieve its reduced goal of three ESS stations within five years. These stations could support one million people each. But they needed continued funding, or their whole vision was at risk.

Paul Manning and Colonel Tibbets sat in a conference room talking with the heads of all the space contractors on Earth.

Morrison from Boeing summed up their feelings succinctly. "What a sea-change! One day we're the saviors of the world; the next, we're the contractors no one wants to finish paying."

Tibbets looked contemplative. "All the world knows right now about Proxima comes from one report from four scientists who went on a scripted visit for two days. Logan is a lot of hype at all times. He is not a scientist. You gotta wonder how safe these new worlds are, right? Most of the worlds that astronomers have found are either 250 degrees Celsius or have storms that make our current hurricanes look like babies. I wonder if he's leading people into a death trap with this fantasy. He was always an idealist that reacted more than he prepared and thought."

A PR guy from Black River who was on the call spoke up, "I can use that. You guys should also talk to the Stick with Earth coalition we started. It's mostly a bunch of rich guys in their fancy homes who have never experienced the effects of the Global Burn, but they align with your cause well."

Paul chimed back in, "All good ideas, let's run with these and stop this nonsense. Every day the world gets caught up in Logan's fantasy is a day we don't get the funding we need to build a real safety net."

Senator Barrister was on the call and finally spoke up, "Paul, we need more than public relations involved in this. Now that the UN is backing Sheltered Refugee, they are a serious threat. As I see it, we have this six-month pilot period to prove Proxima is a bad idea. We need a failed pilot program. To that end, I want you to start working with the director of Black River, Rivio Palmer. He used to be CIA. A good man. And you know about Dr. DeGraff's work to try and create his own gate to Proxima?"

Paul spoke up, "Yes, I met DeGraff briefly. Is he going to be successful?" Paul wasn't impressed with DeGraff when he met him. He seemed too much like a professor who wanted to publish and be famous, not develop technology carefully.

"As a matter of fact, he is making good progress. He was able to send his assistant through to Proxima. He set off a few alarms and came right back, but I think we need to send Rivio through with a team to Proxima as soon as we can. We need someone with first-hand knowledge of what's wrong with the Proxima operation that we can use."

"Sounds great because if we don't get a handle on this, the ESS program will not be going anywhere. And that boils me. Logan has gone too far with his band of merry men."

The senator raised his eyebrow. Hmm, he thought, Paul really resents Logan. Maybe I can use that. Barrister had long since given up emotional responses to setbacks. Emotions led to mistakes. To Paul, he said, "I'm putting you in contact with Rivio and want you to supervise the operation directly. You know what needs to be done. You have my full backing." Barrister smiled. That should do it, he thought.

# Double-Sabotage

*Year:2054 +5.6°F*

  *Earth Population: 10,950,755,113*
  *Population off-earth in Solar System: 520,044*
  *Population in other Star Systems: 1,940,542*
  *Yearly population decrease due to Global Burn: 65,524,552*

While the UN and many sponsor nations were ramping up their operations, Quantum Pioneers continued to migrate people over to Proxima in increasing numbers through Sheltered Refugee's twenty-four facilities. Thousands of refugees were moving their families over to brand new apartments on Proxima. Once they moved, they were automatically full citizens of the colony of Proxima b. They didn't complain about the gravity or the disruptions in getting household items that were not available yet. They just rolled up their sleeves, worked with their new neighbors, and found a common purpose in building a new world together. Without hope just weeks before, the new pioneers were thrilled with their new life.

It was a beautiful summer day in June. Matti and Kira were walking down the ramp to the quantum gate in their Greece facility. They were moving the family's residence over to

Proxima to continue managing operations from the Proxima side. Kira was in the University in Proxima, and Matti and Logan wanted to be closer if there were problems. Kira also had another ulterior motive. She wanted to be the first person to bring a pet over to the new world. Her cat Andromeda was with her.

"I'm so excited, mom. I get to bring Andromeda over to the new world! But I'm also terrified she won't do well in the higher gravity. Are we doing the right thing?" Kira worried.

Matti and Logan had talked with Kira and discussed how they would manage the cat in the new world. Kira asked the veterinarian that had approved all transfers of farm animals to examine Andromeda and approve her for transfer. Cows, pigs, and even chickens were being transferred to the new world, but no pets were allowed until now. Andromeda was the first. Kira hoped if she was successful, it would open the way for other families to bring their pets.

Matti reminded Kira, "The vet said that other farm animals adapted well after only a week. Be sure to watch her for the first week, and hopefully, she will perk up after that. And if not, we can always bring her back."

"It's OK, Andromeda," Kira said to her cat in soothing tones. The cat was in a standard cat carrier. "You might be surprised at first, but you'll be alright."

They traveled to the transfer point and were sharing a carriage with another family who was migrating over. Kira saw a girl who was about ten years old and spoke to her, "Hi, my name is Kira. This is my cat, Andromeda. She's going to be the first pet on Proxima."

"Wow, my name is Sumer Tahir. I'm from Turkey. Can I pet her when we transfer over?"

Kira wasn't sure, so she said, "I think she might be alarmed and need to stay in her carrier when we cross, but why don't you give me your phone number and in a week you can come over to my house, and we can play with her."

"Great, I'd love that," Sumer bumped her phone against Kira's to exchange numbers.

They were crossing, and Kira could see the girl was worried. She took her hand in hers, "I've crossed several times, and it's no problem, a little bit of dark, and then suddenly you're in the dimmer light of Proxima's sun. You'll love it there; everything is brand new. There are a lot of kids your age." Sumer smiled at Kira and pressed her hand tighter as they crossed.

They experienced the usual dark period when they were in the transfer space, and then the dim red light of Proxima's star shown down on them. "Wow," was all Sumer could say, "I can't believe we just traveled so far. This is so alien. Everything is heavier!"

"Yes, it takes about two weeks to get used to being heavier, but then it's ok," she reassured Sumer. "This is where we split up, have a great time settling in, and I'll call you!" Kira waved at Sumer as she and her family joined a queue with others to be taken to their new apartment.

Matti and Kira looked over at Andromeda. The cat was meowing softly, clearly scared. She could tell something very big happened. Kira leaned over and put her fingers in the cage. The cat nuzzled them. "It's ok, honey, we'll be home soon, and you can explore your new home!" Andromeda meowed again. Matti and Kira climbed aboard a special transport for existing residents of Proxima. The carriages were self-driving. As soon as they were settled, the carriage started up and drove them to their new home.

Matti loved that she was going to be closer to Kira on Proxima and wished Logan could permanently move to Proxima as well. She was excited that Kira adjusted so well. She was doing wonderfully at the university and developed a lot of new friends with her classmates. The first class of Proxima University bonded more than average, which was understandable given their circumstances.

Matti just hoped Logan was holding up against the various attacks. It was a critical time for the success of the project on many fronts. Seeing the new families settling in on the Proxima side made her feel like it was all worth it. They helped so many start a promising new life, free from the pending climate disasters on Earth.

The UN migration teams had been impressed and appreciative of Sheltered Refugees' Quantum Pioneer settlements and technology. The pilot program was progressing successfully.

Logan led extensive tours on Proxima for UN delegations of engineers and administrators. It was the fifth time he did so in a week. Logan had never seen visitors taking so many notes. Logan appreciated that this was perhaps the only chance they would get to learn before having to go to the two new worlds themselves and replicate the success. Not an easy task.

On the first day of the tour, Logan took everyone to the new city just past the transfer gate. First-time visitors spent most of the day, getting over the shock of being in a new world. The second day, when people started accepting the new world's reality, Logan broadened their trip to include a view from Homestead Rock, a tall hill three thousand feet high that afforded a great view of the building going on below. The view of a thoroughly planned and sustainable city was impressive.

The integration of residential, commercial, and manufacturing areas was beautifully combined into a functional and aesthetically pleasing city that was expanding itself at a rate of thirty-five thousand people a week. There were twenty-four such cities on Proxima, all within one thousand miles of each other and extending toward one another.

Logan was atop Homestead Rock, explaining the expansion philosophy.

"Over the last year, we have expanded the mining facilities that you can see in that direction," Logan pointed away from the sun toward a mine shaft that had earth movers moving vast quantities of rock to a processing area. "The city is now growing mostly on its own with little assistance from Earth. We are mining the critical materials we need for our building printers, which you can see working over there."

He pointed toward the front-line of expansion, where a cloud of dust partially obscured five immense boxy structures that were the building printers.

"Each printer can print a new commercial or residential building each day, and each building holds one-thousand people."

Proper appreciation came from his visitors. Jamo Wombo, a materials engineer, asked, "What is the total time it took you to be self-sufficient, minus any adjustment for research?"

Logan rubbed his chin.

"Well, it took us two years to build the infrastructure and another two to become self-sufficient. I would say one year of that could be due to first-time experimentation and learning. We have sent you all data chips with our analysis of all construction, including completion times and architectural diagrams. We have also downloaded all of our engineering specifications to the UN, so you all have access to our building program's secrets. All we ask is that we all share any improvements any group comes up with. We'll only be successful if we cooperate."

"A more than fair arrangement," Jamo commented with a nod of appreciation.

Amy Wanaker posed a more humorous question, "Will all the buildings be the same? I can't imagine thousands of the same building."

"Interesting question Amy," Logan responded, "There are twenty-two types of buildings that were designed. A computer was used to randomly vary parameters. So, the core systems and architecture will be the same, which engineers love, but the more decorative features will change. So, we hope that cultural preferences and differences will be preserved as much as possible. And all of you can have a big impact on that process by introducing cultural modifications into the designs. We're counting on you doing so."

Logan was happy with the tours and his work with the UN. The problem was that Western media was being flooded by propaganda against their Quantum Pioneer program. Scary 'what-if' scenarios were going viral on the internet. What if Proxima had unknown creatures they didn't know about. What if a plague hit? What if the gates went down and everyone was stranded? He knew Ruiz's legal and media teams worked overtime to combat the false information, but it was difficult. All he could do was do his part and work to get the truth out. So much was going well, but his biggest fear was that public opinion would be swayed by the lies being repeated on public media.

\* \* \*

Kira and her five friends had spent the last year together in classes and doing practical fieldwork in the hills surrounding Proxima's colonies. They were determined to help the effort on Proxima and so had formed a small exploration team. They called themselves the Proxima Five and were given an ATV by the University to explore new areas to support the construction and farming groups.

Kira and her group would scout for promising areas to build farms or other installations needed by the colonies. Their work was in demand because there was no extra personnel to do scouting. All other personnel were busy six days a week meeting their expansion goals, which always seemed to become more urgent. They carried a sonic repeller on their ATV to ward off large bearhogs.

"Hey Kira, look at this," shouted Max, one of Kira's friends she met when she helped put the documentary together two years ago. Max was walking around a massive structure. Checking their maps, they determined it was not built by the Quantum Pioneer program.

"Narly," Max exclaimed, "it must be an alien artifact. You're like your dad, Kira, finding artifacts!"

Their current trip was a follow-up to a challenge Kira posed to the group several months ago. She asked, "If you were an alien, where would you put the equipment to maintain the gates?" The group quickly intuited that aliens would put such a site precisely in the center where all the gates, and thus cities, on Proxima were forming.

Kira and the other three explorers walked over to Max. They started circling the structure. It was made entirely of rock, but the shape was suspicious. It was too symmetrical.

"It is exactly thirty meters square and appears to extend as deep into the ground," Kira reported. Kira never lost an opportunity to show off her unique ability to automatically measure, zoom, and even take and transfer 3D photos of what she saw with her prosthetic eye.

"Weird," was AJ's only comment as he touched the walls. "Seems to produce a lot of heat as well. Kira, you getting any readings on infrared?"

Kira felt silly; she hadn't thought to switch her eye to infrared as it always read heat signals exceptionally accurately. When she switched, she screamed out, and all her friends looked over with concern.

"What?" AJ shouted.

"Sorry, it just startled me. I've never seen such intense energy. On infrared, the building looks like one bright yellow block, and the energy readings are like what we get from the alien power generators; only this one seems to be putting out two-hundred times more energy than one of our city generators." The city used five quantum power generators.

"What could it need all that energy for?" Miranda verbalized what they were all thinking.

Max, the only cautious one of the group, was backing away.

"Guys, this is where we need to retreat. Let's pull back behind that hill over there."

He pointed to a mound a quarter-mile back from where they were. They all climbed into the ATV and had no sooner arrived at the hill when AJ pointed past the building to a dirt cloud on the horizon coming closer to their position.

"Kira, I thought you said we were the only scouts out here today?"

\* \* \*

Rivio wasn't happy. Dr. DeGraff had taken four months to set up a secret transfer station to Proxima so that it was safe enough to send his team across. It took another month to infiltrate Sheltered Refugee's computer systems and security so they could drive their armored personnel carriers loaded with ammunition around without being detected. One of Rivio's team members, Archie, was a genius hacker and set them up to look like any other pioneer buggy. He has even been able to get them off the detection grid when they needed to, like now.

Rivio replayed the conversation with Paul Manning in his head. They had talked yesterday at Paul's Madrid headquarters about what Rivio found at Proxima in his first few weeks of scouting.

"Something doesn't add up," Paul challenged Rivio. "There must be a primary power source on the planet, possibly an alien construct to keep the gates open, and it's going to be big."

Paul was troubled that some alien civilization set up Proxima to receive transfer pioneers through the gates from just about anywhere. It seemed too easy. For years mankind struggled just to get back into space. Paul was proud that he'd led that effort. The scientific community expected it to take hundreds of years of toil and scientific breakthroughs to develop a faster-than-light drive so that mankind could get to the stars. This alien civilization gave Logan a gift that just opened a door, and people stepped over to another planet?

Paul couldn't accept it. How could someone just *walk* over to a planet? The thought of it was a mockery, an insult, to the toil and struggle Paul and his space-pioneers had gone through to establish the space frontier. Images of the trillions of dollars and the many lost lives opening up the space economy flowed through Paul's mind's eye. They were successful! They were profitable! They were the heroes, not Logan and his amateur band of merry scientists. It was more than a normal man could take.

Rivio was used to military operations sponsored by corporations, but this was different. He recognized the gleam in Paul's eye. This was personal. He could see Paul was being consumed with jealousy. Rivio would have to be careful. Revenge missions were always the hardest since his orders would be based on passion and not logic.

Paul looked up at Rivio, "You have to go back and triangulate the power spikes when people transfer. Take Douglas with you and figure out if there is a central power core. If we find that we will prove to the world just how unstable this whole new world transportation method is."

Rivio took the hint. He was to be the *destabilizer*, a role he rather relished.

"I'll find it, and when I do?"

He left the question hanging.

Paul looked over at him, "Let's show the world just how risky it is to travel to new worlds on technology no one understands. One accident," he eyed Rivio meaningfully, "and everyone will see that it is crazy to pursue this alien magic."

It took two more weeks for Rivio and his team of four to triangulate the power signals, and the final result was so obvious he wondered why others hadn't thought about it yet. The power core was at the exact center of all of the transfer stations on the planet. He bet no one even thought to explore that location, so he didn't expect any resistance.

The small UN teams that guarded the gates on the Earthside never assumed anyone would challenge the pioneers on Proxima from an unauthorized gate. They were confident they controlled the only access to Proxima. All that was on Proxima was a fledgling UN force, pitifully small for the close to two million people that now lived there. They would certainly not be prepared for Rivio's trained combat team. Rivio brought his full gear, just in case, including his favorite missile launchers. He really liked to be prepared.

The combat team crested a hill and saw the colossal stone building.

"Here we go, boys and girls; this is the place. Petra, do you have the charges ready?"

Petra was their explosives expert and was trained in Russia before joining the mercenary team.

"Da," Petra nodded, which was all Petra would usually respond, and all Rivio needed to know. They drove up close to the structure and jumped out, two taking up a defensive posture, scanning the horizon for trouble, while Petra carried her special case up to the structure. She began wiring explosive charges.

Kira and her group were hidden behind a hill a quarter of a mile away from the structure. Kira zoomed in on Rivio's team with her bionic eye. She instantly transmitted pictures to her dad about what was happening.

Logan just finished the command center tour when Kira's message came in with all sorts of flashing red alerts. Just like Kira, Logan thought, until he looked through the images. The army semi-automatics were clear enough in the image. Kira also included the text, 'This structure looks alien to me and gives off a hell-of-a-lot of infrared. Do you know these guys? They don't look legit to us.'

Logan checked the coordinates, and the pieces were starting to fit together. If his hunch was correct, he was both excited and pretty worried. He texted Kira back to stay out of sight and forwarded Kira's message and images to Proxima's UN security command. A small force was nearby at the closest transfer gate. The force was small, with only ten soldiers, but they were more prepared than their size implied and were ready 24-7 to go anywhere on the planet.

"Major Karper," Logan sent an emergency security request and was instantly connected.

"Go ahead, Mr. Conover, we are reviewing your recon now. Do you want a full response?"

"Yes," he responded. "But do not in any way, target the structure in the center. I believe that structure is what stands between us being connected with Earth or not. Protect it at all costs."

"Roger, we'll protect it. Sending in our rapid response team now. Contact time is thirty-five minutes."

Logan hoped that would be enough and commed Kira to stay undercover until the UN troops secured the area.

Kira and her group began discussing what they should or could do when Kira's face suddenly lit up.

"Max, did we bring that fly drone? The one with the camera and drill bit?"

They were used to traveling with a flying construction drone to perform small fixes to problems in the water, communications, or electrical stations they visited. The drone Kira was thinking of was the size of a large fly to get into tight spaces. It had a small drill and other tool attachments.

Max checked his backpack and pulled out the drone.

"Right here, do you want me to send it up?"

"Yes!" Kira whispered. "Link my bionic eye to the controls."

Her eye suddenly switched over to the view from the drone, which was hovering over their group. As disorienting as it was when she first received the eye, she was now used to having a different view in one eye. Kira looked toward the intruders by the alien structure. The drone zoomed over toward where she looked. She sent it toward the armored truck and had it enter the engine. *Now, where is the gas line?* Kira thought.

Petra ran back to the mercenaries' armored vehicle. Rivio gave the word to take cover. Several men ducked behind a large rock. Petra counted down from twenty and set off her electronic trigger. The dust exploded in all directions around the structure, and the earth rocked up to a mile away.

* * *

While Logan was touring the city with the UN and Kira was exploring with her friends, Matti was on Earth monitoring the gates and transfer systems. She developed a keen interest in the rate at which they could increase transfers over the last year. Given the Fuerte Group's warning and their predictions, Matti calculated the pace they needed to achieve so that they could build-out and transfer half-a-billion more people over the next eight years. It was a steep goal, but the motivation for everyone on her Earth-based command team was high. It didn't hurt that most of them moved their families to Proxima and planned on going over themselves.

Lights started to flash in the command center, and their monitors switched to emergency messages. Matti long ago removed any loud sirens because she hated those things and didn't think they served any purpose except to make everyone in the area non-functional.

"Maria, what's going on?" Matti asked her operations day-shift director, who was in charge of all transfer gates across their twenty-four facilities.

"Checking now," Maria responded, clearly working the problem with her other facility operations managers. "That's odd. We have a zero-power transfer reading just now."

Communication lines started flashing with incoming calls from the gates.

Maria spoke to several gate operators and then looked over at Matti, "The gates are *all* down. All at once, twenty seconds ago."

Matti took out her phone, and for the first time ever, she couldn't get a signal from Kira and Logan. Now she was worried. They always assumed the gates couldn't be shut down from the Proxima side. "Restart the systems and send out an emergency conference request to all sites. Ten minutes. Also, run a scan of the latest logs, including any data you have from Proxima. See if there was anything unusual leading up to the shutdown."

Matti was damned if she would let this ruin her program and strand her family four light-years away!

\* \* \*

Right before the explosion went off, Rivio sent an automated signal back to the Black River command post on Earth. Manda Lodhra heard the message and smiled from her Pakistani Black River headquarters. The attack might be modest, but the public relations impact was where Black River shined.

The real purpose of maintaining black ops and terrorist cells within Black River, Manda knew, was that a relatively small terrorist attack could be built into a world-changing social impact through modern media. They mastered the art of creating negative narratives using social media tweets and posts.

As soon as she received the signal from Rivio, she released two-thousand pre-prepared blogs and posts into the mainstream Western media. Tweets through their fake celebrity accounts and the phony video were especially effective. The core message was that there was a fatal accident on Proxima, and it was cut off from Earth with all the horrors of that event spelled out for the public to panic over.

Manda was incredibly proud of the fake video they shot of bodies strewn over the false Proxima set. The video also showed a phony quantum gate that was down, highlighting the horror of loved ones crying and being stranded light-years away from Earth. Within minutes of release, she noticed the video went viral. She smiled again and picked up her comm device. Paul appeared on the other end.

"Our video has gone viral, sir. You can proceed on your end."

"I love it when a plan comes together." Paul acknowledged the message then cut the secure comm call. He made a few other calls and put phase two of the plan into operation. While he felt a twinge of guilt about stranding so many on Proxima, he felt even more like a hero that he was going to expose just how flimsy Logan's solution to save the world was. People were going to flock back to the space program, he felt sure.

\* \* \*

When the dust settled, Kira could see the alien structure was still intact, just a lot dirtier than before. She zoomed in with her eye and did a full scan. There didn't appear to be any damage, but her comm signal was flashing red, saying that the gates were not operational.

Logan was picked up by the UN SWAT team and was en-route to the alien structure when the gate down alert was sent. He swore under his breath.

"Continue on our goal Major, the sooner we neutralize these terrorists, the more we can figure out if we can reopen the gates. Capture them alive Major, we need answers."

Major Karper, a veteran of many actions on Earth, nodded curtly, a rugged look in her eye.

She commed her team, coordinating the assault. "Contact in two minutes. Stand by to deploy and subdue the hostiles. Alpha, you're on point, and we'll bring up the rear."

They were all traveling in two modified Mi-52 gunships, a hearty workhorse that had proven it could operate well on Proxima in the increased gravity. All it took was more gas per mile than usual. Logan made an exception to his no gas vehicle rule for the gunships. Every other transportation mode on the planet was electrically based. He was glad now that they made the exception.

Rivio heard the gunships within a few minutes of the explosion. How had they gotten here so soon? He started looking around. Someone must be out there and saw his team even before the explosion.

"Set up the missile launchers, we have incoming."

As soon as the gunships came within range, Rivio gave the

order to launch. Two Hellfire missiles shot out toward the sky, locking onto the gunships.

Logan could see the launches. The Major shouted, "How the hell did Hellfire missiles get on Proxima?"

The pilots were already doing evasive maneuvers, swerving, and changing altitude. They tried to get a lock on the missiles and started firing 30-mm shells from their Bushmaster guns, but the rockets were tracking them hard. Two seconds from impact, the missiles just ran out of fuel and fell from the sky. Everyone onboard whooped.

Logan shouted, "Nice shooting!" to the pilot who looked over at the Major, "Wasn't me. We were cooked."

Kira and Max, and her other friends were jumping up and down. "Wahoo! Way to show them, Kira!"

Kira was smiling from ear-to-ear. She told the drone to drill as deep as possible into the missile casing when she saw the missiles in the truck. The drone must have hit the missile fuel tank. "More than one can play the sabotage game!" Kira shouted.

Her dad's voice came over the comm, "Was that you, Kira? Did you guys do something down there?"

"Who us? We were told to stay put!"

Logan didn't believe her for a second.

The alien structure's control system registered the initial explosion and put its quantum power system on hold. After it did a thorough diagnostic, a process that took thirty minutes determined there was no damage. It then scanned all of the places on the planet utilizing quantum gate services and restored power and service.

On Earth, Matti and her team suddenly registered all systems operational. She rushed down to the gate on the

Earthside. She told the operators to let her and a small security team through. She knew the head of security was as concerned as she was and nodded to her on the way. They all climbed into an ATV and were the first across the transfer point.

When they emerged on Proxima, a few moments later, the security team piled out and ran to the command center to see if they could assist. Meanwhile, Matti immediately commed Logan and could see from his video cam, that they always shared with each other's comm devices, that Logan was just landing onto the surface near the alien structure.

"We're OK. There has been an attack on what looks like the alien quantum power source we always suspected existed somewhere on the planet," Logan commed Matti when he saw her active signal.

Matti let out a huge breath she hadn't even known she was holding. Logan was OK. So far. Next, she commed Kira and received a video call request. Thank goodness, she thought with immense relief.

"Mom! We found the alien transportation enabler! And, uh, I guess we helped take out the attackers too. We're all safe. The UN is fighting the intruders on the ground now."

"Thank God you're OK. What were you all doing out there? Can you get back now?"

"Yes," Kira responded. "As soon as we get the all-clear from the UN. It looks like a terrible battle. We disabled their armored vehicle with our drone, so they aren't going anywhere."

Matti smiled despite her concern for her daughter and husband and thought that the intruders, whoever they were, clearly hadn't planned on Kira and her friends showing up.

Matti commed back to Kira, "So glad you're safe, honey, but your father is in the middle of that firefight! I'll see you when you transfer back here. All hell is breaking loose on Earth, so it will be good to have a clear story from you and your father. Love you." Matti signed off.

"Love you too, mom," Kira responded and ended the comm with her mom, feeling sober.

She was afraid for her Dad. She hadn't thought about the repercussions on Earth and hoped this wouldn't slow down the migration. She was aware that there were groups who didn't want them to succeed. But what was the alternative? Only a relative few would be able to go up to the space stations that now orbited high above Earth.

Kira zoomed in on the fight. She saw her Dad hiding behind the intruder's trucks. So far, he appeared unharmed. Meanwhile, the UN troops had killed most of the attackers. There was just one left hiding behind the alien structure, and the UN troops were surrounding her. Kira zoomed in on the attacker and was shocked to see the attacker was working on a device, trying to wire it. Kira commed on the UN channel, "Attacker is arming a device!" She sent the picture she had.

Major Karper received the intel and immediately commed her troops, "Pull back on bogie three, chopper one lift and subdue."

One of the UN choppers lifted off the ground and gave air support. Circling around the alien structure, it fired at the last attacker. As the attacker was hit, an explosion went off near the structure. Kira immediately received alerts from the Proxima control center that the gates were down again.

On the comm channel, all of the gate operators on Proxima started panicking again. Logan communicated to Matti that the facility looked undamaged as the latest explosion was smaller than the first. Matti relayed the information to the operators. Still, it didn't bode well that the system went down twice in as many hours.

Major Karper walked over to the attackers that were hit. Two were still alive. She put them in handcuffs and led them back to the helicopters. "We'll take these two into custody and get statements from them," she informed Logan as he, Kira, and her friends boarded the other helicopter, which was going to return them to the gate to get back to Earth.

The UN troops stationed on Proxima were relieved by the new forces and escorted them back to Earth. Logan finally made his way across with Kira back to Earth, and they were all met with a slew of news reporters. There were many conflicting stories in the media, and the reporters were trying to sort out the facts.

Logan was too tired to talk to them but figured he should make a brief statement since he was probably the only one who knew the truth. "I have just returned from Proxima. There was an attack on the alien power center by what appear to be earth-based actors. The attack was unsuccessful." Reporters shouted lots of questions. "How did they get to Proxima?" "Could this happen again?" Logan said, "We'll make a more complete statement later as I'm sure the UN military will as well."

Logan and Kira were tired but were immediately put on a plane to New York, where there would be a special inquiry into the incident on Proxima.

There was still a slew of negative stories and postings on social media preceding the transportation 'blackout'. Some were still stirring up protests in various cities, denouncing the migration as a dangerous folly, with the outage as a prime example of why using the quantum gates led humanity to a death trap. *As if the Global Burn wasn't enough of a death trap back on Earth,* thought Logan. He was amazed at how fear in groups could be stoked.

He caught a headline on BNN, 'Proxima: Salvation or Death Trap?' and shook his head. He hoped the inquiry would expose the truth, but it didn't look like the world was running on truth right now.

Matti, Logan, and Kira were interviewed for two days by UN personnel. Logan and Matti spent the rest of the time with Ruiz and his PR folks. On the morning of the third day, Logan was just getting out of breakfast when one of Ruiz's assistants ran up to him.

"Sir, Mr. Ruiz urgently needs to see you. Could you please follow me?"

Logan nodded and followed the young man to a conference room at the old Millennium Hilton hotel, where they were all staying.

"Logan, there you are." Ruiz was beaming, so something must be going right for once. "The footage of the attack on the alien structure was finally released, and also they identified the militants. Look at BNN." Ruiz pointed to a monitor running in the corner with a breaking story.

"The *New York Times* has just published a copy of a private bank transaction that shows a transfer from one of Paul Manning's shell corporations to an outfit named *Black River*. This company was owned by the ring-leader of the attack on Proxima. The money transfer was for fifty-million dollars."

Logan was surprised, "Well, that was subtle."

He couldn't believe Paul was so sloppy.

Ruiz commented, "The tide is turning against them, so now is the time for you to seal the deal with a UN speech."

Logan was taken aback for the second time in five minutes. "Me?"

"Who else? This is a critical juncture in history. Let's turn the corner on this and give everyone an excuse to be sane for once. The Earth has been hurting for years. You wanted to fully go public before. Well, now is the time to assert leadership. You're our man."

Logan knew he was right. He looked forward to expressing his views for once. It felt right that someone should start holding up a torch and not a sword. Mankind was tired and to the breaking point. The quantum solution was the way forward. Logan had always felt it.

"OK, I'll do it," Logan said with conviction. Ruiz looked over at him and raised an eyebrow.

"Alright. You embraced that sooner than I expected. I think you're turning into the leader we all knew you could be, Logan. Heaven knows we all need a good leader right now. I'll set it up for tomorrow at three pm. It will be a full UN drama event."

"Let's do it," Logan responded. He was tired of all the politics. He would say his peace and make Quantum Pioneer fully public.

Ruiz looked impressed and felt happy that Logan was finally coming into his own as a leader. Fuerte had not made a mistake in putting so much trust in him, Ruiz thought. The world was falling apart. Logan was rising to the occasion.

* * *

Back in his office in Washington, D.C., Senator Barrister closed the file on the ESS program. Paul was a good man; it was too bad he had to take the fall. Once it was clear the attack on Proxima failed, the Senator knew it was time to cut his losses. He called in his chief-of-staff, Karen, and gave her the receipts hiring Black River. Paul's name was on the receipts.

# A Door Opens

*Year:2055 +5.7°F*
  *Earth Population:  10,920,755,113*
  *Population off-earth in Solar System:  650,044*
  *Population in other Star Systems:  30,250,542*
  *Yearly population decrease due to Global Burn:  120,524,552*

The UN General Assembly was more crowded than it had ever been. Ms. Olsen started the session. For an hour she detailed the various events that transpired to get the world to the critical point it was at. She spent time detailing Proxima's attack and who had been responsible, making sure to expose and then nullify all of the false messages that were alarming many on social media. By the time she was finished, there was a definite positive shift in online social sentiment, reversing the negative image of Sheltered Refugee Black River had tried to foment.

Sabine then introduced Logan as the CEO of the Sheltered Refugee organization, the first alien artifacts' discoverer, and the creator of the quantum gates.

Logan stepped up to the podium and looked down at Matti and Kira, who were beaming up at him. He smiled and looked out at the audience with hope and confidence.

"Madam Chairman, ambassadors, citizens, thank you for having me speak at this critical juncture. My lot in life has been discovering and using what our alien friends, and I do mean friends, have given us. Great gifts. We have not met these aliens, but amazing positive results have proven the worth of their gifts to us."

Logan's image finding the first alien artifact was shown on large screens in the room and through-out vid screens around the world. There was complete silence in the hall.

"My path started as a key contributor to the first space mining programs, where you'll all know I, with several others, fortuitously found the first alien artifacts. The artifacts that have led to so many advances in our technology over the last fourteen years, including cheap, clean, abundant energy, something mankind has been searching for, for centuries."

Logan paused, took a sip of water then continued.

"Less known are new quantum gates that have granted humanity access to three new worlds." The screen image changed and showed a quantum gate with pioneers passing through.

"Were these artifacts placed there for us? I believe it was no accident that mankind was given these tremendous gifts at just this time in our development. I have reviewed the history of our solar system with my colleagues, and I would point you to the 2017 event of Oumuamua, the first verified interstellar object that passed close to Earth. I know the objects were placed there at that time by an alien spacecraft because we have recently discovered evidence from 2017 proving this."

Logan then played the video clip that Ruiz had given him and recently given him permission to make public. It was narrated by Matti's father, Dr. Damon Garcia. Matti blinked back a tear when she heard her father's voice. "This is a recording of Oumuamua releasing a probe that landed on Anteros." A screen showed a blurry image of an object coming out of Oumuamua and, in time-lapse, showed it approaching the Anteros asteroid.

"Whoever placed these objects knew we would find them and that we needed them now. My path has been to bring the benefits of these wonderful gifts to mankind, step-by-step."

Logan paused while an image of migrants crossing to Proxima was displayed, showing hundreds making the journey.

"Is it a coincidence that we can now just walk from our soil to Proxima's soil so easily? Why do all of the planets given to us at the alien site on Anteros all have breathable atmospheres? There has been much turmoil about the safety or wisdom of traveling to these new worlds. Some feel we should keep pursuing expansion to low-earth orbit. I say that there has only been one path for humanity over the last five thousand years, and it continues on Proxima."

Logan motioned to the image, and it changed to a series of pictures showing ancient refugees up to the pioneers of the eighteenth century in America's West.

"Our world history is one of migration to better lands when the lands we are in turn inhospitable. I announce to you tonight," another image appeared, a flyover of the colony on Proxima, "that your fellow citizens have achieved a fully sustainable community on Proxima. If the gates were permanently closed, whether due to natural cause or attack, two million people are now living there with their families. They have everything they need to continue to prosper. Mankind has left the cradle."

An image of the first colonies on a world other than Earth

to support man was displayed. The audience erupted into applause.

"Has it been easy? No! Has it been without loss of life? No! A few brave heroes have given their lives so that millions could succeed. Have we been able to bring families to a better life? Yes! We persist. We expand. Millions of pioneers have migrated to a new life. One of promise and possibility, not one of failure, as a small group of criminals have recently been telling the media with no basis of fact. My path has led me to know and feel in my heart, in the soles of my feet as I step on Proxima's soil, that this is a continuation of our destiny, a gift to mankind from a long-gone civilization. They intended for us to progress, not fail under the weight of our developmental pains on Earth."

A new image of ESS One appeared.

"We need a solution for *all* the people of Earth. I still love space, its boundless promise. I think we need to be out in our solar system."

The image changed again to the pioneers crossing to Proxima through the quantum gate.

"But we now have a simpler and more natural way of fulfilling that dream! One that will allow all men and women to have a future. It is important to state the facts. We did the math, and it was heartbreaking. Even with several space elevators, we can only lift a small percentage of humanity to space, even over a hundred years. But, as many have said before me, when one door closes…"

Images of recent devastation on Earth were shown.

"Another one opens."

The image of quantum pioneers appeared for the third and final time. Logan looked with bright and confident eyes out to the audience.

"Let us leave, for now, and give our burdened planet time and space to recover and follow the UN migration initiatives. Let us expand to these three new worlds. Come with your fellow Quantum Pioneers to take hold and mold these great new worlds. The door is open."

Logan paused a full ten seconds, then bowed briefly and left the stage to enormous applause. While a few ambassadors stayed sitting, most rose to their feet. The message was simple, direct, and convincing. The world was finally ready for it.

Two days after Logan's 'Another Door Opens' speech, Paul Manning was indicted on conspiracy and other charges. He was removed from his post at Space Industries Consortium, which announced that all construction was stopping except on the current three ESS stations that had been started. No finish date was announced.

To much fanfare, the UN pronounced the six-month new world migration test period a complete success. Then, in a move that would prove decisive in the fight to save billions of people, the UN officially opened two new worlds to full migration.

The first new world was Kepler 452b, renamed Prosperar, *prosper* in Spanish. It was 1,400 light-years from Earth and slightly larger, with a gravity 1.1 times that of Earth.

Also opened for migration was Kepler 62f, whose surface was seventy-five percent water. This posed a unique problem, as they had to tune the gate entry several times before finding solid ground to transfer new pioneers. The first time they opened a gate, ten-thousand gallons of water came back to Earth from the new world before the gate was closed.

The gate operators then opened their gate to Kepler for

viewing only so that no transfer of water would occur. After much searching, they were able to find a location with solid ground. The Kepler 62 system consisted of five planets and was 1,200 light-years from Earth in the constellation Lyra. It circled its red-dwarf sun every sixty-seven days. 62f was renamed Xinjia, *new home* in Chinese.

Under the UN agreement, North, Central, and South American countries were assigned to Posperar. China, Russia, and other Asian sponsors were awarded Xinjia. European, Middle Eastern, and African (EMEA) countries would use Proxima. There was overlap from existing Sheltered Refugee sites, but that was ok. Ultimately, everyone had the right to petition which world they would settle on, although they were required to stay with their original gate world for at least one year before transferring.

Over the next year, with a vigor that had not been seen on Earth since after World War II, the world started focusing entirely on the migration through the quantum gates to the new worlds. A tremendous amount was accomplished when ten billion people concentrated on a single objective.

\* \* \*

It was a calm Monday night in Shanghai on the last days of November 2055. Xi Chen was broadcasting from the Jinping Gate.

"This is a day that will be remembered through time, the opening of the Xi Jinping Gate, the broadest and largest quantum gate open to Xinjia. Through this gate will travel many millions of Chinese and Asian citizens to the large, fully sustainable habitats that are being built on Xinjia."

The Jinping gate was, indeed, the most massive gate built to date. Of the two hundred gates now in operation, Jinping measured a full quarter-mile across. One hundred Fulton reactors provided the energy to keep it open, the largest of the newest quantum power transfer reactors. The Chinese didn't do things half-way.

"It is planned that three-thousand people will transfer every ten minutes to transfer one-hundred-million citizens per year. This is only one of five gates opening across Asia."

Xi Chen continued the broadcast with the shot of a long line of refugees and temporary housing stretching out from behind the new gate.

"The story that has led up to this opening is a sad one. Severe drought has displaced hundreds of millions across Asia, and over sixty-million people have died over the last two years from related malnutrition, disease, and starvation. Refugees are lined up as far as the eye can see, by a few estimates over twenty million in this area alone, waiting for relief and opportunity in the promise of a new home, Xinjia."

Across the world, in Brazil and all other South American countries similar, but smaller gates opened. In Brasilia, Santiago, Buenos Aires, Panama, and fifteen other cities, gates opened to let people migrate to Prosperar. A network of portals was constructed between Proxima, Prosperar, and Xinjia to facilitate trade. Those who wanted to travel between the new worlds could, but most transportation was one-directional, off Earth.

The mass migration galvanized the imagination of the world as well. Disruption and suffering were now very wide-spread due to the never-ending *Global Burn*. Everyone knew a relative killed in a fire, drought or one of the massive hurricanes or typhoons that were sweeping over the world. But there was also a singleness of purpose not seen before.

The corresponding hope and vision of a brighter, more sustainable world was taking hold. Few pioneers looked back. The millions who made their way to the three new worlds responded similarly. Like the pioneers of old, colonizing a new planet was challenging work and took total dedication. Stories abounded of monumental and heroic efforts by many to get shelters and then permanent buildings erected and moved into.

A unique identity was forming for each world, as well. A more unified sense of modern national identity formed not around their past differences but around working together to make their adopted new worlds successful.

Because success was not a guarantee. Each new world was challenging. On Xinjia, there were enormous water serpents, larger than whales, that killed several ships' crews before they figured how to subdue them.

On Prospera, the radiation was proving more potent than on the other worlds, so they added a three-foot dirt barrier to all buildings to shield the inhabitants. They also created a radiation alert system to warn people to seek shelter when a solar flare was expected.

* * *

Logan was in a meeting on Proxima, where he was spending the majority of his time. His work was on the new worlds to support the intense building program never before seen in the history of mankind. It put the post-World War II building boom to shame.

Chi was now in charge of the coordinated build-out across Proxima and requested more resources, "We need two-hundred trained mechanical and civil engineers yesterday. We finally have the new Proxima-based automated mining and supply chain system feeding material into our 3D building printers fleet. We need competent people to keep it going and ensure a steady supply of material. The one thing we can't afford is an interruption in our schedule or people back on Earth won't be able to transfer."

They were acutely aware that their building program was life and death for people back on Earth.

Matti responded on the conference call, "I'll get our human resources group to scan the transferees on the waiting list back on Earth and expedite the transfer of qualified engineers."

"Wonderful! Yesterday was not an exaggeration."

Matti left the conference call. She had other business to finish.

\* \* \*

Matti Conover walked into prison block one-ten on a late Thursday afternoon with a fierce determination in her step. Paul Manning was resting on his bed in his cell and was startled to see Matti approaching.

"What are you doing here? I'd thought you'd be out overseeing your new world, not coming and seeing the fallen from your past."

The Paul she had known wasn't here anymore. In his place was a miserable and defiant man. She walked up to Paul's cell and spoke through the bars, her expression serious, "Is that all you have to say after trying to murder my family?"

277

Paul was taken aback but quickly recovered, "Is that what you think? What about all the people you're misleading, promising a new world, full of danger and death?"

"You're deluded. But, I don't want to talk about me. I came here to talk about my father, Damon Garcia."

Paul cocked his head to the side. It was clear he had never heard of Damon Garcia. Well, that was interesting, thought Matti. "He was the astronomer who discovered that Oumuamua was an alien spacecraft and had sent a probe to Anteros. You knew all along, didn't you?"

Understanding dawned on Paul. The Senator had been the one to ask him to go to Anteros first. It made sense that the Senator just didn't pick that asteroid by accident.

Matti continued, "He was murdered. My father was murdered for that precious knowledge about Anteros."

Senator Barrister never mentioned how he had gotten the information on Anteros. "I didn't know about that."

"And I'm supposed to trust you on that? The man who tried to strand tens of thousands of people on Proxima?"

"You have to believe me, Matti. I wasn't involved in your father's death."

This was the response Matti had hoped for, "But you know who did. The person who told you to capture Anteros and bring it back to Earth. Who was that? You owe me that, at least. Your friend didn't exactly keep you from getting into here. Where is your friend now?"

Paul blanched. She was right. Barrister used him as a scapegoat for the whole Proxima incident. Why should he protect him now? "OK, I'll tell you on one condition. A ticket to a new world."

Matti had anticipated this condition. She pulled a slip of

278

paper out of her bag and held it up. "One-way ticket to Xinjia. Talk."

Paul took a deep breath, "Barrister. The Senator. He made getting Anteros our first priority as a condition to the funding we received."

"When did that happen?"

"2030, when we received the funding and when you started at Space Industries. It was Barrister who knew."

Matti dropped the slip of paper under the prison cell and walked away without a backward glance.

Paul reached down with anticipation for the paper, his ticket out. His face turned to horror, and his hands started shaking when he saw the location on Xinjia he would be transferred to. A Chinese prison!

\* \* \*

It was January 1, 2056. The world was celebrating the one-hundred millionth person to transfer to a new world. Even more significant than that milestone was the completion of infrastructure worldwide and on all new worlds that would allow the transfer rates to increase ten-fold. The plan was to transfer half a billion over the next year, a considerable increase.

It was a time of mourning and of leaving behind. Everyone felt the massive movement off of Earth, and it created a great sadness for the world that used to be. Their once-beautiful and seemingly boundless world was dying.

On Earth, in just two short years, the effects of the Global Burn increased four-fold. The acceleration rate was truly exponential, and they had hit the steep and painful part of the exponential curve. Skies were filled with smoke from the many fires around the world, droughts were severe and constant on large areas of each continent. Monstrous hurricanes and typhoons left entire areas uninhabited. The oceans lost much of their once teeming life. Many of the world's once most populated coastal cities were now underwater. All of the related disruptions were severely impacting the world's ability to maintain any kind of quality of life. Rationing was common for water and many foodstuffs around the globe. Water availability was now the most pressing issue in countries. Even with thousands of Logan's water desalination plants, clean water was scarce.

At exactly eight in the evening on January 1, a Saturday in most spots on Earth and the other three planets humanity now lived on, people stopped and lit a candle and held it high for one hour. It was an hour of remembrance and of sad hearts but also one of rising hope. Hope that humanity was moving on, expanding into the universe, and wasn't dependent on just one world anymore.

Barry Shindler, the conductor of the New York Philharmonic, raised his baton and started to conduct a world anthem that was composed by the world's foremost musicians. It was broadcast around Earth and on all three new worlds. Candles were held high in Beijing, New Washington D.C, Moscow, London, and in thousands of other cities across the globe, while people listened as the bars of the anthem swelled in sadness and hope in mighty melody. On Prosperar, on Proxima, and on Xinjia, they all bowed their heads, most with tears in their eyes. So many already dead, and still so much more suffering to come.

Gone was any blame. It was too late for that. The primary

emotions were sadness and resolve. There was a plan to transfer and save as many of the world's peoples as possible.

The time-frame was overwhelming. Projections were that a tipping-point of catastrophic proportions was coming. The environment had sustained five degrees of warming, and ecosystems were failing. Everyone could see that now, but it was too late for it to recover, too late by several decades. Like a wrecking ball that already started its swing, it was impossible to stop.

The building program on the new worlds was ramping up so that millions could migrate, but would the effort scale as rapidly as the devastation rate? Most economists shifted their practices to evaluating this problem and suggesting ways the world could increase the building and migration rates to match global deterioration rates. If the world couldn't achieve an exponential migration curve, they would miss their window of opportunity. It was truly a race against time. Ingenuity and determination were the primary weapons.

Humanity mourned and vowed to work harder together, live the best they could, help one another, and put aside centuries-old feuds and prejudices. At least temporarily, racial tendencies faded as the people of Earth were unified by the threat of common destruction. Unified in their resolve and sadness for a beautiful world that was abused for too long and would now require centuries, if not millennia, to heal.

# This Can't Be Good

*Two years later, Bethesda, Maryland*

*Year: 2057 +5.9°F*
 *Earth Population: 10,020,755,113*
 *Population off-earth in Solar System: 720,044*
 *Population in other Star Systems: 450,550,542*
 *Yearly population decrease due to Global Burn: 125,524,552*

Dr. Calum Larkin was a senior scientist at the International Weather Service. He and a team were tracking odd phenomena in the Caribbean and across the Atlantic. He pulled into his usual parking spot on a chilly February morning early in 2057. In many ways, it was the golden age for weather forecasters. Many events related to the *Global Burn* required accurate forecasting in an unpredictable world with lives often depending on their best estimates as to the direction and arrival of storms and droughts—in short, Calum was happy about his team's contribution to saving lives around the world.

He carried his cup of coffee up to the third floor of the weather services building, an old government building located in Bethesda, Maryland. The building should have been torn down thirty years ago but was given to the service when they doubled their staff two years ago to coordinate weather forecasters worldwide. Their goal was to provide an integrated and accurate global weather perspective. He moved from London to take up this position and rather liked Maryland if you could discount the occasional terror of a mega Atlantic hurricane threatening to hit the coast.

It took the first year just to build their model in R+. It was measured as being twenty-percent more accurate than prior models, a considerable increase from a statistical perspective.

After two hours, all of Calum's peers arrived or logged into their daily conference call, which usually lasted from five minutes to two hours, depending on the depth of information to be discussed and the potential for harm from the various global weather events.

Calum's boss, Dr. Arkin Stockbridge, started the meeting with his usual way of cutting right to the important stuff.

"Folks, Dr. Larkin has forwarded his data on the Gulf Stream effects he has been monitoring. I want him to give us the summary then open up for analysis. Let me say upfront that many of us at HQ are disturbed by the trends in the data."

Calum started his summary, "In short, we have observed the Gulf Stream 'hiccup' several times. Sharp spikes in the speed of the Stream's flow can be observed on a regular interval every eighteen days. This severe rate change in the flow has a bullwhip effect across the Atlantic. For several months the flow has increased faster than average than just completely dropped off."

There was silence for thirty seconds as everyone was clacking on their keyboards and bringing up various graphs from the data set.

Geoffrey Rankin, the lead forecaster from Brussels, spoke up, "Hmmm. You know when you mow your lawn, and the motor suddenly revs up and then sputters? It means that you're," and another person finished his thought, "running out of gas."

The same scientist continued after a ten-second pause in which much more clacking could be heard.

"My God, the Atlantic thermohaline circulation, it's stopping. Here is a quick projection based on our models and your new data—circulation flow just flat lines in three months."

Calum leaned over the graphs and saw the analogy of the engine out-of-gas was apt. The projection seemed accurate.

In what would become the longest quoted example of British understatement, he said, "Well, this can't be good."

\* \* \*

Oddly, after the thermohaline circulation stopped, there was little immediate notice given to it. While there didn't seem to be any direct effects yet, forecasters did note an uptick in climate extremes worldwide. Droughts, fires, torrential rains, hurricanes, and tornadoes increased measurably. They were constant and unrelenting. The map that everyone referred to was called the 'Daily Habitability Map,' which was produced in great detail and showed which areas of the world were becoming uninhabitable. It also showed where refugee stations were. Refugee counts exceeded one billion and were the core of those that migrated to new worlds first.

People, more than ever before, adapted. The stock market now measured companies on the extent they had migrated their services or factories to the new worlds. Supply chains became localized to minimize disruption, and everyone focused all efforts on the migration effort to Proxima, Prosperar, and Xinjia.

By 2061, there were five hundred gates, all operating at full capacity. The world was astounded at how rapidly the 3D building printers' army was building out their new communities on the new worlds. Even so, as soon as new buildings became operational, they were filled with migrants.

* * *

Logan was in his office on Proxima late at night, where he could often be found these days. With the rapid development and population growth on Proxima, he took on more and more executive duties, including being heavily involved with the formulation of their new constitution. He was deep into getting a consensus around the form of their governing legislature, which they would be voting for within the next year.

Logan pulled up a satellite photograph of Proxima at night. There were lights centered in twenty-four cities, spaced equidistant from the center where Logan knew the alien power center was. He still marveled that a single power center could support the gate and power needs of a planet. Was there a limit? Was there a risk? Hundreds of gates and power cores all drew power from what Logan imagined was a single quantum source near the Sun. At least, that was Will's theory, and when had Will been wrong yet?

The cities on Proxima were all under seven years old, and the newness brought unexpected benefits and challenges. The benefits were excellent. To achieve sustainability, they eliminated the use of cars and planes to favor efficient electric public transportation. They also co-located people as close as possible to their workplaces. The result was a significant reduction in energy demand and pollution. It helped that there was one-hundred-percent clean energy because of the quantum power generators, but they still reduced consumption by eighty-percent. They recycled water and produced goods designed to be reused or recycled when they wore out—there was only one percent waste. The rest was recycled or reused.

Logan was contemplating these facts because he was attending two important conferences tomorrow after meeting with his executive steering committee at seven-thirty in the morning. He usually spent all of his days working with government representatives to formulate their new constitution. For a few days, however, everyone on the government panels took a break to meet with constituents, so Logan focused on other aspects of Proxima's development.

The first conference was a business conference in the morning. Then a conference of sociologists was having their opening session later in the day and asked Logan to add weight to their deliberations.

Logan arrived at the business conference and was amazed; there were one-thousand corporations and companies in attendance. Matti took over much of the strategic planning for Proxima businesses, and she was running the meeting. Logan was ushered to a seat at the front. He enjoyed not having to run a session for once.

"Welcome to our first Proxima Business Development Conference!" Matti smiled during the applause and looked over the audience, most of whom she knew well. How exciting, she thought, that they would move forward as an independent colony and figure out how to keep the economy healthy.

She continued, "I want to thank Mr. Conover for being able to attend our conference," Matti paused and nodded toward Logan. The audience gave a round of applause for Logan. Matti continued, "we want to support the smooth development of our business infrastructure.

"Everyone here is taking advantage of tremendous growth and investment opportunities as you set up your operations on Proxima and the other New Worlds. But everyone here was behind a push to pause for two days to set out goals for common infrastructure and coordination of our new markets. So, Welcome!" Again, polite applause from the audience. "Krishna, who all of you know by now has his pulse on all the development work on Proxima, will divide us up into sessions to formulate our needs and commitments. In the last session of the conference, we will be finalizing a draft of our joint development plan. On a personal note, I want to acknowledge and thank the wonderful cooperation and generosity I have received from many of you to keep Proxima supplied with basic foodstuffs and goods. It's been a superb effort to provide for our colonists even during chaotic rapid growth. We couldn't increase our transfer rates and save so many lives without your hard work in this regard."

Krishna then took over the meeting and split everyone into sessions. Matti came down and walked with Logan to the first session to outline government commerce regulations and policies. A draft document was being reviewed for approval, and Logan immersed himself in the working session. Matti smiled and thought how far Logan had come from his pilot days. He was an outstanding pilot, but his calling was to lead them all to these new worlds.

After a relaxing lunch session, Logan headed over to another building where the conference on social and economic governance was occurring. This conference's goal was to formulate recommendations to the newly formed legislature that was creating a new government and constitution. The recommendations focused on how to achieve the most balanced and sustainable world from a governance point-of-view. While the new government focused on environmental and resource sustainability due to necessity, they also needed structures that led to sustainable economic and social governance.

The conference was opened by Dr. Jamal, a leading sociologist. His short talk was titled, "Proxima's Social Framework or 'What have we done?'" Dr. Jamal took the podium and looked out over the several hundred attendees of the conference. He began his remarks.

"We all know the excellent resource sustainability and technology applied in building Proxima, and it's a marvelous achievement. But I put forward this question: What has this physical structure of our new community done to our social framework, and what are the vast social implications of this for the future?

"Here is why this topic is relevant. The rapid timeframe and lack of a competitive framework have created our society with few class differences. For instance, take home size. Home size ranges from five-hundred to three-thousand square feet, and homes are assigned based on need and number of people in a family and not how much income one has. Executives tend to get bigger apartments, but there are no million-dollar mansions and ranches, which extends to other aspects of class.

Salaries are, so far, more equal. So, what does the effective elimination of the top one-percent upper class mean for us? Class inequality created enormous political and social issues on Earth. What will the almost total elimination of class inequality lead to?

Another huge related question: Will eliminating slums and poverty bring a radical reduction in crime and drug use? Logan and his team were literally trying to save the world and probably didn't consciously think they were reducing poverty. Still, the lack of slums and a high minimum wage has enormous social implications. We also now genuinely have equal access to education and communication, and online resources. There are no 'bad schools' and 'good schools' based on their nearness to poverty centers. We don't have private and public schools. Other big questions relate to the uniformity of government on Proxima and the apparent lack, as yet, of divergent political parties. The list goes on.

I am not trying to say these things are good or bad, but this conference is important because we wish to state the enormous social implications of what has happened. We need to formulate policy with an awareness of our new social structures. These things will undoubtedly create opportunities and challenges, but ignorance of the changes will lead to inappropriate policies. This social clarity is our goal for the conference."

With that, Dr. Jamal left the podium, and people left to go start the different tracks of meetings. Logan approached Dr. Jamal. Jamal smiled broadly when he saw Logan, "Did I shock you? I wasn't trying to blame your design team for anything. Just open our eyes to what we have done."

Logan smiled, "No, No, I'm just contemplating the new

perspective you've given me. We just hadn't gone that deep when designing. We were just trying to make space to house millions of people decently, as soon as possible, fairly and sustainably. The fact that we achieved more equality or reduced poverty wasn't even on our radar."

"Yet, that is what you have done. Interesting, isn't it? Design has more than physical impact, especially since we have an entirely new society where no building is less than seven years old. It all was designed by a single team over a relatively short period. But there are many good implications, much good that has been done! You have done well. Social scientists are so excited! And it is probably good *you* did the design. Historically, when social scientists design society, it leads to horrors such as eugenics and the creation of master races. Not a good thing. So, your approach is best."

Logan went to one other session and then went back to his office. That night he looked at his satellite photo of the cities on Proxima with new eyes. They were going to have over a billion people on Proxima. So many lives saved, but now that they achieved it, what did it mean? Where would they go from here? Logan's head spun with the amount of work it would take to stabilize this new world and its form of government. Perhaps, he thought, Adams, Jefferson, and Washington felt like this when they created the United States. It was an incredibly humbling thought.

\* \* \*

Later in the month, Logan and Matti walked to Kira's graduation in a rare moment off from their busy schedules. They moved into a permanent home on Proxima when Kira started college, and they made it a point to have dinner and family time together each Sunday. Four years of college flew by, and Logan and Matti couldn't believe their little girl was graduating. They were incredibly proud parents.

It also hadn't escaped their notice that Kira and her peers didn't consider themselves from Earth any longer. They had started their adult lives on Proxima and were the first true Proximins. Kira and her friends were already contributing so much to the new world, it would be fascinating to see how they would lead their generation forward.

Kira was in the first class to graduate from the new Proxima University, where tuition was free for all students. There were many degrees offered in the sciences and engineering. Kira received an engineering and business double-major. She excelled in both. Unlike many colleges on Earth, Kira spent a full half of her coursework on practicums and internships, putting into practice immediately the concepts she was taught. This was good educational pedagogy and practical as there was still an extreme shortage of engineers with many ongoing projects.

Sam, Mike's and Marisa's son, was graduating with a degree in animal husbandry. Sam already contributed a lot by organizing a new approach to raising meat for the colony. He and his fellow students designed a sustainable, humane, and low-water approach to raising beef, chicken, and pork.

Sam and Kira also made recommendations on setting prices for meat that reflected the actual cost of production, something that was non-existent back on Earth. Meat processing was a too high resource-intensive process, and accurately pricing it to include the cost of water and other externalities was only fair. Sam's work helped lower meat consumption to a responsibly sustainable level, one-third of the old-earth average.

The colonies on each of the new worlds were expanding at an astounding one-thousand percent per year. This was only possible using 3D printer technology but had the interesting side-effect of leaving everyone's head spinning from the extreme rate of change. People who started as an apprentice in a field often became senior managers or directors within a single year.

"There she is!" Matti nudged Logan after scanning the graduates. Kira's curly hair stood out among the five-thousand graduates. Also, continuously bouncing up and down in her chair gave her away. Matti waved and caught Kira's eye, who smiled back and waved, super excited that this day was finally here, glad that Earth's first interstellar mass migration hadn't killed her opportunity to get a degree.

Mike and Marisa found Sam and were waving at him. Both sets of parents were proud of their children, not just because they were graduating but also because they were already establishing themselves in their careers and helping their community. It painted a bright and hopeful picture for the youth of Proxima.

For graduation, the speaker was Dr. Olsen, the UN Secretary-General, who hadn't wanted to miss the chance of doing something positive to support Proxima. She also loved visiting the new worlds as trips were rare for her with all of the UN's work.

Logan welcomed the Secretary-General early in the day at the speaker's reception. He couldn't help but notice how much older she looked. No Secretary-General in the history of the UN had to deal with so much violence and change.

She gracefully and successfully kept the world from spinning out of control. There were many open conflicts around the world, but as a whole, the UN provided leadership and kept the migrations going; it was their singular focus now. But Logan noticed it took a toll on Sabine.

The topic of her speech was "You Are Our Hope and Joy." It was a heartfelt speech. Sabine started:

*Graduates! You are our hope and joy. All of the last few years' toils, struggle, dreams, all we have left we have put into your prosperity. Everyone's sacrifices, including many people's ultimate sacrifice, is now focused so the next generations, your generation, will survive and once more thrive.*

*Entire industries and economies, and even ecosystems have collapsed on Earth, whose days are numbered. Let it be said that my generation is, finally and humbly, no longer taking away the hope for you, the future generations. Still, we remain singularly dedicated to launching you into this new sustainable world.*

*Mankind will continue, not just as a stone-age relic of times gone by, decimated by climate disaster brought on by neglect and greed. Still, humanity will continue and spring forward into sustainable worlds with those like yourself at the tip of the spear, with strong character forged by strife and hardship.*

*Many in the past have told graduates, 'you are our future,' but I say you are more; you are our hope and joy. Let heaven judge us all now by what we can accomplish over the next few years that we still have Earth.*

When the speech was finished, everyone was left in tears. It wasn't so much the words as the fact that everyone felt the meaning behind them more now than ever before. Everyone was deeply affected by the Global Burn, but more and more were inspired by global migration. Her speech was broadcast throughout the new worlds and Earth. It was an inspiration for more challenging times to come.

# Cataclysm

*Year: 2062*

  *Earth Temperature Increase: +9°F*
  *Earth Population: 4,890,755,113*
  *Population off-earth in Solar System: 1,820,044*
  *Population in other Star Systems: 3,823,250,542*
  *Total population decrease due to Global Burn: 1,010,123,100*

In the years of renewed focus, the world accomplished much. By 2062 almost four billion people migrated to the new worlds from Earth. Due to migration and death due to climate disasters, Earth's population was reduced to under five billion, less than half of what it was only eleven years before.

\* \* \*

Dr. Calum Larkin, now Director of the International Weather Service, sat at his desk in Bethesda, Maryland, reviewing the combined global long-range weather trends. He was more troubled than usual. The world had crossed the once unforeseen average temperature increase of five degrees centigrade or nine degrees Fahrenheit. Faced with recent data and visuals his team collected, he had felt uneasy for weeks. Inexplicably, Earth was calm across many continents, back in some cases to 2020 levels of disruption. Having fewer people on Earth helped, but it didn't fit any of their models, making them nervous. Calum called his deputy director, Dr. Lucia DeMarcos.

"Hi Lucia, can you come into my office and help me with something?"

"Sure, be right there." Lucia was senior to Calum back when he entered the Service, and they were friends ever since. They had 'weathered' many storms together.

Lucia came in and stood next to Calum. She gazed with him at all of the 3D live-data models visible from Calum's many display monitors. She saw the issue instantly.

"It's so calm," she commented.

"Exactly," Calum agreed. "Like we are waiting. It's like… the calm before the storm or the receding of water before a tsunami. I'm worried, more than my usual level of worry."

"What can we do?" Lucia asked.

"Well, let's just make sure we issue an alert to all stations to look for the development of anything *ominous*."

Lucia laughed.

"Good weather terminology! I think I can phrase that for our teams. I'll run more analysis looking for any pent-up forces we haven't noticed. That energy has to have gone somewhere."

\* \* \*

Within days of starting her analysis, Lucia was beginning to see a pattern emerge. Lucia's team started getting measurements on air and water temperature singularities. She started monitoring their projected trends. Her team updated the group's main weather models with the new data. They found a confluence several months down the road.

With the slowdown of ocean currents over the last several years, gigantic hot water pockets were forming deep within the Pacific and Atlantic oceans. Meanwhile, an extreme arctic cold front formed. The difference in temperature between these two masses was over one-hundred and fifty degrees.

She immediately called Calum, "We have collected summary data that is extremely alarming. Can we all meet in an hour?" She then re-validated the model and her results.

In precisely one hour, the entire facilities' meteorologists were in their main conference room seats.

"Let's just dive into the data," Lucia started when Calum entered and sat at the head of the room.

Her team cycled through several charts of water temperatures and maps, showing the heated masses of water deep in the oceans.

"We have never seen these types of super-heated reservoirs of water. They don't bode well. If they were to reach the surface, say, when the arctic air mass goes over, well, here are our projections for the size and power of the resultant hurricane."

Calum leaned forward to look closely at the data as others groaned.

"Sorry, Lucia, what is that in your long-range forward model?"

Lucia looked up, "That's our monster. We've checked our model assumptions several times. That is a Category 9 megastorm with winds of 350 mph that covers most of the Atlantic Ocean. The ocean surge alone is 150 feet, like a giant tsunami followed by an F6 tornado one-thousand miles wide."

Calum didn't want to jump to panic mode. He spent the next three hours having everyone review and tear apart the data. At the end of the session, they were all either in shock or depressed. Lucia's team was spot on with their results. An earth extinction-level event was on its way within the year.

Calum handed out their marching orders.

"OK, people, give me an executive presentation with convincing data by tomorrow by five in the evening. I'll brief the UN Secretary-General. She can help us figure out what to do with this. Lucia, please set up a permanent monitoring team for this potential event."

*One week later, Proxima, President's offices*

In a landslide vote, Logan was voted President of Proxima. More than even becoming President, he was thrilled at the progress they were making on Proxima. The cities were developing rapidly and were magnificent, full of pioneers with the energy and will to succeed.

His chief-of-staff, Marta, poked her head in the door, "You ready for the all-executive conference?" This would be his second all-executive meeting with the other world presidents and the UN Secretary-General. The first meeting was held a month ago and was convened to coordinate constitutions among the new colonies. It was a big affair, lasting three days.

This conference was more secretive via secure com-call. His cabinet was already on mute on the call. He tapped the screen to join, his face now showing up in the corner of the conference screen.

After only a few seconds, Logan could tell it was an

emergency meeting. Logan was surprised to see the UN General Assembly with all nation's ambassadors in their seats.

The Secretary-General started the session, then invited Dr. Larkin, the head of the international weather service, to the podium to give a critical climate briefing.

Dr. Larkin succinctly summarized the dire weather explosion that was coming. After reviewing all of the data, he ended with, "We have estimated that the two super-hurricanes, one in each ocean, will start and last for over four weeks, wiping out ninety-nine-percent of dwellings worldwide. They are so huge. I'm afraid no one will be untouched."

After he was finished, there was a prolonged silence in the room and on the call.

The Secretary-General broke the silence, "Thank you, Dr. Larkin, for your organizations' excellent work. I have asked three independent weather services to verify Dr. Larkin's teams' findings. Unfortunately, they all concur."

She took a deep breath, "I'd like to devote the rest of this meeting, discussing what we can do ahead of this cataclysmic event. We have just sent everyone a proposal for action that, firstly, details a coordinated world-wide press briefing to our citizens. We want to communicate what we're going to do at that time, not just news of the pending catastrophe.

"In terms of solutions, we are proposing increased migration quotas to the new worlds since escape seems to be our only practical action at this point. The new world migrant quotas go beyond current building capacity rates. This is an emergency evacuation. We have broken down the recommendations by country. Everyone needs to review these with their governments and be ready in twenty-four hours for our conference call. The expectation is that within one week, we will need commitments on our world-wide emergency response action plan." Sabine looked out over the audience with conviction, "We have advanced warning. Let's make the most of it."

The Secretary-General took questions for thirty minutes, then ended the meeting.

Logan's executive team joined him in his office when the meeting ended. He met with them for four hours, outlining short and mid-term activities to ready Proxima for refugees' influx. They would figure out how to provide shelter for as many as possible.

At the end of their research, they estimated they could help another three-hundred million before the storms were due to hit, one hundred million more than planned by converting all new buildings into emergency shelters. It would take all citizens' combined effort, but given that most everyone on Proxima was a refugee recently, Logan didn't anticipate any lack of cooperation. After the emergency, the modified buildings could be converted back to long-term housing. They were, all things considered, astounded at how much they could contribute.

\* \* \*

Senator Barrister was never one to go down with the ship. Dr. DeGraff built a unique gate for him at his ranch. With the gate, Barrister got access to Proxima without others knowing. He spent over two-hundred million dollars building a secluded compound on Proxima away from the cities being built. He was proud of his new estate. It maintained a head of cattle and a garden to supply food for his family and staff. The ranch wasn't environmentally sustainable, but it was grand. He went to great lengths to see that no one knew about it except those scheduled to move over in the next week.

The day he left his Senate office for the last time was a sad one. Everyone else had packed up and already left for one of the three worlds. He sat, tapping his pencil on a blank sheet of a fresh yellow legal pad of paper. How many bills had he shepherded through Congress in his forty-nine years? How many backroom deals saved businesses or sunk his opponents? He sighed and left the note. *We will continue elsewhere.* He put down his pencil, turned out the light, and made his way to the airport to go to his Texas ranch for the last time before migrating.

At his ranch, later that evening, Barrister picked up his bags. All of his people had gone on before him except the gate operator. He walked down to the gate, which sat only a few hundred feet from the front door of his ranch villa. He looked back at his house and thought about the many memories of good times with his family. Oh well, he thought, he would have an even better life on Proxima, away from the Senate's demands.

"Hey, Mr. Barrister, you ready to go?" Larry, the quantum gate operator, saw the senator approaching and got ready.

"Yes, Larry, time to go. Thanks for staying for me."

"No problem at all, Mr. Barrister. Here, let me get your bags. You can just sit here in the golf cart, and I'll drive you right through to Proxima. Dinner is waiting for you at your new estate."

Richard closed his eyes on the way through. He didn't know what to expect. They rolled through the gate, and he could instantly tell they were on Proxima. Everything felt a lot heavier. "Ooof," he said to Larry and opened his eyes. His new estate looked terrific, definitely worth the two-hundred million.

Another servant took Richard's bags. "Good trip, sir?"

"Yes, a great trip…" Richard knew that voice and looked over to look closer at the servant. Who was that? Logan?

Logan smiled, "Hello, Senator. Surprised to see us?" Besides Logan, Matti walked up.

Richard was shocked and looked around frantically, where was his security?

Matti smiled, "Did you really think we wouldn't be able to detect your building effort after the attack when your people crossed over illegally? We've known about your estate for weeks."

Richard smiled back. What a nasty woman, he thought. "And what are you going to do about it? I'll just have my lawyers tie you up for years. You can't kick me off."

"No need," Logan responded enigmatically. He and Matti waved goodbye. As they were walking through a small gate, they had set up to get back to their headquarters on Proxima. Logan called out to Richard, "We just hope you brought your hunting rifles. The bearhogs are pretty awful this time of year." With that, they walked through the gate and were gone.

Right then, alarms started ringing. Richard ran up to his house and ran through the door and into the operations room. A worried attendant looked up, "Sir, thank God you're here, look!" The attendant, a young man in his twenties, pointed to the radar. Twenty blips were approaching from all directions at over thirty-miles-an-hour.

Richard's eyes widened. "Where is security?"

"They were called away to an emergency at the other side

of your property."

"Oh, God," was all Richard could say as he caught the first sight of a giant bearhog bearing down on his property.

Back at the Proxima main headquarters, Logan and Matti walked out of the gate. Logan commented to Matti, "Too bad they didn't know to install bearhog sonic deterrents."

\* \* \*

In what would be remembered as the *Final Migration*, nearly one-billion people transferred to the three new worlds in the six months before the storms hit.

When the storms did form, they were as predicted: two mega-hurricanes, each with winds of over three-hundred-fifty miles-per-hour and over two thousand miles in diameter. These were storms the world hadn't seen in millions of years; prehistoric monsters from another age.

The first to hit went, with a fit of unfortunate navigation, directly through the space elevator. Made to withstand winds of up to three-hundred miles-per-hour, the elevator withstood the onslaught for a full twenty-four hours before all the facilities at the Earth end of the cable were torn to shreds. The main cable lasted another twelve hours, but it too snapped under the storm's continued onslaught. In an age of decimated economies, it would be impossible to rebuild, assuming anyone was left after the storms with the ability to do the work.

The two-million inhabitants of the three ESS space stations watched the elevator destruction in horror. This was their only reliable link to Earth. They let out a collective gasp when they saw the elevator wiped-out. They were on their own.

\* \* \*

Immanuel Esteban was a six-year-old boy with bangs over his eyes. He stood on his family's farm in Guatemala, feeding his favorite young pony. The green-laced sky was frightening. When the sky quickly turned dark as night, his father and mother came running in from the fields. They grabbed his hand and ran into their modest two-room home his grandfather built. They hid in the basement. It didn't matter; all was gone in a matter of seconds when the storm blast hit at three-hundred fifty miles-an-hour.

Sophie Watson, a nine-year-old girl, stood with her hand in her mother's in a doorway in Chicago. She was blown away, still grasping tight to her mother's side.

Samuel Johnson played his cello in a church in Atlanta. Xie Ping looked out from his doorstep in Hangzhou, China holding his two kids' hands. Fábián Regina sang in a church in Budapest. "Mario! Mario!" Lucia shouted for her son from her gated front-door in San Jose, Costa Rica. Reginald Montgomery, age fourteen, from New Orleans, was riding his skateboard down a hill. Alister Grimes from Bath, England, was washing onions from his small backyard vegetable plot. Alice and Tom Philips, married for fifty-two years, with twenty grandchildren, the youngest of whom was five months old. Their daughter was in the house in Wichita, Kansas, holding Archie, their grandson, when the storm hit their home. The wind was indiscriminate and took all in its path. All were lost.

Washington, London, Tokyo, Moscow, Beijing, Chicago, Mexico City, all the great cities of mankind, all the many lives of those who were left, were swept away like dust before the storm wrought of mankind's years of inaction and folly.

As much as possible, antiquities from holy sites and governments were either buried in massive vaults or taken to the new worlds. Even so, many people on the new worlds were sick when they saw Earth's holy cities and temples, Mahabodhi, Pashupatinath, the Golden temples, Mecca and Madina, Jeruselum, and even the great pyramids torn to shreds. They were wiped from the face of the Earth as sand is blown away by the wind.

Even with preparations, the entire power and communications infrastructure of the world was obliterated. Satellites still functioned, but nobody on the ground connected. Those in underground bunkers survived the best of any, but even these sustained significant damage from rocks that were hurdled like cannon shots, digging up the earth hundreds of feet deep. Most bunkers were flooded as the massive tsunamis coursed around the world. The hurricanes raged for weeks, endless destruction in their wake.

\* \* \*

The administrators of the new worlds decided to shut down the quantum gates when the storms hit. On Proxima, Logan was in the control room with Matti as the gates closed, one by one, around the world as the storms passed close or over the sister facilities on Earth. It was a spooky feeling watching them stop. After nearly eight weeks, not one gate reopened. Advanced planning ensured each colony could gate to each other world, but none of the colonies had a working gate back to Earth.

After a full year passed and the gates were still offline, they gave up hope that they would ever come online again.

Armageddon prophesied for thousands of years, finally came. The colonists' great gratitude was that they were given years to migrate and prepare for this day when they were cut off from Earth. Earth was lost for now, but humanity persevered.

# New Hope

*One year later, Proxima b*

*Year: 2063 +8°F*
  *Earth Population: 90,755,113*
  *Population off-earth in Solar System: 2,220,003*
  *Population in other Star Systems: 5,823,250,542*
  *Total missing or killed due to Global Burn: 4,610,123,100*

President Logan Conover and Proxima's First Lady were standing arm-in-arm, in the late evening hour, out on the ledge overlooking an expansive valley below, lit by the bright moonlight of Proxima's two moons and a panoply of stars. They were finally feeling peace and safety they hadn't felt in years.

Matti looked out over the valley sadly, remembering the loss of so many back on Earth. Then she sighed and smiled up at Logan, thinking how fortunate they were. There was a bright new hope given to those who managed to pass through a gate before they were closed. She could see many small children happily running, playing in the fields beside the community buildings. There was even a dog playing along with them.

"What's on your mind?" Matti asked, seeing that Logan was

more contemplative than usual.

"I want to tell you about a secret meeting on Earth before the storms hit. The secretary-general asked all of the presidents to New York City to the UN headquarters two weeks before the storms hit and then swore us to secrecy as a condition of her gift."

Matti looked surprised, "What sort of gift?"

Logan started telling Matti the story, "We were in her main conference room, just the three presidents of the new worlds and herself. No other world leaders were included."

* * *

The Secretary-General leaned back and sighed after swearing the three presidents to secrecy in writing. Logan, she knew well, having worked with him through-out the last five years of building the gates and the migration. The other two presidents she had worked with, but they were only elected to their positions six months ago when Earth found out the timeframe of its pending doom.

Prosperar's president was a woman named Elza Lima Luz, the president of Brazil before being elected as Prosperar's new president. She was tall, unassuming, and accomplished more for countries in Central and South America than anyone before her. She started her career by creating a treaty to stop the Brazilian fires in the Amazon, a problem that had persisted for decades.

Xinjia's president was a short, powerful-looking man named Li Heng. Li was on China's central committee and had extensive experience making trade and peace deals with India and other Asian countries. He created the first All-Asia

Trading Block after President Trump from the US realigned many older trade agreements. Asia was looking to consolidate its regional advantages. Li was the right choice for Xinjia, which supported a ninety-percent Asian populace.

She launched into her most consequential act as Secretary-General and her saddest, "I want to give each of you, as the acting heads of humanities' new worlds, what has turned out to be Earth's most precious possession, the alien artifacts. I will give each of you one of the world Tubes that haven't been used, but all will get the frequencies for all three new worlds. I intend to give access to all of the three remaining worlds to each of you. I'm putting that in a resolution for a vote by the UN tomorrow. The Instructor and the other artifacts will be split-up and handed over to you as soon as you can get teams here to take them.

"My personal wish to each of you," she said as she looked each in the eye, "is that you remain peaceful with each other. Take this horrible time and make mankind better because of it, cooperate with each other as peacefully as possible. We have a historic opportunity to stay united. Please be the great leaders you are and keep us united."

"You sound like you aren't coming with us."

"No, I am not. This position is my life-work. It is where I will stay until the end. I have a place in the Alps, maybe we'll survive. You three and what you can achieve on your new worlds are the new hope of mankind, our new beginning. What a great hope it is!" she said, smiling.

Not being one for long speeches or goodbyes, Sabine had a few private words with each of the presidents. Before leaving, the three presidents set up a time and place to meet for the first New World Conference. They set a date six months after they assumed their independence from Earth. They each were in the middle of forming governments in their new worlds and felt six months was the right time to come together again. Privately, they were all thinking that six months would also give them time to put together exploration teams to travel to each of the three new worlds and start staking their claims.

"What did Sabine say to you privately?" Matti asked, having sensed that Logan was done with his recollection.

"She said, 'I appreciate your selfless work to save as many as we have. It has been good to call you, friend.' Then I told her much the same, telling her that if it were anyone else in her position, I didn't think we would have achieved a tenth as much as peacefully as we did. I wished her and her family well from both of us. I also told her if she wanted a home for her grandchildren, she could send them to us, and we would welcome them."

"Did she? I didn't even know to check the manifest of travelers."

"I checked earlier today. Two of her grandchildren made it over. I left them a note that we were friends of their grandmother and would love to see and welcome them. They happily agreed. They miss their grandmother. She was a great woman."

Logan smiled back at Matti, and Matti put her arm around Logan. She looked back out at their new world. Logan remembered a few lines of a poem he read years before, in a simpler time when all he did was fly experimental spaceships to asteroids. He recited them from memory for Matti.

*When all the stars are shining,*

*in the struggle of memories past*
*we'll remember those that came and sacrificed before us*
*in this long silent spring.*
*Then we'll let the heartbreak of those moments*
*and the rich tapestry before us*
*take us finally to our home.*

They were finally home.

# Epilogue

Kira and Sam were thrilled to be back exploring the surface of Proxima b. They were both hired by the new Ecology division of the government of Proxima. They were on a team responsible for keeping the balance between the needs of the new communities and Proxima's environment. Proxima now supported over a billion people. The rapid expansion hit the environment pretty hard, even with all their sustainability planning. No one wanted problems with their environment after what happened to Earth, so there was a massive effort to stem any migration impacts.

Kira proposed the idea of exploring back out at the alien power station to see if there was any other alien technology at work that might be helpful for Proxima. Since the attack, no one had been back from the science community. The UN security teams had installed a perimeter fence and security bunker near the alien power station to protect it, but no one explored the site beyond that.

Sam and Kira were in one electric ATV. A team of three other researchers was in a second. They had a security escort, which was now required for anyone going out into the wild areas. The escorts' mission was to protect Proxima from exploitation and protect the explorers from harm from any bearhogs. The bearhogs had grown clever recently. They rubbed grass deep into their ears so the sonic deterrent wouldn't bother as much. Who would have thought they would rather be deaf than leave the colonists alone? They were getting bolder in approaching smaller groups of humans when they ventured outside the cities' walls.

"Can you help me with this sensor?" Kira called over to Sam. They were setting up a sensor array around the alien power station to help monitor for any changes. They decided to set up two rings of sensors around the power station, one twenty-feet from it and another one-thousand yards out, to see if there were other phenomena taking place outside or around the station.

"Sure." Sam came over and helped wire the last sensor to their network.

"Ok, let's give this a test." Kira touched a button on her tablet. A diagram of all the sensors lit up. Data started streaming into her system. "It seems to be working. Let me see what the graphs are showing." Kira flipped through a few more screens. She concluded to the team who were standing around her, "Looks good, we're getting good data. Let's go back to camp. Tomorrow we can get the first snapshot of data and analyze it for anomalies."

Sam grumbled, "Sounds great. I, for one, have been thinking about dinner now for two hours."

Walter Horton, another of the scientists on the team, spoke up. "You're always thinking about dinner! Let's go eat, then contact headquarters. They'll want to know our status."

The next morning Sam was up early. He went down to the command tent, where they stored all of their monitoring equipment. Coming into the tent, he was surprised to see

Kira already at the console. "You couldn't wait either, huh?" he laughed.

"No, I couldn't. I've found something."

"Really?" now Sam was interested, "what have you found?" He put his hand on Kira's shoulder and looked over at her screen.

Kira noticed he put his hand on her shoulder. She liked it. Sam was a good friend, but of late, they were seeing if they could be more. Kira hoped for a deeper relationship; heaven knew Sam was her best friend and had been for years. It seemed natural to go further now. She always supposed when it was right, it would just happen. *I guess it's happening,* she thought with a smile.

"This blip right here, it's regular. Look." Kira replayed the last ten hours of data in a ten-second summary. The blip went on and off in a regular cycle every five minutes.

"It's like a beacon," Sam conjectured.

"My thoughts exactly. Let's go find out." Kira grabbed her backpack with her water and camera equipment. She ran out of the tent.

"Whoa," Sam ran after her, "shouldn't we wait for everyone else? That blip is a kilometer away."

"I'm checking it out," Kira put her hands on her hips, defiantly, "you coming?" Kira jumped into a buggy. She started it up. Sam threw up his hands and climbed in, "It's probably a security sensor the UN set up. No harm looking, I guess." As soon as he said it, he didn't really believe it.

Kira threw the buggy in gear. It topped the rise of a hill, toward the anomaly.

Sergi came out of his tent. He saw the buggy go over the hill. Oh, oh. He was also on the scientific team and could imagine what just happened. He ran down to Kira's tent. It was empty. He then ran over to Sam's. It was empty too. Dang! He ran over to the security tent, "Hey guys, Kira and Sam went off by themselves!"

"Not again, those two are brilliant, but they haven't a clue about how to stay safe. Wake the others and get to the buggies. We have to go after them again."

Sergi ran to get the others. He could hear all the security personnel running as they gathered their equipment.

They all flew out of camp and started following the tracks made by Sam's and Kira's buggy. Most of them grabbed a breakfast sandwich and tried to get a bite to eat as they drove over the hill. They were all shaking their heads.

Sam and Kira climbed out of their buggy a kilometer from camp. They were both staring at another alien structure. They went into a cave with a reasonably high ceiling. This is where the signal originated. When they walked inside, they noticed an arch of stone cut so evenly, it could only be another alien structure.

Sam took Kira's hand. They walked toward the arch. "I'm not sure about this," Kira said.

"What? Now you're chickening out after we dashed out of camp? Something is odd about the inside of the arch…" Sam reached out to touch the stone. "It's so cold, I wonder why."

"Maybe we should go back for the others. This isn't what I expected."

"Come on, we have to figure this out." Now, Sam was engaged in the puzzle. Kira knew she couldn't pull him away from a mystery. Sam was always intensely focused on any challenge. Well, she had gotten them into this, so she walked forward with Sam.

Sergi and two security personnel ran up to the opening of the cave. They saw Sam and Kira about to walk into a strange arch. Sergi cried out, "Guys, no!"

Kira and Sam didn't hear Sergi. They put their hands out into the arch and couldn't feel any difference. They walked forward…and disappeared.

Kira and Sam looked back. They couldn't see Proxima. They were in a silver room with no windows and high ceilings. They couldn't see any source of light, but the room was bright. They shielded their eyes and jumped back, shocked.

Not more than ten feet in front of them was an alien. It was tall and thin. It looked up from a silver desk. It stared at them with intelligent eyes, then nodded once.

Back on Proxima, Sergi saw Kira and Sam disappear. Before he could run forward to the gate, it disappeared as well. The entire stone structure just vanished. An empty cave was all that was left. His first thought wasn't of fear for his friends but about what in the world he was going to tell Kira's father, Logan.

# Author's Note

Thanks for reading *A Door Opens.* I hope you enjoyed following Logan's, Matti's, and Kira's journey. And I hope you also found some space to think about the coming climate-change impacts our world will be facing soon. If you could leave a review for the book, I will reserve a space for you on the next buggy over to Proxima b. Alas, if it were only so! But I really, really would appreciate a good review on Amazon.

I was fascinated by the news stories of Oumuamua when they broke back in 2017 and wanted to start this book on the premise that it really *was* the first spacecraft verified to be from outside our solar system. The news articles said it was the first 'object' from outside the solar system, but we all knew better, right? Who would call it an 'object'? It had the shape of a spacecraft, it acted like a spacecraft...

As I was writing the book and doing 'the numbers' on space elevators and space stations, I just couldn't get enough people up to space. It turns out space isn't a near-term savior from climate change. At least not for more than a few thousand people. Not even in fifty years. We seem to think that way, that we could all migrate up to space, right? But the numbers say we migrate to space over hundreds of years...there are *billions* of us.

So, while it will be essential to spread to new planets in our solar system, it looks like we need to find another solution to our climate issues. The book's projections of the severe effects over the next ten to forty years are all from climate change research except for the last hurricanes that destroy Earth. But, global supply chains breaking down, many more wars, floods, fires, and uninhabitable zones on the planet are all possible and happening already. If anything, we've found that projections the scientific community has made have been *understated* over the last few years.

Alien artifacts would certainly jump-start a solution, but humanity *has the* ability to solve our political and technological issues. Surely we can have hope that we will find a solution, involving the help of aliens...or not. But seriously, w*hat are we waiting for??* We've got to get moving on getting these solutions in place. It really needs to be a global, all-hands-on-deck effort.

Stay tuned for the second book in the *Space Knows No Bounds* series, *Hints of Infinity.* It will feature Kira as the main character and deal with first contact. I don't think first contact will be as straight-forward as many science-fiction space opera books purpose. I think it will be complicated. I mean, do we really think when two entirely different intelligent and advanced races meet we'll understand each other at all? I'm more on the side of movies like *2001—A Space Odyssey* and *Arrival* than *Star Wars.* Although, who doesn't like a good space battle, right?

I just think alien races won't be on the same developmental page as us. We will probably be *millions* of years apart with entirely different technological and physiological foundations. That means complicated. It might even explain why we haven't heard clear radio signals from the stars yet, from projects like SETI.

On the other hand, there are sextillions of habitable stars in the universe. Sure, they are far apart, but that is a number with *twenty-one zeros!!* A recent Penn State study using Kepler telescope data estimated ten billion earth-like planets in our galaxy alone[1]. Then there are about two trillion galaxies, so my math says there are a *practically infinite* number of potential alien races out there. So, *where are they?*

Take care in these 'interesting times' we live in. Keep the hope alive for great solutions to our world's most significant problems. And please leave that positive review for *A Door Opens!*

[1] Business Insider. **Morgan McFall-Johnsen.** Aug 16, 2019